ORDER

BILLIONAIRE IN DISGUISE: MAXENCE #2

By: Blair Babylon

Dree Clark thought tall, ripped, thoroughly hot Augustine was her knight in shining armor, until she discovered he was her priest.

Where's the last place in the world evil drug dealers from Phoenix would look for a girl who owes them money?

Nepal.

Dree is on the run. Her dead ex-boyfriend owes a whole lot of money to some drug dealers, and if they can't get the cash from Dree, they'll take it out of her hide. When Catholic Charities offers Dree a mission into the far reaches of Nepal because they need a nurse, Dree jumps at the opportunity and prays she'll be safe.

Until she meets the Catholic priest who'll be leading the mission.

It's Augustine, the sexy guy from Paris.

But he has a new name, *Father* Maxence Grimaldi.

Well, she'd told him to lie to her.

She just never thought he'd lie about *being a priest.*

Now, she's journeying far out into the wilds with the hot priest.

And oh God, they're riding motorcycles, and he's wearing black leather with a priest's collar.

And there aren't enough darned tents to go around.

She's not going to be able to keep her hands off him.

PRAISE FOR ROGUE, MAXENCE BOOK #1

"Maxence is everything I love in a romance novel - a whipsmart man with an anguishing call to serve that conflicts with his love for Dree. I was spellbound!" - New York Times bestselling author Julia Kent

"What a wild and sexy race through Paris! Rogue masterfully combines nail biting suspense with high steam for the ride of your life with Maxence and Dree." ~ USA Today bestselling author JJ Knight

"Another masterpiece from Blair Babylon, who I am convinced keeps getting better and better. Max is not at all as I'd imagined him, and really it's no wonder, since he has been forced to repress who he is. The real Max keeps popping up his head, doing real-Max things that the other Max wishes he wouldn't do. He struggles with his inner demons to be a Godly man, but he hasn't quite figured out how to balance the different parts of himself, and as a result, tortures himself. He is a man searching for himself, impeded by too many bad guys who wish him harm. It's hard to focus on self-actualization while trying to simply survive without getting yourself killed." -- E.C., Goodreads Reviewer

"Blair's stories have always been hot but this one might be the hottest yet." -- Xtreme Delusions Book Blog

"I just couldn't stop reading! This book is addictive!" -- Kat, Goodreads Reviewer

"Rogue is a phenomenal romantic suspense that is sure to delight and entertain as it holds your heart and mind captive. Nothing can prepare you for the roller coaster ride that is Maxence. He will take you unawares and leave you completely breathless and wanting. If nothing else, you will learn why he is so addicting to the women that he meets." -- Words Are The Breath of Life Book Blog

"Good gosh! Author Blair Babylon is a master at building suspense. I have been eagerly awaiting Maxence's story for YEARS. Finally it arrives and I am practically salivating as I tear into the book, excited that I will finally learn the truth about the elusive Maxence. As I am reading, I am finding that Maxence's unveiling is happening at the rate of an excruciatingly slow strips tease. The end of "Rogue" finds me with almost as many questions regarding who Maxence is as the beginning of the book-- but I promise that slooowly he is starting to be unveiled. **One thing that is made abundantly clear is that Maxence lives two polar opposite lives and this results in my finding myself even MORE intrigued by him. Now THIS is what I consider phenomenal writing!"** -- Lil Miss Reads A Lot Book Blog

PRAISE FOR ONE NIGHT IN MONACO

"Holy Maxence! Max hotness! Max suspense! Max everything! Follow your favorite book boyfriends Casimir and Arthur as they try to figure out WHAT the hell happened to Maxence in Monaco, with all the opulence and lavish lifestyle you'd expect from Blair Babylon's Runaway Billionaires. This series starter is hot, hot, hot!"

~~ USA Today bestselling romance author JJKnight

"Blair!! LOVED it! A fun, sexy, fast-paced read that had me on the edge of my seat wanting to know what happened that night!"

~~ Pippa Grant, USA Today BestsellingAuthor

"What I love about Blair Babylon books is the worlds she creates, and One Night in Monaco is no exception. Luxury, power, wealth - all of it beyond your dreams - is a backdrop for our very human, very vulnerable, and often extremely alpha characters who show us how uniquely human we all are -- but Maxence? He's one of a kind. And hot. Whooooo boy."

-- New York Times bestselling author Julia Kent

"Addictively entertaining and full of escapist goodness,this stylish page-turner left me breathless and begging for more!"

~~New York Times bestselling author Annika Martin

"This is *One Night In Monaco*, Billionaires In Disguise; Maxence written by the amazing Blair Babylon! This book has been a long awaited one! I'm so excited to finally dig into the man of mystery Maxence Grimaldi!! He has been in this series as friends of Casimir and Arthur, his sexy as h@ll friends from boarding school. Ms Babylon knows how to string you along and NEED to know about her wonderful characters. She never fails to amaze me with the amount of details and little flashes of other friends that she sprinkled throughout her books. Full of intrigue, sinister associates, mob related activity, utter indulgence of opulence and sexy sexy times! Hurry up with the next one Ms Babylon! I'm about to burst over here!!"

--Goodreads Reviewer

"I knew that I would be drawn into another great series and it definitely got me out of the book funk I was in. Ms Babylon is an author who literally creates a world to escape into thats way out of my normal life, but so totally believable too. This book took me from the monotonous dreary reality of work, and whisked me to the cosmopolitan shores of Monaco and Italy. Max is a character that has been in a few of the other books in the Billionaire world, hes always been a bit of an enigma and I can't wait to read the next book in his series. I haven't read every book in this vast world of European Elite and Royal society, but if you want to get hooked then you can start with a book 1 in a few of the storylines free... What are you waiting for. Get hooked like me. What I thought to One night in Monaco... Well I read it in one sitting, every page was more intriguing than the first. MAX has been a favourite character for a while, he's so mysterious and I can't wait to read the next books."

-- Goodreads Reviewer

"Friends, Casimir, Arthur and Maxence, will do anything for the other. Max is missing...His friends fear the worst, when they look for Max, always coming up empty handed...Until Genoa Italy happened. Maxence, always the gentleman and rescuer, was needed by Simone. He would do anything to help get her home, where she will be safe. I want to thank, Blair Babylon, for bringing Max's story to life. I can't wait until the next episode. This most definitely gets 5 stars."

-- Goodreads Reviewer

PRAISE FOR BLAIR BABYLON'S BOOKS

"The book oozed heart and passion from every page, it was as if it was traveling through my fingers to touch my very soul - I'm gobsmacked at how I feel about it! It showed more than I thought I was going to get it gave me *love and passion in absolute bin loads and moreover it was full of desire, hope, longing, honesty and devotion* - not just from the characters but from the author also because her devotion to her craft was clearly evident in this book - she nailed it!!" -- *Books Laid Bare Blog, (Every Breath You Take, Rock Stars in Disguise: Xan)*

"*Every Breath You Take* was an absolutely stunning and creatively passionate exploration of two lost and lonely people finding

the missing part of their heart and soul in each other. What a breathtaking journey filled with unwanted hope, unwavering love, and unexpected devotion! This series is continuing with such a brilliant depth of heart and soul that I just can't get enough of. I am definitely looking forward to more of these ground-breaking stories." --*Shadowplay Book Blog, (Every Breath You Take, Rock Stars in Disguise: Xan)*

"The writing is great, as usual, and the characters are so well developed. **Author Blair Babylon has extreme talent here."** -- *Sammy's Book Obsession Blog, (Every Breath You Take, Rock Stars in Disguise: Xan)*

"This book brings together two of the author's series, Billionaires in Disguise and Rock Stars in Disguise. Prior to this book, the two were entirely separate. If you haven't yet read any of the books in these series, then what are you waiting for? **You do not need to read them to understand this book, but reading them will give you a broader understanding of the incredible canvas Blair is using as her background. She has basically created these worlds and characters from scratch, and what a world it is."** ~*Fictional Men's Page for Book Ho's*

"**This was one incredible story.** I can't wait to continue with this series." ~*Books and Beyond Fifty Shades*

"**Let me first say WOW... I am seriously addicted to Blair Babylon's books** her imagination whether it be Crime, Rockstar or Billionaire.

She creates a world where you are immersed with colourful and diverse characters and situations that you don't want to escape from." ~*Kat's Book Promotions*

"What a pair! This story had me clutching my chest. **I loved Tryp. His damaged and broken soul tugs at your heart strings.** His need to spiral down into the darkness to escape his past will have you wanting to comfort him and just whisper sweet nothings in his ear. The unlikely friendship was definitely the perfect route for this story. It takes a special kind of person to handle all of Tryp's darkness. Elfie definitely proved herself worthy and I loved her determination and strength even though she has a past of her own that she is desperately trying to run from. **Blair Babylon delivers a truly emotional story that had me on one helluva emotional rollercoaster.** I am definitely looking forward to reading more from this series." ~*Jennifer's Book Obsession, (Somebody to Love, Rock Stars in Disguise: Tyrp)*

"Just believe me when I say you DON'T want to miss this one." ~*Jo's Book Addictions (Somebody to Love, Rock Stars in Disguise: Tyrp)*

"This was my first Blair Babylon book and I was on a rollercoaster. **Tryp and Elfie need to read by all, a raw story of friendship and love.** Truly only the strong survive. I want more of these two."~*Romance Bytes (Every Breath You Take, Rock Stars in Disguise: Xan)*

"**The chemistry Wulf and Raegan have is amazing** and the fact that they are both so stubborn makes their relationship funny at times. The series covers everything from finding out about the good, bad, and ugly of each other to meeting the family. There are raw emotions in these books."
~~*Random Musesomy Book Blog*

"Blair Babylon knows what she is doing. **This is some of the best romance I have read, hands down.** It's got a little bit of everything, for everyone....the story was so well written, infused with sex, humor and drama, that **I would gladly read it over and over again.**" ~*Contagious Reads Blog*

"**If I could give 10 stars I would!** I adore this book, I have read it two times completely and many times parts of it." ~*Katrina's Books Blog*

"**AWESOME!** When I first started reading this book I thought it was going to be your regular romance book and I thought, what kind of spin could possibly be put on this kind of relationship. Don't get me wrong, I am the first person to admit that I love a good relationship. I think it's hot but I was still waiting for a new refreshing spin on romance novels, and this was it for me. So of course you still had the typical kind of damsel in distress and then that sexy as hell man coming to save her. **Well the twist is something that you wouldn't expect....** Wulf also has a secret, and when I mean secret, it's a big secret. No, it's nothing that you might be thinking, like he is married or he is gay. **I mean huge, I was in complete shock when I**

found out. That is one of the things that I loved most about this novel, **everything that I thought was completely wrong and it kept me intrigued the entire time.**" *~Fictional Book Ho's Blog*

"The writing was great and **I loved the way the author "peeled away" the layers** of them and let us really get to know them gradually. I loved the mystery in the characters backgrounds and personalities. **I loved the suspense and action thrown in the story also!"** *~Sammy's Book Obsession*

ALSO BY BLAIR BABYLON

ORDER

Billionaires in Disguise: Maxence #2

BLAIR BABYLON

Malachite Publishing LLC

CONTENTS

ORDER

Billionaires in Disguise: Maxence #2

BLAIR BABYLON

When the Son of Man comes in his glory, and all the angels with him, he will sit on his throne in heavenly glory.

All the nations will be gathered before him, and he will separate the people one from another as a shepherd separates the sheep from the goats.

He will put the sheep on his right and the goats on his left.

Then the King will say to those on his right, "Come, you who are blessed by my Father; take your inheritance, the kingdom prepared for you since the creation of the world. For I was hungry and you gave me something to eat, I was thirsty and you gave me something to drink, I was a stranger and you invited me in, I needed clothes and you clothed me, I was sick and you looked after me, I was in prison and you came to visit me."

Then the righteous will answer him, "Lord, when did we see you hungry and feed you, or thirsty and give you something to drink? When did we see you a stranger and invite you in, or needing clothes and clothe you? When did we see you sick or in prison and go to visit you?"

The King will reply, "I tell you the truth, whatever you did for one of the least of these brothers of mine, you did for me."

Then he will say to those on his left, "Depart from me, you who are cursed, into the eternal fire prepared for the devil and his angels. For I was hungry and you gave me nothing to eat, I was thirsty and you gave me nothing to drink, I was a stranger and you did not invite me in, I needed clothes and you did not clothe me, I was sick and in prison and you did not look after me."

They also will answer, "Lord, when did we see you

hungry or thirsty or a stranger or needing clothes or sick or in prison, and did not help you?"

He will reply, "I tell you the truth, whatever you did not do for one of the least of these, you did not do for me."

Then they will go away to eternal punishment, but the righteous to eternal life.

— THE GOSPEL OF MATTHEW 25: 31-46

CHAPTER 1
DISAPPEAR
MAXENCE

Maxence Grimaldi disappeared.

Maxence Grimaldi disappeared because that's what he always did.

When he'd left Dree Clark sleeping in the enormous bed in the suite of the Four Seasons George V Hotel in Paris, he'd brushed her blond hair with a kiss, showered and packed in the bathroom, and quickly let himself out without waking her up. The hotel had summoned a car to take him to the Orly airport, where he'd boarded a private plane to take him to Kathmandu, Nepal.

A stewardess wearing a scarlet sheath dress with her black hair carefully smoothed back in a French twist leaned down and asked him, "Would you like scotch or wine, sir? Or something else?"

Maxence glanced at his phone, which was receiving a signal from the plane's Wi-Fi connection. "It's seven o'clock in the morning."

She smiled.

Maxence shrugged. "Scotch."

Her smile turned conspiratorial. "Yes, sir. And for breakfast?"

"Eggs. Toast. Something substantial. Thank you, Malini."

She walked back to the plane's galley, her slim figure swaying as she walked between the white leather reclining seats that lined the narrow fuselage of the aircraft.

The engines whined as the small jet drilled through the air, and Maxence spread his hands on the rich, burled wood of the table where he sat. Three more oversized seats, currently unoccupied, also stood around the table. He stretched his legs underneath, enjoying these last few minutes of luxury.

Not minutes, actually. *Hours.* The flight from Paris to Nepal, even with a private plane and with only a short refueling and reprovisioning stop in Doha, Qatar, was still nearly fifteen hours.

They raced south and east, toward the encroaching night, so his day would be shortened by several time zones. The plane would land in Nepal in the early morning of the next day.

Maxence Grimaldi ruminated for fifteen long hours upon the choices he had made in his life.

Some of that time, he read to deepen his thoughts. Several meals were brought to him, which were of excellent quality, and he ate. The two air hostesses tag-teamed Max to keep him company, sitting across from him at the table while they ate and indulging in polite small talk. The three of them played cards for a little while.

It wasn't all charity. Long-haul flights weren't easy on the flight crews, either. They were going to have to turn around and fly this long route again on the way back with an empty plane the next day. Max planned to be in Nepal for at least a month, perhaps two, so there was no use keeping the plane, the pilots, and these ladies stranded at the Kathmandu airport for such a long stretch. His family would surely utilize it in the interim.

As the hours passed, the air hostesses spent less time with him, as they always did, and Maxence spent more time reading and contemplating.

The plane raced toward midnight and the spot on the horizon where the sun would rise.

When it grew dark, Maxence asked for turndown service, and the air hostesses reclined one of the couches into a double bed and laid sheets on it before closing the window shades.

The turbulence of his thoughts would not allow him to sleep. He didn't feel regret. He never did after one of those interludes when he slipped sideways and fell into temptation and his life as it might have been. But his lack of discipline and the depths of his own depravity disgusted him. He should not indulge like that. He should not lose discipline.

Although, if he hadn't met Dree Clark, who had captivated him for those few days, it probably would have been worse.

It certainly would have included a greater number of women.

He probably should have thanked her for keeping him from having to perform even more penance, which was another item he would have to deal with when he reached the rectory in Kathmandu.

Two hours before they arrived in Nepal,

Maxence arose from where he had reclined but not slept, and he took a small suitcase from the back of the plane, where it had been stowed for this purpose. He shooed the air hostesses back behind the curtain that shielded the galley for a few minutes of privacy. Malini wouldn't let the other woman peek, not that Max cared.

Maxence was a large man, six feet four inches, and packed with a generous amount of muscle. For him, trying to change his clothes in a tiny airplane bathroom was an invitation for disaster. He would at least break the mirror when he stretched, if not accidentally tear a cabinet off the wall when he tried to put on a shirt.

He removed a suit of unrelieved black clothes from the suitcase and set them aside. He shrugged off the black Armani suit jacket he wore and unbuttoned the white, silk-blend shirt underneath.

Under his shirt, he wore a slim platinum cross on a thin chain that he didn't take off. He'd hung it around his neck directly before he'd left the hotel and Dree sleeping like an angel in the crisp, cotton sheets.

As he removed each item of clothing, he folded the clothes neatly and tucked them inside the empty luggage.

After a quick shower in the private plane's minuscule stall, he donned the other set of clothes, which was just as finely made and also Armani, but tailored in a more subdued style. He tucked the platinum cross inside the shirt, next to his skin.

The shirt's collar was a high, ecclesiastical band into which he inserted a white tab.

It felt less like a baptism and more like a snake shedding its worthless skin.

When Maxence looked up in the mirror, a Catholic priest—or almost-priest—wearing a Roman collar looked back at him, judging him for the way that he had spent the month since he had last worn ecclesiastical garb.

It was a harsh judgment, as it should be.

Also, his black hair fell in curls over his forehead and around his ears. He really should've made time for a haircut while he was in Paris.

When he returned to his seat, he slipped on a suit jacket that matched the slacks, also in sober black and as well-tailored as everything else he owned.

Back at the suitcase, Maxence removed a fine gold crucifix on a string of black rosary beads from a side pouch of the bag and stuffed it in one of his pockets. He looped a different cross around his neck, a slightly larger one made of iron on a matte, metal chain.

As the plane began to descend to Kathmandu's Tribhuvan International Airport, Maxence took the opportunity to utilize the plane's Wi-Fi to check his messages.

His cousin Alexandre had texted a long diatribe about their family's political machinations and how much of his time these intrigues required. Alex also said he was on his way home because a particular errand required his presence, which seemed menacing, and he suggested that if Maxence wanted to attend their dying uncle's funeral, he might want to start finding his way home because it would happen soon. Alex also mentioned that his wife, Georgie, had been in touch with her college friend who had married the notorious Wulfram von Hannover, and unmentionable plans had swung into progress re: Flicka.

That was even more menacing, but Alexandre had a flair for seeming a bit of a dangerous psychopath. His reputation for the occasional brutal murder had probably kept him alive. The Grimaldi all had their tricks.

Maxence inhaled a steadying breath and, for the first time in days, checked his limited, private social media and the newsfeeds.

He found a picture on his social media feed that stopped his heart.

Max's ex-girlfriend, Flicka von Hannover, the one who got away, stood beside his older brother, Pierre, and they posed for the cameras as the happily married couple they were purported to be. Her smile was not the joyful grin Maxence had seen directed at himself so many times, but she wore the formal, seamless mask she used for important engagements and when she was weeping inside.

A bump of turbulence jostled the airplane, and Max's arm swayed with the phone as he tried to compensate.

Queasiness filled his stomach, and he swallowed hard.

Maybe it was an old picture because Pierre was pulling a PR stunt. Anything was possible.

He sent a DM to his cousin Marie-Therese Grimaldi, *Is Flicka in Monaco?*

He waited only minutes for Marie-Therese's reply. *Yeah, she just showed up out of nowhere. I saw that pic, too. When I asked around, everybody's hush-hush, but* *they said she's in the palace. My dad is *pissed.* He thought she had divorced Pierre. And then, you know.*

No, Maxence didn't know what his Uncle Jules would do in that case, and he sure as hell didn't want to. Jules Grimaldi was a psychopath of the highest degree and a virulent racist and misogynist. Maxence had expected someone to dox him as an actual Nazi for years, but it hadn't happened so far. Jules had probably never made the mistake of committing his intent and manifestos to writing or the internet because he was diabolically intelligent. However, Max had heard Jules's sinister diatribes at suppers and repeated from the mouth of Marie-Therese.

He stared at the picture again.

No matter what, Flicka was out in the open now. Both Alexandre, who was a past and potentially future murderer, and Flicka's older brother, Wulfram, were *en route* to her.

Wulfram von Hannover was one of the most powerful people in the world in his own quiet way and employed a startling number of mercenaries.

In this situation, Maxence knew to step aside and allow the reputed serial killer and the mastermind who owned paramilitary units to take care of the problem. He swiped out of the window on his phone and turned off the Wi-Fi and cellular signal, essentially demoting it to a camera and an off-line e-reader.

Max would have little reason to use the phone while he was in Kathmandu on the mission that would take him into the interior of Nepal. There probably wouldn't be any cellular signal, anyway.

He might as well leave it off.

Plus, turning off his phone was one of his most essential tactics when he disappeared, he'd discovered years ago. Palace security had a much harder time tracking him if he didn't ping a cellular signal everywhere he went.

But the palace and court intrigues and soft, delicious women were behind him now. He was no longer Maxence of the Grimaldi.

He touched the stiff, white square in the collar near his Adam's apple, reminding himself of who and what he was.

There was no reason to torture himself with what might have been with Flicka or what he'd had with the buoyant, bubbly Dree Clark, whom his body longed for even as he sat in an airplane speeding away from her.

His palms remembered the satin of her skin, and his fingertips recalled the silk of her hair as he clenched it in his fist at the back of her head. His skin grew sensitive, and the rough fabric of his clothes rubbed his torso and thighs.

Maxence drew a deep breath and settled his soul. It was unlikely that he'd ever see her again, or at least never when they could be together. Those four sensual days had been stolen time, a moment that could never come again. That life was behind Max, and he packed the sensations and desires into the back of his mind where they could not touch him.

Sitting in the seat wearing a Roman collar and his pocket heavy with a rosary, that stolen time was not his life.

Max sought to do good in the world and commune with God instead of indulging his appetites and lusts, which was the usual lifestyle for members of his family. He wasn't different from them, but he had chosen a different path.

Dawn bloomed like a rising chrysanthemum over the sawtooth horizon, and the irresistible lure of the habits Maxence had cultivated rose within him.

Malini and the other stewardess would be watching, but Maxence would do it anyway. He'd already prayed the Office of Readings in the dark before they'd awakened.

He drew his rosary from his pocket and laid the crucifix so that it dangled over the edge of the table.

In the Liturgy of the Hours—the daily litany of prayers mandatory for Catholic priests, deacons, and religious laypeople—Lauds is the early morning prayer to the rising sun that represents the risen Christ. Praying the Office of the Aurora consecrates the day to Christ.

He consulted the e-book he had stored on his phone months before and scrolled through the text to find the ordained prayer for that morning, Friday, December twelfth.

As always for Lauds, he pressed his palms together, and began, "Lord, open our lips, and we shall praise your name." He whispered the prayers in his deep baritone voice, and quietly sang the antiphons that buttressed the Psalm, an Old Testament Canticle, and the Psalm of praise for that day. He knew he had a good singing voice. A streak of musicality ran through his family.

The practice rolled through him, knowing that laypeople and priests were facing a crucifix and the rising sun as its light moved across the Earth and repeating the same prayers to dedicate that day and their lives to something greater than themselves.

His arms unfurled to his sides, held to the level of his shoulders, and he lifted his chest and his face to the warmth of the morning sun, breathing in a serenity of spirit he found nowhere else but in prayer.

He recited the Lord's Prayer, leaning forward with his heart when he said, "Thy will be done," and finished the praxis with the doxology, "Glory to the Father, and to the Son, and to the Holy Spirit. As it was in the beginning, is now, and will be forever. Amen."

Maxence was made small and humble by dedicating his time and work to that which was good and holy.

His hunger for all that his family held dear—power, wealth, envy toward each other's influence and belongings, avarice for more and worse violent delights, and a gluttony of the soul for the entire Earth and everything in it and to consume every person they could reach—receded. Maxence was a damaged man and a dangerous one, but these moments in prayer restored what was lost and broken for a few moments.

When he finished, he stood, brought the crucifix to his lips, and returned the rosary to his pocket.

The morning sun from outside the plane's porthole window warmed Max's face, and they flew through clouds of molten gold and silver.

Malini approached him, smiling and holding a tray with a cup of cinnamon-scented chai. The air hostess's smile was less conspiratorial, kinder, and entirely unsurprised.

He took the cup, grateful. "Thank you."

"A blessing, Deacon Father?"

Maxence had tried arguing with her that he wasn't a priest yet, but she always just smiled and said that she wanted a blessing anyway. The Catechism of the Church said that every baptized person is called to be a blessing and to bless, so Maxence drew on that as his guide. He drew a cross in the air over her, intoning, "In the name of the Father, and of the Son, and of the Holy Spirit, may the Lord bless you and keep you safe. Amen."

She sighed, and her shoulders lowered as if in relief.

"Are you Catholic, Malini?" He'd never asked before.

"No, I'm Hindu, but we believe that all religions are paths to God. I attend many churches because I feel closer to God. I have been to Catholic Mass many times. The singing is very nice."

Maxence felt compelled to ask, even though it seemed intrusive, "You don't take communion in Catholic churches, do you?"

"Oh, yes. It is very important to partake of prasadam. The plane is on final approach, Deacon Father. You should probably take your seat. I have to go to the crew seats now."

"Malini, communion is different than prasadam. There's an important distinction. You really shouldn't—"

"The captain has turned on the seatbelt sign, and the crew has to go sit down now. You drink your chai and have a good landing." She hurried off.

Maxence stood beside the table, shocked and utterly at a loss as to what to do. To take Holy Communion, one must have been baptized in the

Church and be in a state of grace. She had to go to confession. There were *rules*.

He called after her, "Malini, this is important. It's considered a mortal sin."

She waved him off and sat next to her friend, belting herself into the seat, while Max was relegated to his table for the landing.

After the plane touched down, Malini dodged Max until he had to get off the plane. She obviously didn't want to hear what he had to say. He thought he had her phone number, so he could text her a more coherent explanation later.

After Maxence got off the plane and cleared Nepali customs at the airport, he was met by Father Xavier Kocherry, a tall priest with skin the color and texture of worn mahogany leather, whom Maxence had known from a previous project in the state of Tamil Nadu in India. He heartily shook the man's hand and then hugged him while they laughed.

Maxence hoisted his rucksack onto his back, while Father Xavier picked up the wide cardboard box filled with supplies Maxence had carried off the plane. He said, "Sorry, I could only find one jar of peanut butter in Paris."

Father Xavier laughed. "I am very glad for the one jar of peanut butter. Next time you come to Nepal, plan ahead and make sure to bring two."

Maxence asked him, "Is there Mass this evening?"

Father Xavier shook his head. "There is one tomorrow morning over at Our Lady of Perpetual Help. We will attend that one, but I am then called away to minister in other parts of the city for the week and will be staying at the rectory there. Sadly, we do not have much time together."

"I'm afraid I'm going to need to be reconciled before Mass tomorrow morning."

"*You*, Deacon Father? I'm shocked."

Father Xavier's absolute earnestness as he said that shamed Maxence even more. Father Xavier had never heard one of Maxence's confessions after he'd gotten back from Europe. "I'm afraid so, and it's probably good that I should have sufficient time to do penance before Mass tomorrow morning."

Father Xavier's honest confusion forced Max to look away because he could not meet the priest's eyes. Father Xavier asked, "Have you been having doubts about your vocation? You have wanted to take Holy Orders for years. I would have thought that you would have received that sacrament by now."

"It's complicated."

"God is not complicated. The Divine is not complicated. There is only love."

Despair left Max's body with his next breath. "Father Xavier, that was exactly what I needed to hear today. I brought some of the butter crackers you like, too. Let's go to the rectory and demolish the crackers and peanut butter before I unburden my soul."

He grinned. "I was hoping very much you would say that."

As a significant amount of peanut butter was smeared on crackers and Father Xavier rightfully fretted about sodium-sensitive hypertension and his hypothesized, impending stroke, they talked about the project that Maxence would be leading over the next few months.

"A team of five laypeople," Father Xavier said. "This will be such a blessing, and it is so desperately needed."

"I received the names in an email this morning," Maxence told him while scraping a thin layer of peanut butter on his third cracker. He would probably stop after this one, and he reminded himself to send more of Father Xavier's favorite snack foods once he returned to Europe or the US. "The medical doctor who was slated for this trip dropped out. His mother had a stroke, so he withdrew. Luckily, a nurse practitioner volunteered at the last minute to fill the slot. He'll be arriving in a few hours. I assume it's all right if he stays at the rectory tonight?"

"Of course, of course. He can have my room because I'll stay over at Perpetual Help. Do we know him?"

"I've never met him before, but he comes highly recommended by Father Thomas Aquinas at the Church of the Immaculate Conception in the United States. He's recommended a number of laypeople for projects like this whom I have found to be excellent. Tom is very persuasive at convincing his parishioners and acquaintances to volunteer for missions."

Father Xavier chuckled. "Yes, we don't know anyone like that."

Maxence declined to reply. Yes, he had a knack at persuading people, which was why two of Max's friends from his exclusive childhood boarding school had "volunteered" their time and resources for this very worthy charitable project.

One of Max's school friends, Alfonso, had committed a large amount of money and resources to build NICU micro-clinics all across the hinterlands of Nepal, a surprising move. The charity had approved the project while Maxence had been sitting by his uncle's hospital bed, watching him slowly die, so Max hadn't been available to consult on it. Undoubtedly, the charity's board had properly vetted it. They always did.

The other guy, Isaak, was a good man who pretended he wasn't. He was the diametric opposite of Maxence in so many ways, which was probably why they got along so well.

The whole team would arrive the next morning, the day before the mission officially began.

After Father Xavier had decimated the crackers and peanut butter, he indulgently looped the stole he wore during confession around his neck and, with a crooked smile on his face, asked Maxence what mortal sins he had committed since his last confession.

Maxence couldn't look at the man's dark eyes as he stated that it had been five days since his last confession and he had committed an untold number of sins of a sexual nature with a woman as acts of fornication, at least fifteen acts, impure thoughts, wrath, and an act of violence that was in self-defense.

Father Xavier stared at the swollen knuckles of his hands folded in his lap and was silent for a long moment. His black eyebrows twitched, and he breathed to say something at least once, but caught himself and bit his lip instead.

His dismay and disappointment were palpable in the small room in the rear of the rectory.

Finally, Xavier said, "My dear Deacon Maxence, please say one good Act of Contrition in penance, and let us pray together for grace and to know the true will of God in your vocation."

Losing Father Xavier's respect hurt, and Maxence prayed with every shred of his soul, holding Father Xavier's weathered hands, that he would know the will of God and commit himself to it.

Even as Max prayed, soft sparks glimmered at the edges of his vision: satin skin, hair like shredded silk, a joyous laugh, a glance of blue eyes filled with kindness as she listened to him, and a quiet voice speaking gentle words with him that healed instead of wounded.

Not Dree. Don't think about Dree.

Think about the will of God.

Maxence wrestled with his soul and his thoughts.

Father Xavier sighed, removed the stole from around his neck and kissed the cross in the center, and rose as he wound the small strip of fabric around his hand. "I sense that you have great conflict in your soul, Deacon Maxence. I hope you can reconcile it with God."

"I hope so, too, Father Xavier."

Father Xavier pressed his lips together and shook his head, and then said, "I have heard the ladies in the kitchen, cooking. Lunch will be served soon. I hope you can devote yourself to prayer this day before your mission begins in earnest tomorrow."

After lunch, Father Xavier hurried off to the other church, and Maxence did devote himself to an afternoon of reading and contemplative silence, trying to remedy the trouble in his soul.

His soul did not cooperate.

Maxence slowly conquered his wayward mind. Each time he prayed the hours of the Divine Office, working his way through Sext at midday and None in the midafternoon, he felt stronger in the philosophy and practice of filling his day with prayer.

The clock's hands slowly spun toward five o'clock in the afternoon, local time, and Maxence began to look forward to the evening prayer of Vespers, a prayer of thanksgiving and gratitude for the day, when there was a knock at the front door of the rectory.

Ah, this would be the new volunteer sent by Father Thomas Aquinas in Phoenix, the one with the same last name as Dree, *Clark.*

What a coincidence.

She'd said it was a common surname.

Maxence pulled on his suit jacket, ever careful about first impressions, and brushed the front of it for travel dust before he opened the door to the front garden.

Two women stood in the early evening's fading sunlight.

One was Sister Mariam, a religious sister whom he'd met on a previous mission in India where they had worked together on girls' education in Kerala. She was a lovely young woman, kind and funny. She had excellent taste in tea shops.

The other woman was facing away from him, looking over the careful landscaping in front of the rectory, and she was a curvy, feminine figure. Her short blond hair swirled around her head in the evening's cool breeze.

Before she turned, he knew she was Dree Clark, the sweet and lovely woman whom he'd left in Paris in a bed rumpled by their lovemaking just the previous morning.

As she turned, golden sunlight glowed on her creamy skin, and her wary glance told him that she was just as surprised to see him as he was that she was there.

Sister Mariam introduced them, "Andrea Catherine, may I present Deacon Father Maxence Grimaldi. Father Maxence, this is Miss Andrea Catherine Clark, our new nurse practitioner for the premature infant project."

Dree's expression changed from wide-eyed wariness to the faint gasp of a gut-punch and downward fall of her eyes and mouth, outward signs that she recognized the depth of his deception. She asked, *"Augustine?"*

Yes, he was Augustine, praying to God to *not yet* grant him sobriety and chastity but instead to allow him to resume his life of hedonism and the indulgence of everything he wanted, which at the moment was her, her, *her*.

Maxence reached his hand forward, palm up, beckoning, beckoning *her*.

Dree didn't touch him, and she didn't smile.

He should welcome her off-handedly, and most of all, he should not reveal to Sister Mariam that they were far more than casually acquainted.

And yet he couldn't.

His intensity sharpened.

The sight of this beautiful woman shattered the quiet in his soul that came from prayer.

Appetites raged in him: hunger for her skin, her scent, her touch, and the sweetness of her taste in his mouth.

He was a dark thunderstorm, and his desires formed words. "Dree, *chérie.*"

CHAPTER 2

DEACON FATHER MAXENCE GRIMALDI

DREE

Dree sat on the sumptuous sofa in the rectory's living room, her ankles crossed, her knees together, and her hands clenched in her lap. "This is not my fault."

She wasn't sure that they should have told Sister Mariam that it was okay to go back to her convent quite so quickly. Having some female moral support and a chaperone would have been very welcome just then, especially when she was confronted with her one-night stand who turned into a half-week stand, and who turned out to be *a freaking Catholic priest.*

Or, you know, *close.*

He was a deacon, which meant he had been ordained and had taken the first sacrament of Holy Orders, the Roman Catholic rite that consecrates someone as a priest or a deacon.

He might as well be a priest. Unmarried deacons were supposed to be celibate, too.

Augustine—who Sister Mariam had called *Deacon Father Maxence*—stood by the fireplace and rested his elbow on the high mantle. He had combed through his thick black hair with his fingers, leaving it curling around his face, and was still hanging onto his hair on the back of his head like he thought the top of his skull was going to blow off.

Hers might.

The top of her head might actually hit the ceiling if somebody didn't tell her what was going on *immediately.*

The man she'd formerly known as Augustine said, "I do not believe this is your fault. Indeed, I do not think anyone is *at fault.* I should thank you for volunteering to go on a rigorous mission into the interior of Nepal. That was the first thing I had planned to say, but I don't understand how *you* came to be here."

Dree was still holding her hands clasped in a tight knot on her legs. Adrenaline coursed through her body, screaming at her to fight, flee, or freeze. Freezing seemed to be her best option right now, and yet she had to talk to the man. She would rather blend into the soft, royal blue velvet under her legs and hide.

Her throat was nearly too tight for words. She forced out, "It's not safe for me to go back to Phoenix. I told you everything that happened with my ex, Francis. There is some weird stuff going on there with the police and, I think, other drug dealers. So, I called up Sister Annunciata, the principal of my Catholic high school that I went to in New Mexico, and she called up a friend of hers, Father Thomas—"

"Father Thomas Aquinas from Immaculate Conception in Phoenix," he said with her, in unison.

"The Catholic Mafia strikes again." Augustine shook his head.

Not Augustine, *Maxence.*

And yet, he was still the astonishingly tall, ripped, beautiful specimen of a man Dree had met in Paris.

But, he was named *Maxence.* She had to remember that.

Deacon Father Maxence.

The white tab of the Roman collar on his shirt shone in the late afternoon sunlight streaming through the windows, accusing her.

He had not been wearing that in Paris, and he should have been.

"Yeah," she said. "Father Thomas said he could get me on a plane for somewhere far away from the southwestern US without any questions asked. So, here I am, far away from the southwestern US."

Augustine nodded. "Nepal is very far away from the southwestern US."

"Didn't he or somebody tell you I was coming? Did you *know?*"

"The Catholic Charities division managing the project emailed me yesterday that a person named 'Andrea Clark' had been assigned to us."

He was pronouncing it wrong, *Ahn-DRAY-ah.*

She corrected him, "Andrea." *ANN-dree-uh.*

"I thought it was amusing because you had mentioned that Clark was a very common name," he said, "that there was a university and shoes and department store, and other things also named Clark. So, I thought that the person coming must be yet another Clark. It did cross my mind that they might be a cousin or distant relative of yours, but I assumed the person would be male."

"I can't believe you thought I was a guy."

He frowned. "Well, there's the name, *Andrea.*"

"There you go again, mispronouncing it. I thought it was weird the way you said it when we were in Paris when you were talking about your cousin. I've never heard anybody pronounce it that way, Ahn-*DRAY*-ah. Who even says that?"

He looked up at her, his eyebrows raised in exasperation. "That's how you pronounce Andrea. I've never heard anyone say it the way that you do, *ANN*-Dree-uh. Andrea is a boy's name."

"Andrea is a *girl's* name. It's *always* been a girl's name. It's how you get *Ann*, which is a *girl's* name."

"Andrea is one of the most common name for *boys* in Italy. It's more common than Marco or Leonardo. My cousin's name is Andrea Casiraghi, and I assure you, he's male. Every Andrea I've ever known has been a male. Why would I think it was different now?"

"I can't help the fact that your cousin's parents gave him a girl's name."

"It's *not.* Andrea is a *male* name."

"Well, I assure you I'm not a male."

"I'm well aware of that."

"I should say you are. Speaking of which, why are you wearing a Roman Catholic priest's shirt and people are calling you father? Are you impersonating a priest? That has to be a crime or something. This is *weird.*"

He flipped his hand in the air toward the door. "As Sister Mariam said, I've been ordained as a deacon, not a priest, so I am called Deacon Father Maxence. I have a vocation to be a priest but have not been ordained as one yet."

After being a nurse in an inner-city hospital for years, Dree had a finely tuned bullshit detector. "Deacons are supposed to be either married or celibate."

He shrugged. *"Not yet."*

"Do you mean to tell me that you are *waiting* for *God* to grant you the ability to *keep your pants on?* It doesn't work like that."

He bit his lip, his white, even teeth pressing his full lower lip in a way that Dree had done just two days before.

And wanted to do again.

No. He was a *priest.*

Or *close enough.*

And she was detecting some mighty large bullshit.

She said, "Don't you have to go to confession and enumerate your sins and say penance like the rest of us do, or do deacons get a free pass?"

"Deacons do not get a free pass. I've had to do the rite of reconciliation twice for our time together in Paris."

"Yeah, I'll bet you did." Something rather stupid in her felt pride at that. "You should've told me you were a deacon and supposed to be celibate."

One side of Maxence's mouth rose, and the depths of his dark eyes sparkled with mischief. "I'm rather glad I didn't." He sighed. "And now I'd better go to confession for that, too."

Dree snorted at him. "Having some impure thoughts?"

"You have no idea how impure my thoughts are right now."

"You've got to stop doing that, Augustine.

Speaking of which, what is your *real* name? Is it that Maxence thing or something else?"

"I was baptized Maxence Charles Honoré Grimaldi. Because I have been ordained as a deacon, you can call me Deacon Father Maxence or Father Maxence."

Her tone sharpened. "'Yeah, it'd be too suspicious if I called you *daddy.*"

He winced like she'd slapped him, as he *damn well should.*

She hadn't meant to be quite so sarcastic, but *dang,* this was not some minor thing he'd forgotten to mention. She didn't like that he'd put her in the position of helping him break his vows, either.

She said, "Auggie, you don't even *look* like a Maxence. A guy named 'Maxence' should be effete, skinny, and blond." *Not shredded with muscle and with thick, dark, curling hair and a face like a movie star.* "And I don't know how I'm ever going to get used to calling you that."

He glanced at his reflection in the ornate mirror above the fireplace mantle, and so two gorgeous men were looking at each other. "I don't think I look like an 'Auggie.'"

Dree said, "So, that whole story about you being a *prince* was to cover up the fact that you're *a priest,* or you're *going* to be one, or you *want* to be one. Bravo, Father Deacon Maxence, bravo." She slow-clapped, and for some stupid reason, her heart felt like it was cleaving over and over into a million slices and fluttering as it fell around her.

"It doesn't matter what we call ourselves, and it doesn't matter how we got here. The most important thing now is to figure out what we're going to do about it."

"I think that's obvious. *I'm* a nurse practitioner, and *I'm* going on a Catholic charity mission to help save the lives of newborn preemie babies by building tiny little NICU clinics all over the Nepali countryside. I don't know what *you're* going to do."

He frowned and shook his head. "I've done many of these charity missions all over the world for eight years, from Rwanda and The Congo to Argentina and Nicaragua to West Virginia and the Appalachians. The problem is that we usually slate all-male groups of volunteers for these missions, and I had planned for this group to be the same."

"So, you're saying, *what?* You don't think there's going to be any women's bathrooms where you're going?"

"There aren't going to be *any* bathrooms where we're going. We were planning to stay in rectories with other priests when we can, but there is camping gear that has been rented, and we will be roughing it in the extreme out in Jumla province. A woman would not be *comfortable* in those conditions."

"*Augustine,* I mean *Maxence,* you are a city boy who lives in gussied-up Europe. I am a country girl who was born and raised on a sheep ranch in southern New Mexico. I can guarantee that any 'roughing it' that you *think* you have done is what *my people* would call an ordinary weekend. Do *not* tell me that I don't know how to *rough it.*"

He frowned at her. "I've been on charity missions in some of the most destitute parts of the world, where I lived with families while I built their wells or schools or whatever else it was that they needed.

Nobody was slaughtering the fatted calf for me on those trips."

Dree crossed her arms across her chest and looked away from him. *"Still,* I am a hardened country girl, and I can tell you are nothing but a greenhorn, city-boy *dude."* When she used the word *dude,* it did not have the friendly connotations that surfers have when they say it. "You would get bucked off of a broken-down, hoof-draggin' nag in five seconds flat."

He said, "I can ride a horse."

"Maybe one of those docile, Saddlebred geldings they keep at *dude* ranches."

"This is unproductive. We need to contact Father Thomas Aquinas and tell him to send a different medical professional for this trip."

"I am not *quitting.* I *cannot* go back to Phoenix. If one of us can't go, *you* quit."

"I will not back out of this mission. *You* should quit."

"I'm not going to quit. *You* quit!"

Maxence clenched his fists and looked away from her. "I *must* go on this mission. Besides the fact that I have a great deal of experience in leading compli-cated projects such as this one, these kinds of missions are *why* I am a deacon and want to be a priest."

Dree gasped and pointed at him. "You *do* want to be a priest!"

"Yes! I would've taken Holy Orders years ago if they'd let me. I have *chosen* this life because I want to do good work in the world, because I'm recognized for this because I do good work, and I *thrive* here. When I am out on one of these missions, a sense of

purpose fills me like no other time in my life. This is what I was *meant* to do."

She pointed in the general direction of France. "Then, in Paris, why did you—"

"*I don't know!*"

Dree sucked in a deep breath like when an ER noob resident got hot under the collar at nurses who had far more experience than they did. "*Okay.* We just need to figure this out. So, *okay.* So, this work means a lot to you, but *I* need to go on *this* mission."

"If it's just that it's not safe for you in Phoenix, I can send you back to Paris. I will pay for you to stay at the Four Seasons or a rented house in the French countryside or whatever you want for two months, the same amount of time that you would have spent on this mission. I'll put money in an account for you to spend. You'll be safe *there.* You just can't be *here.*"

"I won't accept charity like that. I *work* for my money. I've worked all my life, first on the ranch and then to pay my way through college, and I won't accept your money to sit around and eat bonbons and fritter away two months."

"You could order *Merveilleux de Fred* every day," he said.

"Oooo, that's playing dirty. But *I* want to make a difference, *too.* When I heard about this mission, it made the rest of my life seem like I've wasted it. Even though when I was in Phoenix, I was working in an inner-city hospital and helping people and saving lives every day, this is even *more* important. I could do something that I'm really proud of here."

He sat in a chair across from her and braced his elbows on his legs, his hands clasped between his knees, a pose that Dree knew was taught to therapists and dorm resident assistants to signal, *I'm non-judgmentally listening.* "We both want to go on this mission."

"*Yes.*"

"It is a problem that you are female."

"Sexist, much?"

"It is inconvenient."

That was worse. "Sorry that my vagina inconveniences you. *It didn't last week.*"

He frowned. "The other four people scheduled to go on this mission are all male."

"You sure about that? Any of them named Chris, or Andy, or Charlie, Skylar, Frankie—"

"Two of them are old friends of mine from boarding school. I've known them for twenty-five years. Both are cis-het males, Alfonso de Borbón y Grecia and Isaak Yahontov. They're tech guys, engineers, and venture capital."

"So, that's two. How about the others?"

"One is a translator, and we asked specifically for a male person. His name is Batsa Tamang. Batsa means 'son,' like a male offspring, in the Nepali language, so I'm going to guess he's a guy."

"You never can tell with names, *evidently.* And there are trans people in Nepal."

"We'll cross that rickety, swinging suspension bridge over a raging river when we come to it. Speaking of which, there will likely be several of those on our journey. If you don't like heights—"

Her words came out as almost a sneer, but he was being an ass. "My cousins and I used to go rock climbing up cliff faces with nothing but Keds sneakers and prayer. You can't scare me."

He cleared his throat. "You haven't seen some of

the bridges that I've crossed in Nicaragua and Argentina. The other guy is purported to be a Jesuit, so he's probably a man."

"Heh. *Maybe.*"

"Right, but it's likely you'll be the only woman on the trip."

"I'm fine with that."

"I'm not. I might not be around every moment to protect you. I have connections to make, business to do, while we're up there."

"Do you seriously think that some of these guys might be Rapey McRapists? If they are, should you be taking them way out in the middle of nowhere, where maybe the police aren't particularly reliable?"

"Alfonso and Isaak are fine. They would never force a woman or do anything untoward. I've never met the translator or the Jesuit."

"I got along *just fine* for twenty-five years before I met you."

"The night I met you, it looked like you were not *fine.*"

She eye-rolled at him. "I promise not to get smashed at the Buddha Bar in the Nepali outback and make stupid pronouncements."

He shrugged. "That did seem like a one-time event. Is there anything else on that napkin bucket list of yours that's going to get you into trouble?"

Dree poked around in her purse and pulled out the napkin she had been writing her craziest goals and ideas for the future on. One corner was limp and becoming frayed. She should laminate it or something. "I promise not to do any of the ones that involve getting naked while on the mission. Going to

Nepal is on the list, so if you hand me that pen, I'll just cross that one off right now."

He handed over a slim pen that had been sitting on the coffee table between them, holding it by one end.

She took the other end of the pen, pinching it carefully, leaving as much space between their fingers as possible.

The heat from his skin warmed the air around the pen, and when she grabbed it, their eyes flicked up and met.

Magic.

Magic like a spark and a crackle and anticipated warmth washed over her, and the dark depths of his eyes pulled her in.

His luscious lips parted.

No, *no*, there was no such thing as magic, and Dree was just taking a pen out of his hand. It was *nothing.*

She leaned back.

He leaned back.

She drew a careful line through the words *Visit Nepal.*

An ink-dot spread from the end of the line and bled into the napkin's paper fibers.

Above where she had crossed out Visit Nepal, the items on her bucket list read, *Play Baccarat at the Monte Carlo Casino, Meet someone royal, Swim in the Mediterranean Sea in the French Riviera,* and *Marry someone you love with all your heart because it's worth it.*

Yeah, well, maybe someday.

She leaned back over the coffee table, offering him the pen back. "Um, thanks."

He took the pen back without looking her in the

eyes that time, keeping his gaze on the pen and the table. "Of course."

If she went on this mission, out into the wilderness of Nepal with this incredibly attractive man who thought he wanted to be a priest, she was going to have blue lady-balls the whole time. Even a waft of warmth from his hand was making her dizzy and distracted. "So, if I wasn't going to go, what would you do for medical personnel?"

Deacon Father Maxence had crossed his legs away from her and was looking out of the front window over the small yard with carefully manicured hedges and bushes, almost like a labyrinth. He rested one elbow on the back of his couch and rested his knuckle on his lips. "I would call Father Thomas Aquinas in Phoenix and a few other network connections and see if they could find a replacement for you and how soon they could be here."

She couldn't look away from where his knuckle touched his full lips. "Could you do that?"

He nodded. "We're supposed to leave on the day after tomorrow, early in the morning. We're having a team meeting here tomorrow afternoon after I assist with Mass at Perpetual Help, and then we will arrange for permits and problems after that. We leave early Sunday morning. I can't imagine that they could get someone here in time."

"You could just postpone the beginning of the trip for a few days until someone got here. Father Thomas was supposed to send someone else. Maybe they could jump on a flight."

"The doctor's mother had a stroke. He had to drop out."

"So, he can't come."

"And the flight time from the southwestern US to Nepal is over a day, sometimes more like thirty-two hours. Even if we found someone as close as India, getting them here and ready to travel would be problematic. Do you have cold-weather gear?"

"Yes, Father Moses in Paris set me up with all kinds of gear—"

"Father Moses Teklehaimanot? Black guy, African, missing part of his small finger of his right hand?

"Yeah, at *Saint-Sulpice* Cathedral in Paris?"

"Yes, and of course, Father Thomas Aquinas sent you to Moses. They're all connected. I think I met your Sister Annunciata in Rome a few years ago."

"Really?"

He nodded. "Nuns and religious sisters choose the best ecclesiastical names. Annunciata. Scholastica. Priests usually don't choose such devotional names, and most keep their given names."

"Anyway, Father Moses set me up with ski pants, a ski jacket, hockey gloves and liners, longies, thick socks, boots, everything. I was wearing half of it when I walked out of the airport in Kathmandu and about had heatstroke."

Maxence chuckled and looked down, his thick eyelashes lying on his skin. "Southern parts of Nepal are covered by a subtropical rain forest. The climate here varies by region due to the altitude. Kathmandu is quite warm."

"Yeah, it's like winter in Phoenix." She coughed because they were talking so much, and her throat felt a little abraded.

Maxence shot her a look. "Are you sick?"

"No, the air pollution is getting to me. It's like Phoenix during a winter temperature inversion, when the air gets bad."

He leaned over to a small dresser and opened a drawer. He removed some white half-domes and tossed them on the coffee table. "Those are N95 masks. Wear them around Kathmandu when you're outside. Once we're out of the city, the air becomes perfectly clean, so you won't need them."

Dree retrieved the masks and tucked them in her purse.

Max said, "Where we're going will be colder, though. Much higher altitude. You'll need your cold-weather gear."

"He sent everything, even space blankets and thermal hand warmers."

"At least you have gear. I'll make inquiries," Maxence sighed, "but I think if we want a medical professional on this trip, it will have to be you."

"At least you know I really do want to be here."

"There is that. I've headed a few projects where people were suckered or pressured into going. Most of them didn't complain, but they weren't happy they were there."

Dree nodded. "So, we're going to be together for a while."

Maxence nodded, his eyebrows flicking up as if Dree had made the understatement of the year.

"I didn't know that you were a deacon or a priest, or whatever you are, or that you wanted to be a priest when we were in Paris."

Maxence's shoulders lowered. "Yes, well, I didn't tell you. That was my failing."

"I'm not the kind of girl who sleeps with priests or even with guys who want to be priests."

"I never thought you were."

"So, that's why you didn't tell me?"

He shrugged, and he still didn't look at her.

She said, "While we are on this mission, we need to keep it professional."

He nodded. "I was just about to broach the same topic."

"I mean, I'm a fun lay for a week or two, but I'm not the kind of girl you give up the priesthood for."

Maxence looked at her first, and then he turned his whole body to face her directly. He leaned again with his elbows on his knees and didn't look away from her eyes when he said, "Dree, *chérie*, I apologize for lying to you while we were in Paris. I should have told you that I aspire to the priesthood, and after I got you back to your hotel that first night, I shouldn't have touched you. That was my weakness and my sin. I take full responsibility for everything that transpired. And even though I have every intention of becoming a priest, I want you to know that any man would be lucky to marry you. Francis Senft is a despicable human being for swindling you out of everything you owned, and he's an idiot because he didn't marry you and cherish you for the rest of his life. He didn't know what he had. You are a beautiful, kind, wonderful woman, and if I didn't feel that I have a real call and a vocation to become a Jesuit priest in the order of the Society of Jesus, I would've swept you up and never left Paris without you. You deserve a husband who will love you with his undivided heart, not a liar like me, and not an idiot like Francis Senft."

~

Dree borrowed a phone and called Sister Mariam so she could spend the night at the convent instead of the rectory. Just because she and Augustine—no, *Maxence*—had come to some sort of détente didn't mean that she wanted to be sleeping in close proximity to him before it became absolutely necessary.

At the convent, she and Sister Mariam sat on threadbare, goose-down cushions on living room couches in the convent and sipped cinnamon-scented milky tea.

Other sisters sat around them, chatting.

Sister Mariam asked, "Did he tell you more about the project?"

"I guess we will be spending most of our time in Jumla province, which he said is west of here?"

Sister Mariam's eyes widened, but her eyebrows went down. "Jumla province?"

Other sisters around them, all of them wearing soft gray saris, turned and looked at Mariam and Dree.

"Yeah, that's what he said. Is that a problem?"

Mariam addressed her sisters. "Andrea Catherine is a nurse practitioner. What can we give to her to take with them?"

With that, the nuns were up and moving. Several of them were dispatched to local hospitals and clinics to confer with other working sisters.

Dree was swept along in the crowd to several storage rooms in the back of the convent. After much discussion, several large cardboard boxes were stuffed full of medical supplies like sutures, courses of antibiotics, gauze and ointment, wound care supplies, a thermometer, stethoscope, ophthalmoscope, a sphygmomanometer for taking blood pressure, and vitamins, *so many vitamins,* single vitamins and multi-formulations, as powders, pills, tablets, and drops.

The other sisters returned, bearing more boxes. Some were taken to the kitchen to be refrigerated for the night.

Mother Superior Maria Devna told Dree, "Before you leave Sunday morning, you will wake us. We will pack the tetanus and other vaccines that have to be refrigerated. They should not freeze and should not get too warm, but you know this because you are a nurse."

Dree pulled Sister Mariam aside and asked, "Am I going to need all these things? Are there hospitals where we're going?"

Mariam shook her head sadly. "Jumla province is very poor. The cities are, of course, like cities everywhere, smaller versions of Kathmandu. There is an excellent training school for doctors and nurses near Chandannath, the Karnali Academy of Health Sciences. However, once you get out into the countryside, it is very bad. Some people do not see doctors for years, and many people die of things that they should not. You will take the supplies?"

"Of course, I will. I'm a nurse. I took an oath to treat people and save their lives."

Mariam patted Dree's hand. "It is much like the vows that we take. Indeed, a great number of nurses are also sisters because this desire to help someone is very close to God. I know you will be with Deacon

Father Maxence, but he may not be with you every moment of the day."

That was uncomfortably close to what Maxence had said. Dree suddenly had a little more trepidation about going out into the wilds of Nepal, even though she had grown up near the Mexican border in southwestern New Mexico.

Sister Mariam continued, "I can give you a veil to wear, so people will think you are a religious sister, and they will leave you alone. They will also respect you more. Do you have a cross?"

"Um, no. I'm sorry. It was stolen. I wasn't wearing it when I went to work on the last day when I was in the United States. None of us nurses wear jewelry. You never know when you're to be standing next to an MRI scanner and have your earrings ripped out of your ears. Anyway, everything I owned got stolen while I was at work."

Mariam frowned. "May I ask what happened?"

Dree swallowed hard, trying to clear her embarrassment out of her throat and her voice. "One day while I was working a fifteen-hour shift, my fiancé stole all my money and every single possession that I owned, and he sold everything for whatever he could get for it because he owed a lot of money to some criminals. When I got home, I had *nothing. Everything* was gone. After I fled the country and freaked out for a few days, I called the principal of the Catholic high school where I'd gone to school, and she hooked me up with people to get me here, where my ex or some other people who are looking for him won't be able to find me."

Sister Mariam's eyes had gone wide, showing

white all around her very dark brown irises. "I just wanted to get away from home and leave Kerala."

Dree laughed. "It's a stupid thing that happened to me. I still can't quite believe it."

Mariam shook herself and blinked a few times. "Nevertheless, we are very happy that you are here, and we honor and respect you for doing a mission for Catholic Charities. If you ever want to become a sister in our order, we would happily accept you. Wouldn't we, Mother Superior?"

Mother Superior Maria Devna nodded. "Although we would appreciate it if you would gossip less and not lead Sister Mariam into temptation."

Sister Mariam blinked, and Dree got the distinct impression that she was working very hard not to roll her eyes or glare at her mother superior. She said, "Come with me, Andrea Catherine. We will find a veil for you."

Before they could go, the mother superior asked Dree, "Did Father Maxence mention if he was saying Mass at Our Lady of Perpetual Help on Sunday?"

"He didn't mention Sunday, and I think we're leaving too early that morning," Dree told her. "But he said he would be assisting and preaching the homily there tomorrow morning, Saturday."

A shiver ran through the group of sisters, and they all glanced at one another.

Mother Superior Maria Devna said, "I will reserve the school bus for tomorrow morning."

Dree stuck her tongue between her molars to keep from cracking up. She certainly understood why they were all excited, though.

She'd been on her knees in front of Maxence, and it was spectacular.

After giggling with Sister Mariam half the night because she really did know all the gossip about every religious person in Kathmandu, Dree sat in a pew the next morning at Our Lady of Perpetual Help with the rest of the sisters, all of whom wore perfectly pleated dove gray saris and shining faces.

Thank goodness Dree had made her confession to Father Moses just a few days before, so she didn't have to ask Sister Mariam to find her a confessor because she'd been having relations first with her boyfriend Francis for months and then with the almost-priest-guy for four glorious days.

Oops. Impure thoughts. She didn't need any of those on her conscience, especially while she was actually sitting in church and could finally take communion again.

It felt good to be able to receive communion and have a clear conscience. Francis had always made fun of her for being upset and not wanting to go to church because she was too embarrassed to admit she'd slept with him and upset because they weren't going to stop, and then there was the whole birth control issue.

But she and Maxence had agreed not to indulge ever again, and so they wouldn't.

With an open and honest heart, she'd told Father Moses in Paris that she had no intention of sinning anymore.

Heck, at the time, she'd believed she was never going to see Augustine again.

And now the spectacularly gorgeous Augustine —*Maxence!*

Dang it, she had to remember that guy's name was *Maxence,* though she had told him to lie to her about his name.

She hadn't told him to lie about being a priest, however.

Anyway, the spectacularly handsome Maxence, with his full lips and dark eyes and black, softly curling hair, was standing in deacon's robes at the altar, assisting a priest at the Mass.

Yesterday, even though he'd been wearing a Roman-collared shirt, a part of Dree hadn't truly believed that Maxence was a deacon and planning to become a priest. His black suit had been fashionable and not altogether dissimilar to the clothes he'd been wearing in Paris. His shirt had been black, but he might have been a mafia hitman, which was more plausible than that energetic, enticing, tantalizing, intensely sexual man with a streak of kink wanting to be *a priest.*

He'd edged her for two days, denying her an orgasm.

He wanted to be edged and denied *forever.*

Now, that was pretty dang kinky.

Impure thoughts.

No impure thoughts in church.

Dree glanced at Sister Mariam sitting beside her in the pew, but Mariam didn't seem to have sensed Dree's immoral musings.

She made a concerted effort and controlled the tempestuous thoughts rising in her mind until the gospel reading, when Deacon Father Maxence ascended the pulpit on the left side of the sanctuary.

Every eye in the church turned toward him, including Dree's.

Morning sunlight streamed through the crazy-quilt stained glass windows, showering the sanctuary and the nave with trembling light.

Maxence was bathed in a sunlit glow that glistened on his dalmatic robe, purple for Advent, and was surrounded by gold glimmering in the air like angelic fire. He touched the page of the Bible in front of him and whispered a prayer before he began to read that day's prescribed Scripture reading.

His rich baritone voice filled the church, which had gone unusually silent without even the common crinkling, sighing, and fidgeting of so many people sitting on wooden pews. Even the ladies wearing rustling silk saris didn't move and barely breathed.

Dree listened to him read the passage, barely aware of the church around her or anything beyond the otherworldly radiance of the beautiful man standing before her, the music of his voice in her ears, and the taste of his words like honey in her mouth.

At the end of his reading, Maxence intoned, "The Gospel of the Lord."

The congregation roused, and everyone replied with voices as shaky as if they had fallen into the depths of their very souls, "Praise to you, Lord Jesus Christ."

Dree realized that she was clutching the back of the pew in front of her with her hands. Her knuckles were white and ached.

Every minute that Maxence had spoken, his

voice had found her and filled her mind and spirit as if he had only been speaking to her.

From the rapt expression on Sister Mariam's face, she had felt the same way.

And the rest of the sisters, too.

Dree twisted and looked around the church. Everyone seemed to be coming to terms with the experience they had just had, blinking and swallowing, while some had their eyes closed and head bowed as they pulled themselves together.

That was *not* hypnosis, that thing that Maxence had done. Dree's parents had taken her to a hypnotist when she was eight to get her to stop biting her fingernails. Hypnotism was a very specific, knife-like form of meditation where the hypnotist invaded Dree's thoughts and supplanted them with her commands. It hadn't worked. Dree finally stopped peeling her nails down to the quick with her teeth in high school.

No, what Maxence had done was not hypnotism.

He hadn't *done* something.

Maxence had *become* something.

His reading reminded Dree of a rock concert, one of the best ones, where even though you'd only been able to afford tickets up in the nosebleed sections and you were jammed in with thousands of other lost souls in the thin skim of smoke near the ceiling, the bass and drums pounded in your veins, and the music flowed through your body, and the lead singer's dark eyes bored into yours as he sang directly to you about love and loss and connection, and you screamed your adoration back at him with the multitudes.

When you remembered it afterward, it seemed like—

Air puffed through Dree's lips.

It seemed like a religious experience.

In that wooden church in Kathmandu, God or something divine had poured through Maxence. It wasn't a trick or technique, but something innate inside him had focused the light of heaven and allowed them to experience it, together and with him.

When he looked up, radiance shone in his face.

Dree's legs were shaking, and she lowered herself to sit on the pew without letting go of the one ahead of her.

Other people were doing the same thing.

It wasn't that Maxence *wanted* to become a priest.

She saw why he *had* to be a priest.

CHAPTER 3

MISSION TEAM

MAXENCE

The initial team meeting for the rural NICU micro-clinic project was held Saturday afternoon in the rectory's living room.

Deacon Father Maxence leaned on the fireplace and rested his elbow on the mantle.

Dree sat on the far end of the couch near the windows, which seemed to be as far away from him as she could get and still be in the room.

Maxence was aware of his effect on people when he read the Scripture section or the homily at Masses or even when he channeled his soul into what he was saying. He'd been able to do it to some extent all his life, though he hadn't understood what he was doing as a child. When you can convince your nanny that you should have candy, ice cream, or some other kid's toy anytime you wanted it, your parents ship you off to boarding school when you're five.

That was how he explained it to himself for years until he realized that they'd also shipped his older brother off to the same boarding school when he was the same age, and Pierre wasn't nearly as persuasive as Max.

Not that boarding school had stopped his eloquence or even slowed him down.

Dree huddled in her chair over by the windows, looking over the front garden. Winter afternoon sunlight showered her with golden light.

After they'd shaken hands when she'd arrived, she hadn't looked at him since.

At Mass this morning was the first time Dree had seen Maxence open his heart and his voice, except for that very quick, light moment at the charity ball at the Palace of Versailles in Paris.

And now she was sitting across the room from him, and she couldn't even look at him.

Maxence considered her to be smart from the moment she'd sobered up. This confirmed it. Being around Maxence was flying very close to a flame.

They should discuss this before it became a problem.

But just then, Max had a roomful of people and an orientation to run.

Rather than stand at the fireplace and lecture them the whole time, Maxence suggested they go around the room and introduce themselves.

The first person to talk was a tall, white guy who was at the end of the couch nearest Max. Alfonso's hair was dark blond, and when he looked up at Maxence, his eyes were a clear shade of green. He sat with his feet placed evenly on the floor together, his knees tight, and his back ramrod straight with his fingers laced in his lap.

Alfonso had always been *uptight.*

He said, carefully pronouncing the Spanish

words precisely, "I am Alfonso de Borbón y Grecia. Maxence and I met at Le Rosey boarding school when we were five years old, and he's been dragging me along on these charity missions ever since."

Alfonso sounded like he was making a joke, but his voice was a bit flat like he wasn't sure he could pull it off. He stole glances at Dree while he spoke like he wasn't paying attention to his own words.

Unease swirled in Maxence. He'd never considered Alfonso to be untrustworthy before, but the way he was looking at Dree seemed predatory.

Alfonso continued, "I have a master's degree in mechanical engineering from the Massachusetts Institute of Technology, and I live in my native Spain. I have been on several trips with Maxence with Catholic Charities over the past decade. We traveled together on charity trips on holiday breaks from school, too. I am pleased to be of service again. I have two nieces, Princesa de Asturias Leonor and Infanta Sofia."

Maxence rubbed his eyebrow and temple. Alfonso had managed to speak volumes about who he was without actually saying it, which always amused Max. Anyone who didn't know what they were listening to would probably wonder why parents would name one of their daughters something so long and unwieldy and give the other the first name of "Infanta," not realizing those parts weren't names at all.

When Max had the choice, he chose to say nothing at all about who he was.

As Dree had discovered to her chagrin, he mused.

It could have been worse.

There was more.

Alfonso continued to watch Dree out of the corner of his eye, and his hands tightened on his legs.

Yes, Dree could distract anyone who liked beautiful women, and Alfonso did. He was just grossly inept at talking to them, no matter how much Max and his other buddies tutored him in the fine arts of flirting and tried to play wingman for him.

The next guy across the room, Isaak, was another exceedingly tall man. He was leaning back in his chair, and his long legs stretched toward the middle of the room, at ease to the point of being too casual. His pale blond hair was rumpled, and his ice-blue eyes missed nothing.

Every time Dree so much as twitched, his glance found her.

Like he was hunting her.

Maxence repressed an inclination to stand between Isaak and Dree.

Isaak said in a deep voice with inflections of French and Russian, "I am another of Maxence's boarding school classmates, but my degree is in electrical engineering. I have a concentration in medical devices. I am from Nice, France, and I am Isaak Yahontov."

"Oh, like the vodka?" the Southeast Asian guy to his left asked. Yahontoff Vodka had dethroned Smirnoff's a decade before as the bestselling vodka in the world.

"Yes," Isaak said, fixing his icy blue gaze on the man who'd spoken. "Exactly like the vodka, except that we changed the spelling of our name when we moved the distillery to Nice after the Communists destroyed our buildings in Moscow."

The Communist Revolution and the entire history of the Soviet Union were still sore spots for Isaak's grandfather, who drank only White Russians because that's what he was.

In many other contexts, Isaak's grandfather would be considered a war criminal, which meant Isaak Yahontov was the grandson and heir of a war criminal.

Max didn't like the way Isaak was looking at Dree. Isaak's cold eyes looked like he might be a serial killer, even though Isaak had never so much as gotten into a fistfight in thirteen years of boarding school or indulged in anything more violent than light sarcasm.

And yet, Maxence felt as though he could not trust Isaak around Dree.

But Max had to run the meeting. "And Batsa?"

"I am Batsa Tamang," the Southeast Asian-looking guy said. His hair was cut corporate-short. "I am the translator, and I did not go to boarding school. Who would do that to their kids? I am thirty-two and speak Nepali, Hindi, Tamil, and English. I was raised in Kathmandu until I was ten, and then my parents moved us to Iowa City, Iowa. My bachelor's degree is in English Literature. I am a registered insurance agent for life, health, auto, boat, and farm. I have business cards if you would like to discuss your insurance needs. I have had my picture taken with George W. Bush, Barack Obama, John McCain, and Hillary Clinton when they were campaigning for the Iowa caucuses, like everyone else in the state. I have a wonderful wife whom I married in both a Catholic wedding with a full Mass and a three-day Hindu wedding, and so I am the most thoroughly married man in the world. My dear wife is the love and light of my life. I miss her so much right now. We have five children under eight years old. Three boys, two girls. I can also play the trumpet."

Dree grinned at Batsa, who smiled back at her and laid five business cards on the coffee table between the couches.

That guy was trouble. Max could sense it. He was practically shoving his phone number at Dree by offering his business cards so freely, probably to send her a dick pic. Any man with so much testosterone that he'd fathered five kids by the time he was thirty-two wasn't safe around a beautiful woman like Dree.

Max would have to watch him.

The last guy on the trip was sitting over on the other couch, his muscled arms crossed over his chest, watching the others. He wore a black Roman-collared shirt like Maxence that was only a few shades darker than his ebony skin, and one of his iron-gray eyebrows seemed perpetually raised. His accent was American and sardonic, and his voice was sonorous and deep. "My name is Father Booker Jackson, and I am a member of the order of the Society of Jesus, founded by Saint Ignatius of Loyola in 1534. I was born on the South Side of Chicago sixty-eight winters ago, and I speak with this deep, regal tone because I trained to be an opera singer before I found my true vocation as a Jesuit priest."

Such a voice might attract Dree. Father Booker was a good-looking man, with high cheekbones, a serious gaze, and silvery, shining hair. If he made a play for Dree, she might go for him. Maxence had never met Father Booker before, but a stated vocation and call to the priesthood didn't always make a man celibate.

Maxence knew that.

And just because Booker was the priest didn't mean he was a saint, and just because he was sixty-eight didn't mean he was dead.

Max would keep an eye on Father Booker as well.

Maxence looked up at Dree, sitting curled up in a chair by the window. "And Miss Andrea Catherine?"

Dree looked up at him, her blue eyes wary. "I'm Andrea Catherine Clark, but I go by Dree. I'm a nurse practitioner from the southwestern US. Nice to meet y'all."

Isaak perked up, and he glanced at Max, over to Dree, and back to Max. "Wait, the girl is going with us? We get to take a girl this time?"

Maxence growled, "Andrea Catherine Clark is a highly skilled medical professional, and she will be accompanying us—"

Alfonso suddenly seemed far more interested in the proceedings. "We've never taken a person of the female persuasion on any of these trips before."

Dree shriveled in her chair. "I don't want to cause trouble."

"No trouble at all," Batsa told her, seeming to pat the air with his hands.

Isaak heaved a sigh and said, "Thank God." He shot a guilty glance at Maxence. "I mean, thank the Lord our God and all that is holy, or whatever."

Alfonso was grinning at Dree. "It will be very nice to have you along for the trip."

Father Booker's expression softened. "A woman is always welcome on our missions. The price of a good woman is far beyond rubies, and I find that missions that include women are more efficient and the scope more wide-ranging than missions that only include men."

Maxence said, "If anyone has a problem with this, we can speak privately."

Isaak leaned toward where Dree was sitting as if he were trying to whisper something privately to her. "These charity trips tend to be sausage fests. These guys are all assholes."

Alfonso echoed the sentiment, "Assholes."

Isaak continued, "I'm delighted you're coming on the trip. Maybe these jerks won't act like hyenas."

Dree looked a little bit more hopeful, her blond eyebrows raised and a smile playing on her lips. "Is it really okay with all of you guys?"

The room filled with male laughter.

Maxence considered punching each one of the other guys in turn.

"Is it okay?" Isaak repeated. "It's more than okay! It's brilliant!"

Alfonso nodded enthusiastically.

Father Booker said, "I thank you for your dedication and your spirit."

Batsa said, "It is very nice to have a woman along. I am supposed to buy a sari and Nepali prayer flags for my wife, and I would very much like your input."

"I really don't know that much about saris or fashion or anything," Dree said.

Batsa continued, "When we are camping out, I will cook dahl and pakoras and anything else that you want. My mother taught me to cook very well because she thought I would never find a wife, because I had only an English literature degree. You will like my food."

Dree looked up at Maxence with wide eyes, like she needed rescue.

Maxence said, "Dree has kindly consented to fill in the role of a medical professional because our assigned person dropped out at the last minute. Everyone needs to behave professionally and with great restraint." He added with a growl from the depths of his black heart, "You assholes stay away from her."

The other guys all laughed again, and from their easy laughter, Maxence surmised they thought he was joking.

Yes, he probably needed to allow them to think that.

Maxence joined in the laughter, even though he did not feel any particular mirth at the situation of these four men eyeballing Dree Clark.

After a moment, Maxence had had enough of the men attempting *banter* with Dree, and he pulled out his tablet and said, "There are a few things we need to go over before we leave tomorrow morning."

Dree fished a pad of paper and a pen from her purse, clicked the ballpoint, and prepared to take notes. She looked up at him again with her gorgeous eyes, sparkling in the winter sunlight.

Maxence thought he would drown.

Instead, he sat down on the hearth in front of the fireplace and said, "The goal of this mission is to identify sites and best practices so we may build small neonatal intensive care units as micro-clinic units in the Jumla countryside. Essentially, there will be an incubator and some medical supplies. Over half of the premature babies in this area die before they can reach medical attention because the hospitals are so far away. Transportation is often unavailable, and the journey can take up to four days on foot. Small NICU's that are much closer would enable some of these infants to survive."

Alfonso also had out a computer tablet and was swiping with a stylus and thumbing notes into it. He announced, "In addition to being an engineer, I own a medical device company. I will be designing and my company will manufacture micro-NICU units for these miniature clinics. We will provide these units to the charity at substantially less than the cost to build them, though we are not able to donate them outright."

Maxence said, "I have rented a helicopter to ferry us to the Jumla district of Karnali province tomorrow morning at ten o'clock. We will arrive in Chandannath soon after. Taking a bus would have required at least a full day, perhaps two. Once we arrive, we will proceed to the rental depot, where the charity has reserved three jeeps for us. We also have camping supplies for when we evaluate smaller communities, though we intend to stay in inns or hostels whenever possible."

Maxence bit his lip for a moment. They had reserved six pup tents for sleeping, but many of the inns they'd planned to stay in had only two or three rooms, total.

Since these rural excursions had always been all-men, he'd assumed they could pair up and bunk together. With Dree along, she would need one room alone, and the five of them would need to share the other room or two.

At least some of the guys would probably end up sleeping in the tents more often than not. He would volunteer, of course, but he wasn't sure which of the other guys would have the stamina to rough it for so long.

Max continued from where he sat on the brick step in front of the cold fireplace. "It is quite likely that we will build several micro-NICU pilot projects with supplies that will be helicoptered in. We will be in the field at least six weeks, perhaps as long as two months."

Everyone was nodding, and the people who were taking notes scratched along as Max spoke.

Dree piped up and asked, "So, there really aren't medical personnel in the smaller communities?"

Maxence shook his head. "Some of these people won't have seen a doctor in years. In many of the small villages, no one owns a vehicle, not even a motorcycle. People live there the way they have for centuries, planting one crop per year of cold-tolerant rice, wheat, barley, or potatoes because the growing season is so short in the foothills of the Himalayas. Trucks come a few times a year to resupply a small store and buy excess crops."

Dree nodded and wrote quickly on her notepad. "I'm assuming no Wi-Fi or internet service."

Maxence nodded. "Maybe at some of the inns, but many of the towns do not have electricity or any infrastructure. When we go on these trips, sometimes I'm incommunicado for months."

Alfonso lowered his tablet. "That hasn't been the case on the trips that I've gone on with you."

"You've gone mostly to South and Central America," Maxence said. "Our missions there tend to be in the larger cities because local priests with a better knowledge of the area take the more rural missions. Nepal is mostly Hindu and some Buddhists. There are very few Catholic priests here. Therefore, when we want to do something in an area like this, we send groups like us who have no local knowledge, and then we hope for the best."

"This sounds like quite a mission you've dragged us on." Isaak grinned at Max and gestured to his cup of coffee on the low table. "You have anything stronger?"

Maxence shook his head. "Father Xavier doesn't keep alcohol at the rectory."

Isaak blew air through his lips in a raspberry and flipped his fingers at the ceiling. "First, you tell us no Wi-Fi, and then you tell us there's no booze? Did you really ask the heir to a vodka fortune to accompany you on a dry trip?"

Maxence tried not to roll his eyes, and maybe it worked. Maybe it didn't. "I said there wasn't any alcohol *in the rectory.* There are plenty of bars in Kathmandu, and I'm sure there will be liquor at the inns where we will stay."

Isaak smiled bigger. "Now you're speaking my language." His glance slid toward Dree, who was industriously taking notes on her paper tablet and didn't notice.

Anger surged through Maxence, and he stood.

Isaak looked up at him, cold humor in his blue eyes. "Something you wanted to say?"

Maxence returned to his seat, brushing imaginary dust off his black pants as he did. "Are there any questions about the schedule or the accommodations?"

Everyone shook their heads, but Alfonso seemed to be eyeing Dree as he did.

Maxence said, "We leave tomorrow morning. Make sure you're here at the rectory by six o'clock because Father Booker will offer Mass for us before we leave. I'll be spending the rest of the day bribing officials for the requisite permits. Alfonso, Isaak, you'll come with me."

axence sat in the Minister of Immigration's parlor and sipped the milky tea the man's wife had provided. "Yes, Minister, but this mission through the charity was not planned months in advance. Mr. Alfonso de Borbón y Grecia, here," Maxence indicated his longtime friend with a gentle hand gesture, "recently designed the innovative micro-NICU unit. It still needs some development, and Nepal is lucky that he and his company have decided to allow Nepal to participate in the development process."

The minister, who was a tiny, skinny man, slurped his tea and gave the cup back to his wife, who hovered around the group. "The permits should have been acquired months ago. Perhaps even a year."

"Mr. Borbón y Grecia had not even conceived of the micro-NICU unit several months ago. He only designed the most integral parts a few weeks ago, and Catholic Charities began looking for a site for the pilot project soon after."

The minister shook his head, squeezing his mouth together into a recalcitrant, unimpressed dot. "The Nepali government does not allow permits to be expedited."

Beside Max, Isaak leaned forward and placed his tea on the small table, clasping his hands between his knees and looking the small minister directly in his eyes. "It's imperative to place some of these micro-NICU's in a country where they are likely to be used, and it's a great opportunity for Nepal to have access to such innovative medical equipment. Surely, there is some *small fee* we could pay to make sure we have the necessary permits to go into Jumla territory."

The tiny minister bounded to his feet. His dusky skin turned an impressive shade of scarlet. "We do not do bribes here! If we did bribes here, hundreds of people would die on Mount Everest every year instead of the stupid few who do."

Maxence smiled at the minister, allowing his breath to flow smoothly. He summoned his sincerity and considered the importance of their mission, and he said, "These micro-NICUs are a beautiful way to save children's lives. It's vital that we construct some as soon as possible because children are being born prematurely across Nepal, and many of them can't get the medical help they need." The importance of it, the sheer gravity of what he was saying, filled his voice, and his soul expanded to fill the room. "We need your help. You can help the premature babies of Nepal. Will you help us obtain these permits so that we can leave tomorrow morning?"

Isaak was watching Max warily, but Alfonso was watching the minister's reaction.

Fifteen minutes later, the three men left the minister's house with a handful of signed and stamped permits.

CHAPTER 4
JUMLA
DREE

The helicopter blades pounded against the air.

Gravity forced Dree farther down into the seat's cushion as the vehicle lifted away from the Earth. Hearing-protective headphones were clamped on the sides of her head.

A four-point seatbelt cinched around Dree's waist and over her shoulders like a backpack, buckling where the four straps met over her pelvis. Her hands clenched into fists around the two woven straps by her shoulders.

She'd managed to finagle a center seat on one of the two couches of three seats each that were facing each other and attached to the walls of the helicopter's fuselage.

Flying was still scary for her after twenty-five years of never having done it until she'd endured two international plane flights in the last week, and this was her first helicopter ride. She wasn't planning on grabbing anyone around the neck and screaming, but she wanted two big male bodies on either side of her so she would feel safer. Also, from the center seat, someone large was between her and the windshield in front and the porthole windows in the back, so she would feel less like she was going to topple out of the oversized mechanical dragonfly.

The chopper climbed in altitude and sped away from the airport, banking to the left. She shifted forward in her seat. Her body hung in the harness.

Dree did not loosen her grip on the straps, though her knuckles ached.

She wasn't going to scream. She *was not* going to scream.

She ground her molars together, not screaming.

Alfonso, the Spanish engineer with dark blond hair and eyes of the clearest green Dree had ever seen, sat on one side of her and had turned his head away to look through the cockpit and out of the front windshield.

On her other side, Maxence was reading something on his phone and whispering to himself.

Max's thigh pressed against the outside of hers. He was trying not to man-spread, but three rather large men occupied the seats facing them. Max's long legs just didn't have anywhere to go.

Batsa, Father Booker, and Isaak sat in the seats across from them, and all of them had rather long legs, too. There had been some careful, unspoken negotiations about whose leg could go where without touching each other too much, which Dree had found hilarious until the helicopter had lifted off and all her attention had been diverted to not screaming.

Father Booker had his hands folded in his lap and his eyes closed, leaning his head back against the seat, either resting or praying to keep the helicopter up in the sky.

Everyone wore hearing-protective headphones over their ears, but the roar of the engine and the rotors beating the air were still deafening in Dree's ears.

Both Alfonso and Isaak casually looked out of the windows and kept glancing at her.

Isaak winked at her.

Dree hadn't planned on picking a bed partner while they were on this little charity mission. She hoped they realized that.

The helicopter climbed in altitude, which meant that the seats that Dree and Max were sitting in felt like they tipped sideways and toward the helicopter's tail.

Gravity forced Dree to lean against Maxence's shoulder just a little bit even though she was hanging onto her straps for dear life.

Maxence closed his eyes and continued whispering. She couldn't hear what he was saying over the whine of the laboring engine and flapping of the rotors. Warmth from his muscular body seeped through their clothes, and gentle heat radiated over Dree's thigh. His shoulder was higher than hers by several inches. Her arm was pressed against his triceps, again separated only by a few paltry layers of cloth.

Even though the interior of the helicopter had a particular smell—sweat from many previous passengers and dirty motor oil—Dree was sitting so close to Maxence that his subtle aftershave wafted toward her nose. It wasn't the same cologne he had been wearing in Paris, which was a bit more like the grass growing on white cliffs over the ocean. Now, with just a turn of her head, she could smell darker musk and the far-away thoughts of a cinnamon and vanilla sweet in a Hindu temple filled with sandalwood and incense.

This was the closest she had been to him since he had left the bed in Paris without waking her up.

Really, the last time she had been this close to him, she'd been sleeping in his arms, naked.

The sun was still quite near the eastern horizon, but light flooded the helicopter whenever they turned. Even though they had met at the rectory at six o'clock, the helicopter hadn't taken off until after eight. The winter sun had been up for over an hour, and while it was quite cool, Dree had removed her heavy coat before they had boarded the helicopter because she'd been overheated.

Every time the helicopter tilted, either she rolled against Maxence, or despite him bracing his legs against the floor and holding onto the arm of the seat, his muscular body pressed hers.

Alfonso was sitting on her other side. She kept bumping him, grinning sheepishly, and resumed trying not to slide out of the harness and die.

With every shift of the helicopter, every bump of turbulence, her body became more attuned to Maxence sitting right beside her. Every time she thought she had controlled her mind, his scent like cinnamon incense would fill her nostrils. When she tried to settle her body so that she wouldn't react to him, the helicopter would roll, and then she found herself draped over Maxence, no matter how she tried not to move, or else his shoulder and chest would lean against her.

The pressure of his body on hers brought back memories of their skin sliding together in Paris, the chiseled crevasses of his skin and muscle as he moved, and his effortless grace and satiny skin.

Her body warmed, anticipating his touch.

The fabric of her clothes felt rough against her skin over her chest, back, and between her legs as her flesh grew more sensitive.

Maxence didn't look at her except for the occasional glance and apologetic smile when they jostled. After about fifteen minutes, he tapped a few times on his phone and settled back to read.

Dree wished she had loaded a book onto her phone, but she didn't know when she'd be able to charge it again. The outlets in the convent had different prongs than the hotel had in Paris, three thick prongs instead of two round ones. At the convent, she'd borrowed a converter from a sister who had one of every type of converter in a box. As soon as Dree had plugged it in, the electricity went out for two hours, and the phone had only gotten about fifty percent charged before she'd had to leave. She'd just turned it off.

Dree looked out the front windshield. Foothills crumpled the fabric of the land ahead of them, but the flight seemed to be skirting the larger mountains.

Turbulence rattled the helicopter. Dree gripped her straps and squeezed her eyes shut.

Warmth and a hard male body flopped across her, but from the wrong side.

When she opened her eyes, Alfonso was half-turned in his harness, and his arm crossed her body, grabbing onto her seat. His far leg pointed toward the cockpit, and his green eyes expanded with surprise. He mouthed, *So sorry*, but Dree couldn't hear anything over the helicopter noise and her protective earmuffs.

His foot must have slipped from where he'd been bracing himself, and he'd fallen over her. She mouthed back, *That's okay*, and gave him a thumbs up.

Alfonso smiled a happy smile at her like she had made his day for not taking offense.

He was really good-looking when he smiled like that.

Like, *really* good-looking. Impressively so. His teeth were white and perfectly even, and he had a shy smile. His cheekbones and jaw on his oval face weren't as pronounced as Max's or even Isaak's, but he looked more refined, more European, maybe.

Dree had noticed earlier that both of Max's school buddies were uncommonly handsome, but this was, of course, a mission with the charity. Hooking up was not on the agenda. She should not be calibrating the relative hotness of her fellow charity workers.

Alfonso tilted his head a little like he might be about to say something, not that she was going to be able to hear even a lick of what he said, but he glanced above her head.

His smile faded, and he sat back in his seat.

When Dree turned back to facing forward, Maxence was turning to look back at his phone.

Had he just—

No, surely Alfonso had just realized that speaking would be futile and decided to wait until they got down on the ground.

The helicopter ride lasted a little over two hours.

By the end of it, Dree was desperate for the cooler air of the mountains in the Jumla district. The heat from Maxence's body continually washed over her, and her skin was so used to seeking his that she had to keep her hands clenched around her harness's straps to keep herself from accidentally reaching for him every time a bump in the atmosphere made her panic.

Finally, as the helicopter crested a low mountain range and turbulence jostled the seat under her tush, a long runway cut through a ragged grid of crop fields in a lush valley. As they neared, houses dotted the fields and sprung up around the small airport like a ring of mushrooms, many capped with vibrant blue roofs.

The helicopter settled onto a helicopter pad at what appeared to be a tiny but functional airport, and the whine of the engine descended as the blades slowed.

Dree jabbed the buckle of her seatbelt to release it and lunged toward the door, dancing over Batsa, who hadn't moved fast enough.

When she glanced back, Maxence had also gotten out of his harness and was braced against the back of the helicopter. Fire filled his eyes, and his set jaw looked like he might be grinding his teeth.

He must hate flying, too.

Dree fled from the helicopter and pretended the reason she'd run was to oversee their backpacks and supplies being unloaded from the rear compartment.

The guys stumbled off the helicopter after her, blinking in the late morning sunlight and establishing their bearings.

Isaak leaned over and braced his hands on his

knees, panting. Father Booker absently patted him on his back while he examined rows of mountains in all directions sawing the sky beyond the buildings of the town.

The town and small airport lay in a broad valley within the foothills of the Himalayas, which seemed far taller than the tail end of the Rocky Mountains that surrounded the Salt River Valley of the greater Phoenix Metro area.

Chilly air seeped through Dree's clothes, and she grabbed her jacket to pull on over her shoulders. It wasn't cold enough to zip it up, just *brisk*.

Maybe she was already acclimating to the cooler temperatures.

Batsa and Maxence talked for a few minutes, pointing at the mountain ranges surrounding the town.

The two ridiculously tall blond guys sized up their surroundings with casual glances but didn't say anything. Isaak seemed to have recovered, though he was still inhaling deeply through his nose.

The small Jumla airport had a short runway and helicopter landing pads next to a low concrete building. A few people wearing light blue coveralls scurried between the helicopters and a small plane that stood beside the terminal. A diagonal staircase led from the plane's exit to the ground, and a dozen people disembarked from the plane and walked into the airport. The women's saris and scarves waived like vibrant flags in the wind funneled through the mountains and scraping across the valley.

Batsa grabbed one backpack and whipped it around, settling it on his shoulders, and he trotted toward the terminal.

Maxence gestured to the other guys. They began to hoist the backpacks on, sling the duffel bags onto their shoulders, and balance the boxes on top of each other to carry them in.

Dree started to grab the backpack she knew was hers, but Isaak already had one hand on it. "That's okay, Andrea Catherine. I've got it."

Maxence whipped her backpack out of Isaak's hand. "I'll take it."

Okay, that was weird. Dree started to lift a box of the medical supplies the sisters had packed for her to take.

Alfonso lifted the cardboard box out of her hands. "I'll take that for you."

Okay, she got what was going on. "Guys, I can carry things."

Just as Dree was seriously going to fight for her equal rights to carry heavy luggage into the airport, Batsa zoomed back over the rough asphalt, pushing a luggage cart, and they piled all the supplies and most of the backpacks onto it.

Okay, she would let the guys push the cart.

Batsa said something to Maxence, who raised his arms from his sides and yelled over the taxiing airplane's engine and the whine of another helicopter landing at the far helipad, "We have to get off the tarmac. More helicopters are coming in."

They all double-timed it toward the terminal.

Dree caught Maxence watching her as if he might have to carry her if she couldn't keep up.

Dree kept up.

As a matter of fact, Dree beat them all to the terminal and held the doors open for the boys to push the cart inside.

Once in the doors, Maxence turned to Batsa and said, "Seriously? There's a problem?"

Batsa told him, "I don't know if the driver is correct, but he said there are no more jeeps this week. He said other people asked for the jeeps. They were all rented to other people since Friday."

"Then what was the point of a reservation?"

Batsa shrugged. "Sometimes, things like this happen."

"What do they have? Do they have pickup trucks or a small van with good suspension? Or a mini-bus?"

"We have to go talk to the men at the rental lot, but he said that they are all out of vehicles. He said that many people have come home to Jumla this year for Divali and stayed very long because Divali was late this year. Many of the people who work in Kathmandu are still here after the Divali holiday."

Maxence glanced at Dree, and his expression was worried. He said to Batsa, "We've got everybody here. This mission has to happen."

"The driver is here with a truck to take us and our supplies to the rental lot so we can look over what they have left."

Maxence waved the rest of them over and told the two blond guys and Father Booker what Dree had overheard. He shrugged and said, "Sometimes, unfortunate things happen on charity missions. We have to figure out how to do it anyway."

The guys fell over each other to get in the bed of the pick-up and insisted Dree ride in the cab. Maxence climbed in right after her, and she thought she saw him scowl at the four other guys.

The ride over to the rental lot was twenty bumpy minutes.

Maxence laid his arm on the back of the bench seat of the pickup truck during the ride, so Dree was essentially snuggled under Max's arm. She held onto the seat beside her thighs as they bumped over the rutted road. Maxence had a firm grip on the door handle with his other hand, probably so he wouldn't flop on top of her as the truck bounced over the road.

That cinnamon and smoke new aftershave of his was the sexiest thing she'd ever smelled, like it was both something she wanted to eat and to take to bed. Dree refrained from grabbing his face and biting his neck only because her fingernails were digging into the fabric of the truck seat.

The truck lumbered down the rutted road for what seemed like hours but was probably closer to twenty minutes, and then it pulled into a dusty lot surrounded by a chain-link fence topped with a coil of barbed wire. The shack standing in one corner had an open window in front like the clapboard booth out in the desert where Dree and her cousins used to rent ATVs by the hour for boonie bouncing.

Maxence stepped out of the truck, and he turned and held out his hand as she prepared to climb out.

Dree hesitated.

She'd almost instinctively reached out and grabbed his fingers to steady herself as she climbed out of the rickety pickup truck, but she had not touched him, like their skin actually touching each other, since the last time they had screwed in Paris. When he'd held out his hand when she'd arrived at the rectory, she'd barely slid her palm over his and shaken him off.

He was turned away from her, surveying the empty parking lot and their driver talking to somebody over at the shack. He twitched his fingers impatiently and then looked back at her. One brow lowered as if he were confused about why she hadn't grabbed his hand and climbed out of the truck.

Because if she grabbed his hand, she might leap into his arms.

Neither of them wanted that.

Right?

Maxence frowned a bit more and didn't drop his hand. "Come on."

Dree reached. Her fingers trembled as they neared his palm, and then their hands clasped.

The skin-to-skin contact was like silk sliding against itself and sparking an electrostatic current that almost made her let go. Her arm twitched, and her nervous system lit up with wanting more of him.

Maxence didn't seem to feel it. He raised their joined hands to steady her as she stretched her toes toward the gravel and dust of the parking lot, her foot dangling in the air as she reached. He glanced back over at the shack, still holding her hand and steadying her. She jumped the last foot and landed on the dirt, wobbling a little, but she was fine.

Okay, she was down.

He hadn't let go of her hand yet.

If anything, his fingers firmed around hers.

Batsa climbed carefully over the tailgate of the pickup truck, steadying himself by standing on the bumper while holding onto the back.

Isaak and Alfonso vaulted over the sides and landed on the ground.

Father Booker unlatched the tailgate and let it crash down, then gingerly extended his legs over the side and lowered himself to the dirt.

Batsa walked over to where the two Nepali guys were talking, and then the three of them pointed to the mountains. Their argument became louder. Amid the hand-waving, Batsa saw them standing by the truck and waved them over.

Maxence was still holding Dree's hand.

The contact of his flesh on hers drew all her attention to her palm, her fingers, and the way that his thumb rubbed across the top of her knuckles just once.

Batsa yelled, "Hey! You guys! Come over here and talk. We have a real problem."

Maxence grumbled, "Yeah, there's a problem. There aren't any jeeps here. There were supposed to be three jeeps."

He loosened his grip on her fingers.

Dree tried to do the same, peeling her fingers back to open her hand.

Maxence's fingers slipped away.

She balled her hand into a fist to hold onto the warmth of his skin for just a minute longer, but the chilly breeze stole it away.

The five of them walked over to where Batsa was arguing with the two rental shop guys. The wind picked up, blowing their hair around.

As they approached, Batsa called, "They don't have any trucks or any vehicles at all."

Father Booker muttered, "Obviously."

Batsa said, "The only vehicles they have are

motorcycles. They have six Royal Enfield bikes, which have enough horsepower to get us up the mountains where we want to go. They have helmets for a small additional fee."

Maybe it was just because when the tourists were running around New Mexico in the winter and prices for everything ostensibly doubled just for them, but she was skeptical about the "small additional fee" for the necessary item.

Maxence gathered Batsa back into the group and lowered his voice. "How many of you can ride motorcycles, and by that, I mean that you've ridden them often and know how to."

Five men looked at Dree.

Oh, no. She was not going to be the lame one, here. "I grew up on a sheep farm in New Mexico. Horses went out in the early eighties. Everyone, including me, herded stock to new pastures by riding an ATV or a dirt bike. We also drove dirt bikes out on the sand dunes for fun. I can ride a dang motorcycle."

With this, the men lifted their heads and regarded each other.

Father Booker intoned, "I have performed missions in South America, Asia, and Africa where motorcycles are the most logical conveyance. I have been proficient for decades."

Batsa shrugged. "My family went to India every summer when I was growing up. I can ride a scooter in Delhi or Kolkata traffic with the best of them. Surely, I can handle a larger bike."

Isaak said, "My family makes vodka. I can drive anything from a race car to a motorcycle and everything in between."

Dree did not see how that correlated, but no one else challenged it, so okay.

Alfonso said, "I own five."

His statement seemed a little more logical than Isaak's, so Dree did not quibble.

Maxence shrugged and said, "I can ride a motorcycle, of course."

No reason given.

All right, but Dree wasn't going to quibble about that one, either.

Maxence continued, "So if we want this mission to proceed, we will be riding motorcycles. We'll have to divvy up some of the supplies into the saddlebags, but we'll probably be wearing backpacks while we ride. Is everyone okay with that?"

All the men guffawed and assured him they were more than fine with that.

That was not the proper way to phrase a question where the answer might have people's lives riding on it. Dree had learned medical questioning techniques in nursing school.

Dree spoke up. "So, it looks like we're going to be wearing unwieldy backpacks while we're riding these motorcycles. I saw a lot of unpaved roads barely cut into the sides of mountains while we were landing. It's going to be mountains on one side of the road, sheer cliffs on the other. Does anyone feel uncomfortable with the thought of riding a motorcycle while wearing an unwieldy backpack over roads that might be rutted, or maneuvering around large obstacles like fallen rocks?"

Father Booker folded his hands in front of himself as if in contemplation, and then he made purposeful eye contact with Dree. "I am more than proficient at riding a motorcycle, and I believe that my expertise is valuable on this mission. However, if it comes to a point where I feel that I am unsafe or endangering others, I will return to Jumla and then Kathmandu. I assume everyone will do the same?"

Dree liked Father Booker. He was sane.

And so, under the wan winter sunlight, the six team members unpacked the medical supplies from the cardboard boxes and stuffed them into the saddlebags that some of the motorcycles had, and then they found room for the rest of the supplies in the extra pockets of the backpacks.

Dree asked Maxence, "You said something about tents?"

His breath puffed out, and he scowled. "Dammit. Batsa! Do they have the damn tents?"

They did indeed have tents, but they only had three.

Dree could tell from looking at the tiny little sticks and scanty amount of fabric that they would only sleep two people each.

And even then, those big guys had better be pretty good friends.

She told Maxence this, muttering under her breath so the other guys wouldn't hear.

Maxence nodded and whispered back, "We're staying in an inn tonight. We'll figure out how to do this later. I can sleep in a tent with Isaak and Alfonso. We went to boarding school together. We have no secrets."

Dree mounted her motorcycle and figured out how to turn it on, making sure she engaged both the clutch and front brake with the levers on the handlebars to ensure the bike didn't go anywhere in case it wasn't in neutral. The other guys also managed to start their bikes without running themselves over, which Dree took as a hopeful sign.

Batsa asked for directions to the inn where they had planned to stay that first night before setting out into the wilderness of Jumla, and he turned out to have an excellent memory and eye for directions as they rode to the inn. Plus, he could read the signs in the Nepali language.

Father Booker and Batsa were steady on their bikes.

Maxence and Alfonso seemed more than adequate.

Isaak wobbled a lot, but he knew what the handles did.

The inn that Batsa guided them to looked like pictures that Dree had seen of houses in New Orleans with porches on the first and second floors. The roof was painted the same lapis lazuli color as many of the other roofs that they had seen from the helicopter, and the plaster was white with emerald patches of moss. A small shrine to an elephant-looking idol out front had prayer flags hanging from cords that formed a little tent around it.

Batsa went inside as the advance guard and talked to the people who ran the inn. When he emerged, he said, "The good news is that the rooms are free as long as we promise to buy supper at the inn because it's the off-season. They're thrilled to see any guests."

Isaak asked skeptically, "I thought tourists rented all the cars?"

Batsa laughed. "There aren't any tourists, just people who are here for the holidays. Everyone stays with their families and sleeps on the floor when they come home for holidays. They flew or rode a bus to get here."

As Dree was a girl who had grown up in what was gently called reduced circumstances, though reduced from what she never figured out, Dree doubted this. She speculated that there were never any jeeps at all, or that the jeeps went somewhere else for some other reason.

Maxence asked Batsa, "If that's the good news, what's the bad news?"

Batsa sighed, and his sour expression looked like he didn't want to say what he had to. "They only have three rooms."

Alfonso chuffed a laugh. "Considering it's almost Christmas, I suppose we should be grateful there are any rooms at the inn."

Father Booker looked at his feet. "I guess we know who Mary is, but which of us is Joseph, and which are the three wise men?"

Isaak glared at the two-story building and said to Batsa, "I thought you said there were no tourists."

"They only have three rooms for rent in the entire inn. That's it. Jumla isn't a tourist area, especially in the winter. If we want to try to find some other hostel, we could. It would probably mean splitting up because I don't think we're going to find anything bigger."

Dree volunteered, "I can sleep in one of the tents in the yard."

Maxence shot her a disapproving look. "If anybody is sleeping in the yard, it's one of us. In the meantime, Dree, you can have one room. The five of us will split the other two rooms. All missions have some unexpected setbacks. We will figure out how to do this."

Dree saw why it was easier to have only one gender along on these missions. Trying to figure out how she could maintain her modesty, as those five guys probably thought about it, was cumbersome.

An even split of men and women would have worked better than one girl and five guys. She should note that to Augustine at some point.

Maxence, not Augustine.

Still weird.

CHAPTER 5

A DEMON IN HER EAR

MAXENCE

That night, Maxence Grimaldi slept on the cold floor of the hostel room with a folded blanket as a pillow. He wished he'd laid out one of the sleeping bags piled in the corner, but he was too tired and fading in and out of twilight sleep to get up and grab one after he'd lain down.

Isaak and Alfonso hadn't snored when they were all in boarding school together as teenagers, but now they did.

A lot.

Seriously, he worried about their adenoids.

It didn't help that right after they had turned out the lights to go to sleep, Alfonso had quipped, "If you're uncomfortable on the floor, Max, I volunteer to go bunk with Nurse Andrea Catherine."

"You're pronouncing it wrong," Max had told him from the floor between the two beds. "It's *ANN-Dree-uh*, not *Ahn-DRAY-ah.*"

"How did she get on this mission, anyway?"

Max gritted his teeth. "She's a nurse practitioner. Our peds doctor backed out, and she volunteered."

"But, how did she come to volunteer? Did you know her from your previous drunken debauchery before you took Holy Orders?"

Not from before, no. "Her Catholic high school principal knows Father Thomas Aquinas of Immaculate Conception Church in Arizona."

"Oh, Catholic Charities mafia."

The wooden floor rubbed a sore spot on Maxence's tailbone, and he shifted over to his side, pulling the two thin blankets with him. His butt became cold. "Yes. Quite."

Alfonso said, his voice rising wistfully, "She is very beautiful."

Max growled, "This is a Catholic Charities trip, not a hook-up cruise." He coughed so that it sounded like he had something in his throat.

Isaak said in the dark, "I didn't take a vow of celibacy, and neither has she."

Max breathed slowly, feigning sleep.

Alfonso and Isaak hadn't taken vows of celibacy, and neither had Dree.

Max reminded himself that, while he may be there to keep Dree safe, he was not there to be her chaperone, and he was not her father.

But if either one of those two assholes laid a finger on her, Max was going to kill him.

They would be out in the wilds of Nepal.

No one would find a shallow grave covered with rocks.

That was rather further down that line of thought than he had meant to go. He wasn't going to kill anyone and bury them in a shallow grave.

No one in Max's family had done that for at least a few generations. His ancestors definitely had, but those were different times. His father probably hadn't. Neither had his uncle, most likely.

Maxence's older brother Pierre, however, was probably a tossup.

And then there was his cousin, Alexandre, but Alex hadn't *buried* anyone in a shallow grave.

That Max knew of.

But if Alex had killed someone and successfully buried them in a shallow grave and no one found them, Maxence wouldn't know about it.

Alexandre was probably an outlier.

Max's thoughts flopped and scurried around for six hours until daybreak. He blamed his utter lack of sleep on the floor and the blanket for a pillow, not on his mind grinding over what those two bastards had dared to say.

The next morning, Maxence dragged himself downstairs to the small lobby of the inn, exceedingly ill-prepared for a four-hour motorcycle ride on a dirt road with a slightly off-centered backpack.

Overnight, snow had dusted the town and mountains, covering everything with white. Their boots crunched the crisp layer like they were walking on a giant, delicate eggshell laid over the earth.

The farmland beyond the town was a monochromatic landscape of white canvas sliced by the black-ink pen strokes of stone walls delineating the fields. The mountains around the valley grew more imposing when covered with ice because only the largest, most dangerous boulders jabbed through the snow.

They didn't leave too early in the morning

because they wanted to give the sun a chance to warm the air, and the delay of an hour spent idling over sweet, milky chai made the four-hour ride more tolerable.

As they were loading up and getting on the motorcycles, Maxence glanced over Dree's winter gear she'd brought from Paris. She appeared to be wearing ski clothes, like a bib and a jacket, all filled with thick down and seeming to be water-resistant, and her boots came up well over her ankles.

It was red and white, practically a diamond checkerboard like his tattoo on his forearm, and Max wondered if Father Moses had done that on purpose.

Good, he'd been worried about her.

When he'd summoned the private plane, he'd had his winter gear packed and loaded, and thus he'd retrieved it when they got to Nepal. Maxence was well kitted out in black leather winter motorcycle gear and boots, as were the rest of the guys because they'd had time to plan and pack for this contingency, too.

Batsa consulted the innkeepers about the best route to the first village they planned to visit, a tiny settlement in the hills that was not too far away. He seemed confident as he led the caravan of six motorcycles out of town.

They sped under a square arch that had been painted red. The city's name was painted on the top in white, and Hindu religious symbols were inscribed down the sides. Once out of town, they opened the throttles and sped out into the countryside.

Maxence herded Dree's motorcycle to take the second position behind Batsa, where he could keep an eye on her. She rode the bike very well, leaning into the turns and keeping up with Batsa easily.

After about an hour, the paved street ended, and the rest of the way was a gravelly dirt road clinging to the sides of the mountains. The noise of their motorcycle engines thundered on the sheer rock walls to their left and blasted into the empty air over the straight drop down to rivers winding between the mountains on their right.

In the warm seasons, these steep valleys would be lush.

In the winter just before Christmas, however, the dead scrub revealed the rock walls and fallen stones of the landscape.

With the motorcycle growling between his legs and the wind rushing over the padded leather he wore, Maxence fell into a rhythm of watching Dree and Batsa ahead of him. He drove slowly to steer around fallen boulders that had clattered down the mountain and hadn't quite made it across the road to plummet down the cliff on the other side.

When they met oncoming trucks or buses, Maxence took Batsa's lead and stuck to the side of the road next to the mountainside as they maneuvered around each other. The trucks ate up the majority of the narrow road. A driver could easily force a motorcycle off the road and down the cliff by accident.

The buses and trucks were jubilantly decorated with bright paint and fabric flags, reminding Max of Hindu and Buddhist temple elephants painted with red and yellow turmeric and saddled with ornate gold-fringed blankets. Many of the trucks that supplied the tiny grocery stores of the mountain villages had fringe hanging around the ceiling of the cabs, with icons of Ganesh, Shiva, and Ram in a tiny shrine on the dashboard. Slogans, many of them in English, were painted in white on the red trucks, such as *Enjoy Today like It Is Your Last,* or *Make Today Count,* or *Bud Light.*

After two hours of death-defying riding, they stopped to stretch their legs. Dree wrenched off her helmet and shook out her blond hair. Her cheeks were rosy but not cold-chapped, and her eyes were bright with glee. "This is awesome!"

Maxence couldn't help but laugh with her. "It's quite an experience."

"When will we get there?"

"A few more hours."

"Is there an inn there?"

"We'll scout the village first, but this will probably be our first day of camping. In another day or two, we'll reach some larger towns that may have an inn. This area isn't a tourist destination like the Annapurna circuit. That's a very long hiking trail that can take weeks, but every hour or so, there's a little town with tea shops and restaurants, and there are lots of inns and hostels along that road. The Jumla district isn't like that, so we're going to have to take what we can get."

Their group of six motored to their destination, which was a small clutch of thirty houses or so and a population of about a hundred and fifty souls.

When people heard the roar of their engines and the sputtering of their tires on the gravel, they came out to look at what had arrived in their town.

Batsa talked to them, obviously explaining that they were on a charity mission by the English words sprinkled into his quick speech to the people who came out.

One young man had a lumpy bandage held in place with rags wound around his forehead. Blood ran into his eye, and he wiped it away impatiently.

Dree stepped forward, removing her helmet and pulling gray fabric out of her pocket that she whipped over her head. The cloth was a veil like the Little Sisters of Charity in Kathmandu wore, and she tucked her hair behind it. "Let me take a look at that."

Batsa translated for her and must've continued to explain that she was a nurse or other medical professional, because he talked for about three minutes before the guy allowed Dree to gingerly unwind the makeshift bandage and look at the wound beneath.

When she got down to his skin, Maxence heard her gasp. "You've been walking around like this?"

Batsa translated what she'd said, but Dree was already yanking medical supplies from the saddlebags on her motorcycle.

Maxence leaned down beside her. "Anything I can do to help?"

She drew a deep breath through her nose, and her eyes fluttered closed for a minute, but she said, "I'm not a doctor, but I know how to suture a wound. It's not going to be pretty. This guy should've had professional medical attention days ago. I can see a lot of his skull."

Maxence said, "If he could have gotten to a doctor, I'm sure he would have. I see horses and yaks here, but I don't see any modern vehicles."

Dree shook her head. "Even in the poorest parts of New Mexico, at least some people have trucks. If you don't have a vehicle, at least your neighbor can drive you into town for medical emergencies like this one. He should see a plastic surgeon, not a nurse practitioner."

"He can't. Can you treat him competently, if not at the level of a plastic surgeon?"

"I can pull those muscles and skin together and sew a few stitches into him. I'm worried about him being able to chew. All those big muscles up the sides of your head are there to move your jaw."

"If we hadn't come along, he wouldn't have even that."

"So, he would have been like that until spring when they could get to town?"

Max paused for a moment. "No, he would've been like that until he got an infection, and then he would've died."

"Okay," she said, staring at her neatly packed gauze and other supplies. "At least I can suture him up so that won't happen."

"You're giving him a second chance at life."

"Don't they have doctors who ride a circuit and come out to see these communities?"

"Some areas do, and sometimes they come in the spring through the fall."

She swallowed hard. "Oh."

"Just one more question. Is there a reason you're wearing the veil of the Little Sisters of Charity?"

"Sister Mariam said that people would respect a woman who had taken religious vows more and told me to wear it."

"And, did you take vows?"

She blinked for a moment, and then the question in her blue eyes turned into anger. Her voice had a cold, steel edge when she said, "No, Deacon Father Maxence. *I'm* not the one who took religious vows."

"I apologize for that, and for everything. Let's go back to how I can help you."

Dree shook her head. "Let's find a place out of the wind where I can lay out my instruments. You can hold his head still while I give him a shot of local anesthetic, and then I'll suture him up."

They commandeered one of the larger houses to use as a makeshift clinic. Dree set out her supplies on a wooden table that had been scoured perfectly clean before they'd arrived. With Maxence standing behind the man's chair and holding him still, Dree numbed the area, disinfected the wound, sewed him up, and then dressed the wound properly.

She turned to the man's wife, who was hovering while Dree treated him. She handed over some supplies and began to explain to Batsa what to tell the woman.

Maxence leaned down and whispered, "Give his wife what he needs, but not any extra. We need to conserve supplies because we're going to be out here for a while. There're going to be a lot more people who need your help."

Dree's jaw set, but she nodded and continued detailing wound care instructions to Batsa.

As soon as Dree was done treating the man's head wound, a woman carried a little girl up to Dree and said something in Nepali.

Batsa translated, "My girl has a demon in her ear."

Dree examined the child and told Max, "She has an abscess inside her auditory canal. Can you hold her? I can numb the area as much as I can, but this little girl *needs* treatment. Batsa, I'm going to need you to translate to the mom how to give her a course of antibiotics."

Dree continued to treat people young and old, working efficiently and continuously to help them, moving from one to the next *to the next* without so much as a breath.

Maxence sent Isaak and Alfonso out to the edge of town under the guidance of Father Booker to set up their camp for the night. He heard Alfonso chattering about what he was going to cook out of the supplies they had brought with them in the backpacks.

After a few hours, Dree's hands and speech were slowing. She strained to lift kids onto the kitchen table that served as an examination table.

Maxence pulled Batsa aside. "Can we get her something to eat?"

Batsa fluttered around and arranged for a late lunch for Dree and them, which was a savory lentil stew and thick naan-like flatbread.

Dree sopped up the stew with the bread and shoved bites into her mouth between patients.

When Father Booker returned to report that the campsite had been assembled, Maxence sent him and the two other guys off to scout possible locations for the planned micro-NICU buildings.

He looked at the stone house they had commandeered, too, and considered the construction and space.

Maybe they didn't need to *build* new construction.

The house had no utilities, though. Sunlight streamed in the windows. The lady of the house was boiling water from a village well on a charcoal stove.

When the sun wilted behind the tall mountains at about three-thirty in the afternoon, shadows spread over the town, and Maxence declared an end to the clinic.

He told Dree, "You're down to treating minor cuts and scrapes with antibiotic ointment and Band-Aids. They can do this. It's twilight now, but the sun will be going down in about an hour and a half. We need to get to the campsite before it gets dark."

Batsa led them to the tents and the other guys, where indeed, a pot of something that smelled delicious bubbled over a small campfire. Alfonso had procured more fresh bread from one of the women in the village.

Maxence fashioned a cushion for Dree out of a sleeping bag and made her sit down by the fire and eat.

She wolfed down the food. "This is so good."

Alfonso beamed at her praise, smiling at Dree and flirting with her with his bright green eyes. He was solicitous, asking her if she wanted more and making sure she had it.

Maxence wanted to slug him, but the lentil stuff he'd made was good. It reminded Maxence of *mesir wat,* an East African lentil stew, and he missed the injera flatbreads that Auntie Ndaya and Auntie Disanka cooked. He would be back home in The Congo in six or eight weeks or so. He didn't need to become morose. He'd managed to video chat with the aunties, Majambu Milandu, and Mpata Majambu while he'd been at the Our Lady of the Assumption rectory, which had been a rare treat due to his hectic schedule, the difference in time zones, and the frequent power outages in Kathmandu.

Dree elbowed Maxence while she scooped the lentil stew with the naan and popped it into her mouth. Her luscious lips puckered as she chewed.

A memory of her red lips tight around his cock intruded on whatever he was going to say or had been anticipating she would say because, oh God, *those lips of hers.*

She elbowed him again.

"What, yes?" Max asked.

"So, this was just a small village that hadn't seen a doctor in a while, right?" she asked him.

"That's true."

"And the villages where we're going after this are larger than this one, right?"

"At least some of them," he allowed.

"And they'll have better access to medical care than this one, *right?*" she demanded.

This was the direction he'd suspected the conversation would be heading. He'd suspected Dree had a soft heart. "A few of them."

"How few?"

"Very few. Most of them will have a significant number of people with medical issues that, in other locations, would be seen by a doctor."

"In rural New Mexico where I come from, there are a lot of poor people. A lot of people live in shacks their granddaddies built that only recently got running water and utilities. I didn't have internet until I lived in the dorms for college. In some of the far parts of the state and out on the reservation, things are a lot more dire. Many people out there still don't have any utilities. But if somebody had that little girl with the ear abscess or the little boy with strep throat, I like to think that all of them would have ridden their horse or an ATV or a freakin' tractor over to a neighbor's who does have a truck to take them into town to see a doctor."

Maxence sighed. "As you can see in this village, no one's neighbor has a truck."

"I guess what I'm asking is, *why* don't they? Or why didn't their parents ride on one of the supply trucks to a larger place to get help or find some more of their people who do have a truck? There is a small store in the town. The trucks have to come here."

"The supply trucks that make rounds to many of these smaller towns might only stop once a month, and they might not reach someplace larger for a week after that. The drivers wouldn't let them on, anyway. They'd become a bus. The people in these villages have no options."

Her voice cracked. "I can't imagine watching my child suffer like that."

Images of chubby cheeks, joyous gummy baby smiles, and hands like tiny starfish clutching his clothes rose in Maxence's mind. "Me, either."

"It's not fair," Dree said. "They should have a way to get into town. Someone should have helped those kids and those adults. That guy's broken leg isn't going to be okay. He needs surgery."

"You fashioned an excellent splint and cast for him. He'll be much better off."

"I know, and it'll probably be able to bear his weight, eventually. He won't be a hundred percent, though."

"You did what you could."

"People need to do *more.*"

"Right, they should. We should. They don't even have the most basic necessities. Alfonso, you boiled the drinking water, right?"

Alfonso glanced at him just as the campfire popped. Sparks soared into the air. "Of course, I did. When I was making the fire, I boiled the water first. Why, do we not need to boil the drinking water here?"

"Yes, we should boil the drinking water here."

"We have on all the other trips like this one. I just assumed—"

"When in doubt, it's safest."

Alfonso leaned back on his arms, shaking his head. "This is not my first rodeo, as you say."

Dree cracked up at him. "Yep, not your first rodeo."

Alfonso smiled at Dree. "I would not let the intestinal parasites get to you, Andrea Catherine."

"Oh, well, thank you. I'm glad you're running interference between me and the intestinal parasites. Thank you for your concern about my colon."

Alfonso continued, "Access to clean water is very much a problem for the communities on charity missions like the ones *Deacon Father Maxence* takes us on."

Maxence noted Alfonso's subtle emphasis on his religious title and stuffed bread and lentils into his face before he could say something stupid.

From across the campfire, Father Booker watched him and ate steadily.

Maxence lowered his head and concentrated on his food.

Dree turned back to him. "So, why are we *only*

doing micro-NICUs here? Why aren't we airlifting in supplies and medical personnel and doing some sort of a village make-over right now?"

Maxence swallowed. "That's the age-old question, isn't it? Why are some people poor, what can be done for the poor, and with the riches of certain geographical areas, social strata, and the Church, why aren't we doing more to help the poor?"

"Right!" Dree exclaimed, bobbling her plate but recovering before it spilled.

Alfonso reached toward her leg in case he could help.

Max wanted to slap his hand away but did not move.

Dree said, "I may have mentioned that I went to Catholic school all my life—"

Maxence smiled at her. "It's come up."

"—so, the sisters and teachers told us that on the Day of Judgment, God will ask each person what they did to help the poor and needy. It's that whole Matthew twenty-five thing, 'whatever you did for one of these least brothers of mine, you did for me.'"

Father Booker stretched his legs. "See, Deacon Maxence? American Catholic schools aren't entirely in disarray."

"Oh, jeez, the sisters hit us with that at *least* every year," Dree told him. "When Sister Ann taught catechism class in junior high and high school, it was once a *month*. There was always a chapter on social justice in the textbook, and she hit them *hard.*"

Max just bet that Sister Annunciata did hit the social justice chapters *hard,* and he smiled as he ate.

Father Booker said from across the campfire,

"Yes, as Christians and other people of beliefs, we have a *personal* responsibility to help the poor."

Maxence heard the challenge in Father Booker's voice and met his insistent stare over the fire. That was the Church's official stance on the matter, that helping the poor is a *personal* mandate for Christians.

"But that can't be all," Dree said. "One person can't do anything big. I mean, individual people like me, anyway. I'm just a farm girl who managed to go to nursing school. People like Bill Gates and other billionaires could do more, I guess."

"Ah, *billionaires,*" Father Booker said as if he found something distasteful.

Three of the six people sitting around that campfire had at least a theoretical claim to that social class.

Alfonso and Isaak shifted where they sat and stared at their food.

Maxence lifted his head. "And yet, most billionaires' net worth pales when compared to governments who could tax them and help far more people. Even here in Nepal, some people are extraordinarily wealthy. The Shah family, who were the Nepali royal family before they were all killed in the massacre—"

"*What!*" Dree half-stood. "Like when Tsar Nicholas the Second and his family were executed a hundred years ago in Russia?"

"Except that it was in 2001."

"*Seriously?*" She glanced behind herself as if regicides might be lurking in the dark hills.

"It was in the middle of a civil war that lasted for ten years. The entire immediate family of the king was mass-murdered in exceedingly odd circumstances. Ten people, including the king, the queen, all their children and their spouses, and most of the king's siblings and their spouses were all murdered, except for one of his brothers. That brother decided not to attend the supper that night. His wife and son were minorly wounded, just winged. So he became king. They blamed it on the crown prince 'accidentally' killing everyone and himself with an automatic weapon."

"That's unbelievable," Dree said, her voice squeaking.

"Oh, yes," Maxence said. "It's *absolutely* unbelievable. No one believes that's how it happened. Anyway, the king's brother who 'decided not to go' was king for a while before he was forced to abdicate."

In the warm light of the fire, Dree pointed to the sky and far, dark mountains. "But—but—didn't he have something to do with it?"

Maxence shrugged. "Like I said, no one believed that the crown prince killed his parents, himself, and everyone else who might have had a claim to the throne except for that one brother of the king, and somehow only lightly wounded his family."

"Right," Dree said, staring at the fire and shaking her head as she processed that.

"Palace coups still happen. The massacre sent a chill through every royal family in the world. When there are billions of dollars and actual power at stake, people will do shocking and terrible things. Anyway, the king's surviving brother and his family, the Shahs, retain an excessive amount of wealth, considering the poverty of many Nepalis. And then when the civil war finally died down, the earthquake happened."

"Earthquake?" she squeaked.

"In 2015. Practically leveled some regions and damaged buildings everywhere."

"Jeez, this poor little country!" Surprise had turned to empathy in her voice.

A lot of the people Maxence knew or was related to would not have been so affected by Nepal's plight. Dree and himself were more kindred spirits than different. "Indeed, those are some of the reasons we're here. Nepal has just had blow after blow. The government should do more to help these people. The *world* should do more to help these people. The moral test for any society and civilization is how it treats its most vulnerable citizens."

Father Booker looked up from his food at Maxence and studied him, holding his bread pinched in his fingers but not eating, because Max had just thrown a theological bomb into the conversation.

Maxence continued, "Because of Matthew, Chapter Twenty-Five, right?"

One of Father Booker's silver eyebrows twitched, and he went back to eating.

They spent the rest of the evening talking about less controversial things—things that wouldn't get anyone laicized or excommunicated—until the fire burned down to coals and darkness crept over the stony ground, encroaching on their little camp.

The plan was to get up the next morning early and survey the areas that Isaak and Alfonso had scouted that afternoon before pressing on to the next village.

Where Dree would undoubtedly work herself to exhaustion again.

Maxence would need to watch over her.

Isaak was standing, stretching his fists into the air and groaning, which sounded uncannily like the way he snored.

Maxence was not looking forward to these nights when he was bunking with the two of them. Maybe he should ask Father Booker and Batsa if they had room in their tent for one more. Batsa was skinny. There was probably more room in that one.

Well, he'd evaluate after tonight. Maybe those two would snore less sleeping on the earth instead of the saggy beds at the inn.

He stood and stretched, his long legs a bit cramped from sitting cross-legged near the fire. The tops of his feet were warm. He grabbed his flashlight off the ground beside his foot and switched it on. Father Booker, Batsa, and Isaak did the same, and the beams strobed in the darkness of the country night.

Isaak and Booker kicked dirt over the coals. Enough dried vegetation covered the ground that they couldn't leave the coals unattended.

The mountains chopped black voids out of the horizon around them, but stars crept out of the darkness above as the fire burned down.

When the fire was mostly out, Alfonso poured water over the last traces of red glow to extinguish it. Steam hissed into the air, clouding their flashlight beams.

Stars salted the sky.

Dree said, *"Oh."* A sigh lifted her voice like when Maxence trailed his mouth over her shoulder to her throat, though he stood several feet away from her in the dark.

An errant flashlight beam crossed her face.

She was staring at the sky, enraptured. "The stars were always bright out on the ranch, but this is amazing."

Maxence and the other guys clicked off their flashlights to see the stars better.

The pinpricks of light grew brighter as his eyes adjusted until the galaxy blazed around them, innumerable trembling motes flooding the heavens.

Yet, even as Maxence gazed across God's creation, the stars and the deep and the world without end in a moment of pure wonder and awe, awareness of Dree's nearness drew his attention.

The pale silver light of the stars touched her nose and her cheek. A faint blue reflection from her eyes sparkled in the night.

"It's so beautiful," she said.

"Yes," Maxence agreed.

"It's—like Heaven. You can see how people back before there were artificial lights must have looked up and seen this," her hand waved in the darkness, "this world of crystals and diamonds in the sky and conceived of Heaven."

He wanted to see the heavens and the world through her eyes.

Max waited, but she didn't say any more, and neither did the other guys.

Eventually, they flipped on the flashlights again. The light scoured the stones and earth, blinding him, and he squinted.

The other guys spoke, and Dree's soft voice lilted in the night.

Maxence trailed Isaac and Alfonso as they

walked back to the tiny, tiny tent standing on pebbly ground.

Just before Max crouched to duck into the pup tent, he looked back to where Dree was crawling into her tent, the flashlight beam filling the fabric prism and reflecting back onto her supple form.

His longing for her was not entirely physical, and Maxence didn't know how to think about that.

CHAPTER 6
CHOICES
DREE

L ater that night, Dree awoke to the sound of a table saw ripping through rough wood, the screaming rustle of slithering nylon, and angry masculine grunts.

Her tent wasn't particularly near the other two. The three tents clustered around the cold fire pit, but the guys had purposely set them apart a bit so disturbances would be minimized.

And yet, the scuffling and growling were definitely human and male in timbre.

She wrestled around inside her mummy-style sleeping bag and stuck her arm out into the chilly air. Her flashlight was right beside her bed, and she clicked it on to the lowest brightness and squinted in the glare.

The tent lit up around her, revealing cardboard boxes she'd stacked at the far end. The temperature outside was below freezing, so she'd brought the boxes of vaccine inside where the air wasn't quite so bitterly cold due to the little bit of her body heat escaping from her thick bedroll. The alpine-rated sleeping bag was so warm that she'd left it partially unzipped because she'd started to boil. Considering that the outside of the bag was burgundy fabric, she would've ended up looking like a steamed shrimp.

The pup tent was constructed to accommodate people sleeping in it and not much else, and she could only sit upright near the very middle where the tent poles raised the center to a triangle. Dree tugged her coat and boots on, not bothering to zip or lace them, and crawled to the far end of the tent with the opening. She unzipped the tent flap and stuck her head out, swinging her flashlight beam in the darkness.

The crisp air nipped her nose and cheeks. The rocks glistened with a crystalline film of ice.

The tent to her left where Father Booker and Batsa were sleeping was still and dark.

To her right, however—

That tent was undulating like three raccoons fighting in a burlap sack.

Dree belly-crawled out of her tent in the cold air, stretched to her feet, and walked toward it. A chill crept into her loose boots and jacket and trickled around her ankles and tummy.

More rustling, more scratching, and a very masculine whisper, *"Hey. Seriously."*

"I'm allergic to something in Nepal. I took an allergy pill."

"But if you move over there—"

"I can't sleep curled up in a ball."

"Well, I can't sleep with my head hanging out of the tent, either."

"Roll your sleeping bag that way. Keep rolling. I'll try sleeping over there. Roll. *Roll.*"

"I haven't been on the bottom of a pile like this since a theater-department cast party in college."

"Maybe if we slept head-to-toe."

"We *were* sleeping head-to-toe. That's how I got kicked in the eye."

"Move over. You're hogging the tent."

"Me? You need to move. Your ass is in my face."

"Bite me."

"It smells like an open cesspool in here. Did someone trump?"

"Alfonso's lentils upset my stomach. We French have delicate digestive tracts."

"Yeah, right. That's why you eat eels and old cheese and stuff. Keep moving. You're lying right on top of me."

"Hey! That had better be your elbow."

"No, just happy to see you."

"Isaak, keep your hands to yourself and try wedging under that tent eave some more."

"I can't. There's a big rock over there. Make Alfonso move over."

Her flashlight beam lit up the side of the tent.

"Shit," said one male voice, probably Isaak. "You woke someone up."

Another masculine voice—and Dree was pretty sure she recognized Augustine's, no, *Maxence's* voice —said, "It's no one's fault. I'll apologize to them."

Dree settled to her knees and whisper-asked, *"What* is going on in there?"

"Nothing," Alfonso's tenor voice said.

Dree shook her head. "My feet are getting cold. I'm coming in."

All three of them said, *"No!"*

Alfonso said, "No, Andrea Catherine. There is no room."

Isaak's deep, French-accented voice teased, "I'm willing to share."

Someone in the tent actually growled like a bear.

She unzipped the tent flap and stuck her head inside, shining the flashlight under her chin like she was telling ghost stories and then turning it on the men.

Their burgundy mummy bags piled on top of each other in the tiny tent, tangled, and they looked like a cup of nightcrawlers with men's faces.

She said, "Jeez, *guys.*"

Maxence said, "We were merely adjusting."

"This is crazy. This tent isn't big enough for three grown men."

"That is what I was saying," Isaak said, grinning hugely. His bright blue eyes sparkled in the flashlight beam. "But if you have room in your tent—"

She sighed. "Yeah, one of you should bunk with me. Come on."

"I'll go," Isaak said and started slithering toward the tent flap.

"No," Maxence said, glowering. "Dree should choose. Who would you be comfortable with?"

She sighed. "Fine. I'll take Deacon Father Maxence."

"I'd be more fun," Isaak said, still grinning. His fingers wiggled by his cheek, peeking out of the face hole of his mummy bag as he waved to her.

She told Isaak, "Yeah, but I need to get some sleep tonight. Maxence is an ordained deacon, so he's harmless."

The other two guys cracked up, their deep, masculine laughter ringing in the night.

Maxence glowered. "I'm not harmless."

The two guys laughed as Maxence gathered up his sleeping bag and followed Dree into the night.

Back in her tent, Maxence kneeled and flipped his sleeping bag over the tent's ground fabric. "Thanks for getting me out of there."

"It's okay. Sounded like there really wasn't enough room."

"We tried all sleeping on our sides, but Isaak rolled over and knocked Alfonso and me over like dominos."

"I can see that happening." She shucked her coat and boots, and then she wiggled back inside her sleeping bag. The fluffy bedroll was still warm inside. *Ah.* She placed her flashlight back where she could reach it and clicked it off.

The glare in the tent subsided, though Max's flashlight still lit up the back wall.

"But you were right," Maxence said, zipping his bag up to his chest. He reached out with one hand and extinguished his flashlight.

Darkness snapped into being, instantly filling the tent to the center peak. Dree couldn't see her own nose, let alone if she'd wiggled her fingers in the dark.

She said, "Of course, I was right. What about?"

"That I'm the harmless one."

She scoffed, "I've got four nights in Paris that say different."

"That wasn't really me."

"Sure, it was. It was *all* you. It was *every last inch*

of you. As a matter of fact, I'll bet it was ten inches. Felt like more. We never did do butt stuff."

"Dree, *please.*"

"I understand there are all kinds of personal conflict going on up in your noggin, but that was *you.* You weren't *faking* it."

"I wasn't faking it, no. But it's not who I *want* to be."

She said into the dark, "Sure seemed like you wanted to be there."

"That's not what I meant. Of course, I wanted to be there. I desperately wanted to be there."

"I'll bet if I offered, you'd crawl right inside this mummy bag with me right now."

His voice lowered still further. "You're not making this easier."

"Hey, it's not my problem. I'm not the one who took an oath of celibacy."

"Dree, I'm doing my best. Don't make this more difficult, okay?"

"Hey, Mr. Deacon Father Grimaldi, you're the one who's supposed to be celibate. But since you can't keep it in your pants—"

He muttered, "I can keep it in my pants. Can you keep your sleeping bag zipped?"

"Oh, I can keep my sleeping bag zipped up tight, but it doesn't matter if I don't. You're the one who 'slips' every chance you get."

"Yeah," he sighed. "I do."

His voice sounded choked.

Oh, jeez. She'd wanted to piss him off, not make him feel bad. "All right, fine. I'll quit sexually harassing you, but the point is that Paris was not my fault. This is between you, your conscience, and the

Big Guy upstairs. I'm just the woman you didn't mention your ethics conflict to."

"I am sorry about that," he said, his voice low.

"You should be. I mean, I knew we didn't have a future together, that it was just those four days and then we'd go our separate ways. You didn't lead me on. But I think the fact that you'd taken Holy Orders, even if you're not exactly a priest, should have been in the conversation before we knew each other 'biblically.'"

"That first night, things were a bit of a blur."

"Yeah," she admitted, "and they were even blurrier for me, but you should have told me the next day. We shouldn't have *kept* doing it. I didn't know you were breaking sacred vows. I just thought I'd had a wonderful four days with an incredible man."

His whisper slid through the dark and around the curls of her ear, "I think you're incredible, too."

Dree paused, gathering herself, and she whispered, "I don't know why we did what we did in Paris, but I can see why you should be a priest."

Maxence's sleeping bag susurrated on the nylon tent floor like he was turning over. He whispered, "Why?"

"I was at the Mass on Saturday. I saw you do the Scripture reading."

Again, silence, until he whispered even more softly, "And?"

"When I told Sister Mariam and Mother Superior that you were going to be officiating at the Saturday Mass, Mother Superior said that she would reserve the school bus so all the sisters could go. I thought it was just because you're hot. I mean, what het-leaning woman doesn't like to fantasize about a hot priest? It's *so* naughty. And a hot priest can take you to Heaven because he knows the way, am I right?"

"I don't know what to say to that," Maxence muttered.

Dree said, "But that wasn't it. That wasn't why they were there. When you read the Scripture, everyone was *enthralled.* Your voice went *through* us. No one could *breathe. That's* why they went. I couldn't *believe* what I was feeling. It felt like encountering God."

She needed to gather herself.

His breathing didn't change to the soft rhythm of sleep, and he drew in a breath like he might say something, and then sighed, and then did it again.

Dree sucked a deep breath for courage and asked the darkness, "Are you—*something else?*"

"—Like what?" Confusion filled his voice.

"Like—" She felt stupid saying it, so she rushed. "Like a saint. Or an angel. Or part-angel, like I'm one-eighth German."

"No," Maxence said. His voice was firm. "I'm just a guy. I'm not anything else. There isn't *anything else.*"

"What does it *feel* like to you?" she asked, a creak of desperation in her voice.

Again, the inhale, a sigh like his breath brushing her shoulder, and he said, "It's like light rolls through me. Or love. Maybe it's more like love. When I'm in it, I can feel the whole church. Not individual people. Not like reading minds. I'm looking at the Bible page and the verses, and I'm breathing air and projecting my voice, but I *am* my voice. I *am* the air that moves through me. I *am* the vibrations of sound that reach people."

Dree stared into the darkness. "And that's why you have to be a priest."

He paused again. "It's part of it. But it's this. I can feel when I'm doing it. Sometimes, when there's something important, I can make it happen, like with that Black English baron at the charity event at the Versailles Palace last week, Sir Marvin Meriwether-Stone."

"Yeah," Dree said. "The investor guy who was with your friend Micah, the one who was *suddenly* very interested in Micah's business deal."

"Right. I did it then for Micah because he wanted that investment and Meriwether-Stone would have missed an excellent opportunity if he hadn't done it, but sometimes it just happens. Sometimes, I don't know I'm doing it until afterward. There have been times that it's happened, and I convinced people to do things when I didn't realize that I was influencing them. Sometimes, I make people do the wrong things."

The thought of a person like Maxence being able to influence a crowd to do the *wrong* thing stilled Dree. It was terrifying.

"When I think about people who could influence other people as I can, who had this skill or innate ability or whatever because I don't know what I'm doing, the names that come to mind are Charles Manson, Jim Jones, Osama bin Laden, and even Hitler."

"But … those guys were all evil," she said slowly, though cold air seemed to be seeping inside her sleeping bag and chilling her skin. "They were psychopaths who had no empathy and treated people like objects that were fun to manipulate. You aren't like that, right?"

"That's not the reason. I *know* I'm not a psychopath. My brother is, and I *know* I'm not like him. Living with an actual psychopath teaches you exactly what they are. He's an empty pit of nothing with no human emotions except a taste for violence. He paints on a mask when he talks to people. He betrays people who think they are his friends, and he does not notice if they are hurt or if they are no longer his friends. He has the soul of a great white shark."

"So, you aren't like that," Dree said. The chill was making her tremble inside her sleeping bag.

"But I *should* be a priest," Maxence said, and his voice in the cold dark air had an anguished edge. "I should be *assigned* to do good works by a hierarchical organization that knows what they're doing. I should be *told* what to say and what to do. If not, I am a deadly virus. I am a brandished gun."

"You don't trust yourself," she said.

"It's more than that. I should be *anonymous.* I should be just another interchangeable priest in a black soutane on the street or wearing vestments during Mass. If I'm someone important, I could be used as a weapon or fashion myself into one. I guess I don't trust myself because *no one* should trust me."

Dree said, "It's not hypnosis. You're not hypnotizing people, right?" It had felt different than hypnosis.

"It's not. Father Moses calls it 'the divine gift of charisma.' My friend Casimir says that I'm 'just really persuasive' because he's a lawyer, while Arthur calls it 'a regal bearing.' I'm not sure what to make of that one."

She chuckled, relaxing a little. "Well, you're a prince of Monagasquay, right?"

He chuffed a laugh. "Yeah, *Monagasquay*. Maybe that's why. But the current sovereign prince doesn't do it that I know of, and my brother, Pierre, certainly doesn't. He convinces people to do things with blackmail or threats."

"You talk about Monagasquay like it's a real place."

He laughed. "I must have a vivid imagination."

"Or you've been describing real people this whole time."

She could hear the smile in his voice when he said, "Maybe that's it."

"Your brother sounds creepy."

Maxence laughed again, a little lighter this time. "Yeah, he is. I'm worried about what will happen to Monagasquay after he takes power, but I'm out of that. I plan to become a Jesuit. I *will* be a Jesuit. It's best for me, and it's best for the world."

She waited for him to speak again, but his breathing slowed. The local time must have been after midnight, maybe much later.

Hours passed before Dree fell asleep.

When she opened her eyes, the tent sides glowed with morning sunlight, and Max was gone.

CHAPTER 7
MONAGASQUAY, AGAIN
MAXENCE

J ust after dawn, Maxence was awakened by the sunlight on the fabric walls of the tent, and he'd quietly unzipped the mummy bag and struggled out of the tiny tent without waking Dree, who was still sleeping. Her lips were puffy and pink like she'd been kissed, and he tried not to think about that.

Father Booker had crawled out of his tent and bounded to his feet, his dark eyes bright and snappy, though one white eyebrow had drifted toward the clouds when he'd seen Max slowly emerging from Dree's tent instead of the one where he was supposed to have slept.

The sun drifted above the horizon into the cold air. The sun's warmth seemed to fade out somewhere in the pale sky, never reaching the black leather motorcycle gear Max wore. Wind whipped at his clothes. He didn't feel the breeze because the leather was windproof, but the clothes lay cold on his skin.

Father Booker and Maxence knelt off to the side

of the camp and prayed the Office of Readings and the morning prayer, Lauds, together. Priests and deacons are obliged to "fill their days with prayer," and the Divine Office or Liturgy of the Hours is the prescribed form of those prayers. In this case, the word *office* is a holdover from Latin, where *officium* means service, duty, or ceremony. The Holy Office is all of these. It is the work and ceremonial form of prayer for priests and other people who have devoted their lives to the Catholic Church.

While Maxence and Booker were off to the side, murmuring and reciting the prayers to each other from their phones, Batsa scrambled out of the tent and set to acting as a sous chef for Alfonso, who'd already started to cook breakfast. Maxence watched with his peripheral vision while Batsa interpreted for a lady who delivered warm naan at the crack of dawn in the hopes they would want to buy more. They did.

After they finished, Maxence and Booker approached the fire, warming their hands in the chilly morning.

Alfonso offered them breakfast sizzling in his skillet, which appeared to be scrambled eggs with onions and peppers and smelled delicious. They dished up.

Max ripped off another piece of flatbread and used it to pick up a morsel of fluffy scrambled eggs. "Seriously? These are the *powdered* eggs? They're perfect."

Alfonso nodded from where he squatted beside the campfire, tending a gently simmering pan of coffee. "I didn't want to put too much strain on the villagers' supplies. It's early winter, and nothing is going to grow here for a while."

Dree still hadn't left her tent.

Isaak had slithered out of the far tent, took an offered plate, and set to eating breakfast without speaking. Max remembered from boarding school that Isaak was not a morning person. Indeed, he was barely an afternoon person. A lot of fun at night, though.

"We do need to be careful how much we ask for or buy," Batsa agreed with Alfonso, flinging his arm at the barren, stony mountains around them. "Nothing has grown here since early October at the latest. The growing season in the foothills of the Himalayas is even shorter than in Iowa."

"Yes, we should try to tread as lightly as possible in these people's lives," Father Booker said in his bass operatic voice. "Is that coffee ready yet, by any chance?"

"Give me your cup, Padre," Alfonso said. "How do you take it?"

"I don't suppose we have milk?"

"The lady who brought the bread also brought fresh milk with her this morning. I think it's yak milk."

"If you please," Father Booker said. "Maxence, do you take milk?"

When Maxence was in the field, he usually took his coffee black to conserve resources. A few times in his life, he had endeavored to mortify himself by drinking nothing but black coffee and water. He hated it. It tasted like privation. "If you have milk of whatever source, I would appreciate it. And sugar."

Just as Alfonso was handing Maxence his cup, the third tent rustled.

Dree's light voice fluttered in the air. "Breakfast smells good."

Maxence and Alfonso turned.

She stood in front of her tent, blinking in the sunshine and ruffling her pixie-cut blond hair with her hand. Her puffy ski clothes camouflaged her hourglass figure, but Max could trace her shape under it with his memory.

"Good morning," Maxence said.

Last night's midnight confessions had not been good for Max's soul. Indeed, he wished he'd rolled over and gone to sleep without a word. She must think he was a freak.

Alfonso crowed, "Andrea Catherine! I have saved a plate for you from these rabid dogs."

She stretched and staggered a little as she approached the campfire. "First, you saved me from the intestinal parasites and now from starving to death in the wake of rabid dogs. I declare, Alfonso, you're my knight in shining armor."

Alfonso looked far too pleased.

Maxence ate the remainder of his food, stuffing himself because he'd spooned extra onto his plate to give Dree in case Batsa and Isaak ate everything in the pan.

"Do you take coffee, Andrea Catherine?" Alfonso asked.

Golden sunlight shone on her pixie face. "If you please. I heard there's milk and sugar?"

Alfonso prepared a plate and a cup for her, which Dree took and ate. "This is good. Where'd you get eggs?"

"Powdered," he assured her.

"Amazing."

Maxence could cook. He should have cooked for her.

Dree elbowed Maxence in his triceps as she scooped up scrambled eggs with pieces of naan. "I didn't even hear you get up."

"It was early. After your impromptu medical clinic yesterday, you must have needed sleep."

Dree squinted in the sun that was still quite near the horizon. "What time is it?"

"Just before eight. The goal for the day is to examine the sites Isaak and Alfonso discovered yesterday and take pictures of them for the charity's board of directors."

Max didn't mention that he was on that board of directors, though they'd decided to fund this project in his absence. When he'd found out the idea of NICU micro-clinics had been accepted and funded without his or any outside input while he'd been sitting by his uncle's bedside in Monaco, he'd not been happy.

Packing up after breakfast took only about twenty minutes, and they roared away on their motorcycles with Isaak and Alfonso leading the way.

Again, Maxence kept Dree ahead of him so he could keep an eye on her. She seemed to ride the motorcycle exceptionally well, but he just wanted to make sure she was all right.

The first spot the engineers had chosen to eval-uate for one of the planned NICU micro-clinics was about halfway between the middle of the village and the edge, a small plot of land with a previous dwelling's stone foundation. Maxence kicked a small piece of wood that bore the black scorch marks of fire.

Isaak said, "It's centrally located, but again, we have the problems of no utilities, no running water, no electricity, nothing that the NICU would need to be able to function."

"The architect and industrial engineer assure us that the solar panels and catchment cisterns will provide sufficient electricity and water." Alfonso's voice was a bit peevish like he'd said that too many times.

Isaak Yahontov, the electrical engineer whose company designed environmentally sustainable power sources, scrutinized the pale sky. "The sun rose above the mountains for only a few hours yesterday near the center of the village." He spread his hand, letting the darkness of the mountains' shadow where they stood fall on his palm. "Even though there's plenty of light to see by, the sunlight is not direct. The sun is behind the mountains and won't crest for a few hours. We'll have only five hours or less of direct, usable sunlight before it descends behind the mountains on the other side of this valley. We can't make solar power with indirect sunlight. The rays have to *hit* the panels. And that river that runs beside the village will slow to a trickle soon. In February and March, it won't run. We'll need water here, too."

Batsa scratched the side of his cheek, where even two days' growth of beard was beginning to look luxurious. "If I remember right, and I'm pretty sure I do, it doesn't rain in Nepal like it does in the States. In Iowa, it rains steadily a few times a week all summer long. Here, there's a monsoon season, like much of Southeast Asia. India is just south of here. A great deal of rain falls during the monsoons, though I think we are on the dry side of the Himalayas and thus in a rain shadow. The problem is that very little precipitation falls during the rest of the year. They have a problem with water supply as well as safe drinking water in these villages. The catchment cisterns would overflow during the monsoons and run dry a month afterward, and there wouldn't be any more rain for months after that."

Dree frowned and glared at her feet.

Maxence sighed. The board of directors hadn't considered this situation, and that was the problem with sending outsiders in to do pre-determined charity projects.

While the intention might be good, the outcomes could be harmful.

He had lived in The Congo for four years. This project would have worked in Rwanda or The Congo, both with lush, verdant farm fields that produced crops much of the year due to a consistent supply of rain and long hours of direct sunlight.

While the six of them were musing on the inherent problems, they mounted their motorcycles. They rode over the rough roads to the next village they'd planned to evaluate, which was eighty miles farther into the Himalayas and a few thousand feet higher in elevation. His ears popped dozens of times under his helmet.

The eighty miles took four hours, guiding the bikes carefully around small boulders that had careened down the mountain.

Again, even though they rolled into the center of

town as unobtrusively as they could, people ducked out of their houses to observe the commotion.

Isaak and Alfonso already knew that they were tasked with assessing locations for NICU micro-clinics and setting up the camp, so they rode off on their motorbikes. Father Booker, Batsa, Dree, and Maxence dismounted to peruse the village's general situation.

Maxence removed his helmet and breathed a deep draught of the crisp air, which was colder as they climbed higher in the mountains. The chilly breeze slid through his hair and over his scalp, and he unzipped his black leather riding jacket to cool off. Riding the motorcycle in leathers with an engine burning gasoline between his legs had overheated him, even though the cold air had essentially become a wind that had howled between twenty to fifty miles an hour as he rode.

Beside him, Dree twisted off her motorcycle helmet and flipped the gray veil over her hair. Almost immediately, she spotted a boy with a skin infection crawling up the side of his neck and commandeered Batsa to translate to his mother what must be done.

Maxence saw the proverbial writing on the wall, so he appropriated a house with a sizable kitchen table for her makeshift clinic. After that, he assisted her where he could, wiped down the table with lye soap between patients, and made sure Dree had lunch when the time came.

People crowded into the "waiting room" area, which was the rest of the small house. Each patient had not only a parent or other caregiver, but also several aunties, uncles, grandparents, or older cousins with them, as the mother should not lack for moral support nor be lonely in her errand.

Such camaraderie and community cohesion were similar to the way of life where he lived in The Congo, and Maxence missed it anew. He missed his people there.

Father Booker prayed with people who requested it and looked after the other children of the mothers who brought their small children to be seen by "Lady Doctor Dree," as Batsa called her.

When Dree had demurred that she wasn't a doctor, Batsa had shrugged and said it was easier to translate that than to define the difference between a physician and a nurse practitioner.

Max and Booker triaged patients as best they could, bringing to the front a small girl gasping for breath while telling people with superficial scrapes who just wanted to see Lady Doctor Dree to wait.

In the early afternoon, three young women arrived at the clinic, kicking the door open as they carried in a fourth young woman wrapped in a blue and orange paisley bed sheet. The long black hair of the woman they carried trailed on the floor as they struggled with even her light weight.

One of the women called out, "Doctor! Doctor," and then a long explanation in the Nepali language.

Batsa hurried over to them and spoke for just a second before he called back to Dree and Maxence, who were over by the table, "Lady Doctor Dree! It's urgent."

He urged the young women toward the table with hand motions and short, insistent words as he grabbed the young woman under her shoulders. "Father Booker! You are needed here!"

Father Booker was already on his way to help. He reached the group of women carrying her. Despite their worried protests, he gathered the sheet-wrapped woman up in his arms. Her arms and legs trailed limply as he dashed for the kitchen.

Dree handed the child on the table to his young mother and ran.

Maxence reached across the kitchen table and lifted the young woman from Booker's arms so they could place her gently on the table. The young woman, barely more than a girl, fluttered her eyelids and rolled her head away from him. He met Father Booker's frightened gaze as they started to unwrap her from the sheet.

Her friends began yelling at them, slapping their hands away.

Batsa said, "They are saying that they promised her they would preserve her modesty."

Maxence lifted his hands from the girl's arm, but he didn't step back. Giving into protestations of modesty seemed ridiculous when this young woman might be dying right before their eyes.

Dree crowded past Maxence and began shining her penlight at the young woman's face, pulling down first her eyelid and then her jaw so she could look inside her mouth. "Her skin and gums are so pale. She's either horrendously anemic or—"

The other women accosted Father Booker, pushing him away from their friend.

Father Booker took his hands away from the girl at the insistence of her friends, and his hands were dark with blood. A drop fell from his fingers and splashed on the bedsheet, turning an orange paisley scarlet. He recoiled, holding his hands out in front of him and striding toward the bucket holding cold water and lye soap.

Dree cast a glance at Father Booker and yelled, "Batsa, tell me what's going on!"

Batsa had been listening to what the girls were saying. One girl spoke rapid Nepali at him, her dark eyes flashing and her hands floating in the air as she exclaimed.

Batsa said, "Your patient has had a baby, two days past. She is bleeding, and she will not wake up."

"Where's the baby?" Dree asked him.

After a quick conversation with the women, Batsa said, "The baby was very small, not any bigger than their hand and fingers. It would not suck, and the mother was bleeding very much. The baby died the first night after it was born."

Dree flinched forward like she'd been punched, and she blinked before she began tugging at the bedsheets that wrapped the woman. "I have to see what I'm working with. Let's get the sheets off of her."

Maxence grabbed the paisley sheet and began to unwind it, but one of her friends grabbed his arm and yanked him backward.

Batsa said, "They are insisting on the woman's modesty. They have only come because Lady Doctor Dree is a woman."

Maxence asked, "Otherwise, they would have let her die?"

Batsa said, "That is not for me to say."

Dree was trying to take the sheet off of the woman, too, but another woman grabbed her arm, throwing glares at Max and Father Booker as she loudly begged Dree.

Batsa told them, "She did not want the men to see her unclothed. Her friends promised her they would protect her."

Maxence glanced up. The house where they had set up the clinic was filled with people, some women, some men, and boys and girls of all ages.

Dree said, "She's dying. We don't have time for this."

Maxence had lived in the midst of half a dozen very different cultures over the last decade of his life. He told Father Booker, who had also traveled the world for missions, "Let's get the sheets off the beds."

The old priest didn't bother to nod but sprinted for the pallets on the other side of the room. They stripped the thick blankets and coverlets off the beds and returned with their arms filled with the large pieces of fabric. "Batsa, we need your help."

They didn't have time to string a cord across the room to hang the sheets from, so each of the men took corners of the sheets, faced away from the dying woman on the table, and made themselves into makeshift tent poles with sheets as curtains between them.

Batsa called something back over his shoulder even as they faced out into the room, and the women's voices calmed.

Maxence sneaked a glimpse backward to make sure this was working.

Dree and the other women were bent over the woman on the table. The young woman's long brown limbs splayed off the edges of the table. Dree was muttering and using hand signals with the women, placing their hands on her patient's legs and patting their hands to indicate that they should hold the woman's legs as Dree examined her.

The orange and blue paisley bed sheet lay on the floor.

Dree occasionally called for Batsa to translate something, but for the most part, they had it under control. At one point, Batsa said something to a woman in the waiting room, and she came and held the sheet aloft as he walked backward for some more intricate translating.

About forty-five minutes later, during which time Maxence again had a lengthy opportunity to review all the events in his life that had led him to this place and observe the interactions of parents and children in the waiting area, Dree announced, "Okay, guys. You can lower the curtain now."

Maxence turned back. "Did she make it?"

Dree nodded as she scrubbed her hands with a small brush in a bucket of clean water. "For now. She had a fourth-degree tear of her perineum. I gave her a local anesthetic and sutured her muscles and skin. I gave her friends my strongest antibiotics for her. I did my best, but she should have been in an operating theater with general anesthesia and a real surgeon."

"We only have motorcycles. I don't see how we could've transported her to a hospital in less than six hours."

Dree blinked hard as she scrubbed up past her wrists to her elbows. "She didn't have six hours, especially sitting upright on a motorcycle. I think she might be okay, but she lost a lot of blood." She blinked again, and a tear dripped down her cheek. "She doesn't know the baby didn't make it yet. They told her that they'd given the baby to a wet nurse until she was better."

Maxence prayed in his mind for the soul of the baby, and his heart contracted with deep sadness for what the woman and the world had lost.

She said, "We have to get these NICUs up and running or something. From their description, that baby could have survived in a halfway decent NICU. It sounded like he was maybe three pounds. He could have made it."

Max stood beside Dree and stroked her back down her spine. Her body quivered like her lungs were fluttering.

She asked, "How do you deal with it?"

"I'm not," he said, his throat tight. "I'm devastated. I've just seen it so many times that I can feel it without falling apart."

She turned and grabbed his shirt, burying her face in his chest.

Maxence wrapped his arms around her, one palm on the back of her head under her gray religious head covering.

Her arms were tight around his waist, and he stroked her back lightly.

After a minute, her arms loosened, and Maxence opened his arms so she could step back.

She wiped the tears off her face with both palms. "I have other patients to see."

Maxence helped her with the rest of the patients, again deciding who needed to be seen quickly and who didn't need to be seen at all. A light bruise doesn't need to be seen by an exhausted nurse, no matter how much the status-conscious father wants the privilege and honor of his child being examined.

As darkness fell, Maxence and Batsa evaluated the few remaining people and decided that none of them needed any medical attention. One older man was obviously just interested in the proceedings because his complaint kept changing from headache to an imperceptible wound on his hand to a vague stomach complaint with no diarrhea or vomiting to a ringing in his ears. He'd chatted with every other patient and parent in the waiting area all day, listening to their complaints with animation and then describing his variable maladies. Batsa had been watching him and giving them updates.

At the campsite that night, the fire at the center blazed merrily in a hastily constructed fire pit and warmed them all.

Just after Max and the rest had gotten back to camp, the three women who had carried their post-partum friend into Dree's clinic arrived, bringing food.

One pressed a tiny idol with a womanly figure into Dree's hand, and they all touched Dree's feet before they left.

Dree thanked them but still seemed subdued.

Batsa identified the various dishes they'd brought and seemed excited. The steel plates that they'd carried contained a lentil stew, a different chicken one, rice, a pickle made of greens, various side dishes, the usual flatbreads, and some steamed dumplings that were fantastic.

Dree stayed quiet as she ate, no matter how much Alfonso tried to cheer her up with quips and banter.

Maxence knew better. He'd worked on this type of mission for nearly a decade. Sometimes, you just had to sit with the disquiet it causes. He made sure she had plenty to eat and that her tent had been pitched on the flattest spot of ground, though he wasn't sure whether he was sleeping there tonight or not.

Isaak sat beside Dree at dinner that night, and he offered her a silver flask from his saddlebags. "My family's finest. It looks like you could use some."

Dree took a long gulp, her throat working as she swallowed. She passed it back to him. "Thanks."

Father Booker passed around some candied nuts he had brought along as dessert, and in the flickering light of the campfire, Maxence watched as Dree ate exactly one and then passed the pouch to Isaak.

She stared into the fire during most of the conversation and finally stood. "I need to turn in, guys. Max, I need a few minutes. Did you guys put his sleeping bag in my tent?"

Isaak pointed to a bedroll over by one of the other tents. "We didn't want to presume. We figured we would ask where his sleeping bag should go."

Her voice was flat. "These pup tents aren't big enough for three grown men to sleep in, especially you three. Max, you can sleep in my tent, but I just need a few minutes to change clothes and have a sponge bath."

Alfonso leaped to his feet when she said that. "I will warm some water over the fire for you. Give me five minutes. I will do this for you."

Dree sat down while Alfonso warmed her water and wrapped a towel around the pot for her to carry it.

He said, "Just put the pot outside the tent when

you are done. I will clean it. You should go to sleep immediately afterward, so you don't get chilled."

Maxence considered that Alfonso might be cock-blocking him by suggesting Dree go immediately to sleep before Maxence got there, but then Max remembered that he could not be cockblocked because he was a harmless deacon who had already taken vows and wanted to be a priest.

He *should* wait until she was asleep before he crawled into the tent.

Dree said, "It'll take just ten or fifteen minutes, and then you can come in."

"Take your time," Max said. "I'll be there after a bit."

He waited by the campfire, talking quietly with the other guys about the technical requirements for solar panels and catchment cisterns.

Isaak looked up from the fire. "Oh, wow."

Maxence glanced at Dree's tent.

In the dark night, she'd left a flashlight on so she could see while she washed herself with the pot of warm water. A perfect silhouette of her curvy form graced the side of the tent as she lifted her arm like a ballet dancer and pressed a small cloth to her shoulder and smoothed it down and over the round, generous peak of her—

Maxence turned back around and stared at the campfire. "Isaak and Alfonso, *quit looking at the tent.*"

Isaak and Alfonso slowly turned back and trained their eyes on the campfire.

Batsa frowned at them until he looked over and saw her shadow. His gaze instantly zoomed back to the fire, and his eyes were wide as he purposefully stared directly into the flames.

Father Booker was leaning back against a rock with his eyes closed, half-dozing, his face turned up to the stars.

Maxence focused his eyes on the coals and dancing flames of the campfire, watching the glowing embers and the gases burning brightly in the darkness. A drop of sap popped, and sparks rocketed upward into the night.

Batsa removed a small book and a tiny clip-on light from his backpack and began to read. His focus sharpened on the book almost instantly.

Father Booker remained reclined with his head tipped back.

That left Isaak, Alfonso, and Maxence, himself.

The three guys occasionally made eye contact over the fire, maybe in solidarity for their restraint, maybe just making sure no one was cheating because then they could all enjoy the show.

Except then Max would have to kill them or gouge their eyes out or something.

He chastised himself for those violent thoughts.

No, if they turned to watch, he would merely remind them that Dree was a human being who was not on Earth for their titillation and deserved their respect.

And if that didn't work, he would shake them until they took their filthy eyes off her tent.

He had to stop this. This was not his way. Respect and restraint were his obligations, but retribution was not.

Max waited, practically counting minutes as the stars drifted overhead.

His mind returned again and again to memories of the curves of her body, the swells and dips of her breasts and waist and hips, and images of his hand stroking her satiny skin, her fragrance lifting from her body as he breathed, and the shivers that ran through her when he ran his tongue over her breasts and sucked on her clit.

Maxence focused on the fire, trying to listen only to the crackles and pops of exploding sap because he could swear that he heard the fabric of her clothes stroking her flesh.

Eventually, Father Booker lifted his head and squinted across the campground. "Her light is out."

The three guys sighed, and their shoulders fell in relief.

Batsa glanced up from his book and went back to reading.

Maxence slapped his knees. "It has been a strenuous few days. I think I'll turn in."

He collected his bedroll from beside the guys' gear and followed his flashlight beam through the night, careful of the stones and dried bushes on his way.

Unzipping the tent flap sounded like ripping a tarp in half in the dark countryside, and he turned his flashlight down until it glowed like a dim votive candle to sneak into Dree's dark tent.

The rear area was heaped with her boxes of medical supplies again, and the lumpy sleeping bag that was Dree lay on the right side of the triangle-shaped tent.

Her face was turned to the side of the tent, so Maxence crawled inside as quietly as he could, closed the tent flap, and unfurled his sleeping bag on the other side. He took off his black leather jacket and riding pants and slipped into his sleeping bag, zipping it all the way up to his neck before reaching out and clicking off his flashlight.

Dark.

The tent fabric overhead shut out even the meager light of the stars, crescent moon, and campfire that his eyes were used to.

Outside, pebbles and sand grated under boots as the guys stood and kicked small stones as they walked around. The campfire *hissed* when they doused it.

On the other side of the tent, Dree was not breathing the deep, even exhalations of sleep.

Her breath sounded like little hiccups and mews, and his heart was breaking. "Dree—"

"Don't be nice to me. It makes it worse."

He considered touching her shoulder, and he considered gathering her into his arms and holding her until the pain all went away, but neither of those was his place in her life. Instead, he asked, "What can I do?"

"—Tell me more stories about Monagasquay."

"That was all a fairy tale. I made it up."

"Tell me anyway," she said.

"I can tell you the story about how my ancestors became the sovereign princes of Monagasquay."

"Okay. All my ancestors have been New Mexican sheep ranchers as long as there have been sheep ranchers in New Mexico."

"Sounds like centuries," Max said.

"More like eighty years. My great-great-grandparents moved there from Oklahoma in a covered wagon pulled by oxen."

"Really?" He tried not to sound like he was laughing at her. "A covered wagon."

"Yeah. How did your people get to Mona-gasquay?"

"I hadn't thought about it, but I suppose they didn't drive Maseratis. Horses, I would think, and ships for the sea."

"Ooo, *horses.* Fancy."

He laughed. "They moved from Genoa to the coast of France a few centuries ago or so."

"So, were they French?"

"Italian."

"Are your people farmers, too?"

"More like pirates."

"Huh. Exciting. My other great-grandfather was a cattle rustler who went straight and became the sheriff of a little town in Southern Arizona because he knew where all the cattle thieves kept their stolen herds. So, he cleaned them out and gave everybody their cattle back, and they kept electing him sheriff after that."

Maxence summoned information and stories he'd heard all his life. "A thousand years ago, my indirect ancestor was a lord of the Italian city-state of Genoa. At the time, there was a civil war raging across Italy between factions who supported the Pope and other people who supported the Holy Roman Emperor, because those two men were fighting for control of all of Europe. This wasn't politics like we think of it today. Politics back then meant that noble lords raised armies by paying peasants and mercenaries and fought each other for control of the cities of Italy, which meant the right to tax citizens and the trade that went through those cities. Controlling a city meant you and your family and your descendants would be extremely wealthy for generations, especially if that city was a seaport on the Mediterranean Sea."

There was a sound of shuffling, of fabric on fabric. Maxence thought Dree had turned to face him but couldn't tell in the absolute blackness.

He said, "Genoa is on the coast of Italy, south of France. Today, the airport there is directly on the coast. The airstrips are right beside the harbor where yachts and other ships dock. Back then, of course, it was more important that it had a natural harbor for the trading ships of the Mediterranean."

"But that's not Monagasquay," she said, her voice still husky from crying.

"Monagasquay is north of Genoa and south of Nice, France. It was much less prosperous than Genoa and had many fewer people and rich people, so it wasn't a prize unto itself. Monagasquay has an amazing natural harbor, though, and a stone headland that was ideal for building a fortress to guard that harbor. We call it 'The Rock of Monagasquay.' By holding that fortress and harbor, one could use the small city-state to launch attacks at Genoa."

"Ah, it was tactically important," Dree said.

Maxence nodded in the dark. "Exactly. Whoever controlled the fortress and harbor of Monagasquay could attack Genoa until they controlled it, too. So, if you controlled Genoa, it was important that you also controlled Monagasquay, or you would eventually lose Genoa."

Another small rustle issued from the other side of the tent.

Maxence went on, "On January eighth in the year 1279, Francisco Grimaldi was the leader of the political factions who supported the Pope and wanted to control Genoa. However, their enemies controlled Monagasquay and continued to launch attacks which would have eventually succeeded in taking over Genoa. So, they knew they needed to capture the fortress and the harbor of Monagasquay."

"Is this where the action movie happens?" she asked, and her voice sounded a little stronger and cheerier.

Maxence smiled. "Not so much of an action movie. More like a thriller and maybe a horror movie. My indirect ancestor, Francesco Grimaldi, the Lord of Genoa and leader of the Guelph forces, led the assault on Monagasquay personally, which was as stupid as the captain of a spaceship going with the away team to a dangerous planet, or a king riding a white stallion at the front of his troops and leading the charge. It was honorable and noble, but we lost a lot of relatives that way. It does sound more like a movie plot than history, full of plot holes."

"But you're making this up, right?" she asked him, sounding puzzled.

"Of course. That's why I keep stopping and having to think about what happened, because I'm making it up, not because I can't remember what year or names of the cities and stuff. Anyway, the Guelph Army commanded by my ancestor Francesco Grimaldi and his cousin, Rainier the First, the Lord of Cagnes—"

"Wait, Rainier? Where have I heard of him?"

"The current sovereign prince of Monagasquay, Prince Rainier IV, is named after him. I might have mentioned him earlier."

"Oh, right. Okay."

"Anyway, Francesco Grimaldi and Rainier I, Lord of Cagnes, assaulted the fortress on the headland above the harbor for weeks, but it was a really strong fortress. They couldn't fight their way in, and they just kept losing soldiers. So Francesco Grimaldi came up with a plan."

"Ooooo, a plan." Dree's voice sounded perkier still.

"His plan was treachery. Francesco Grimaldi's nickname was *il Malizia*, which means 'The Malicious.'"

She chuckled. "So, like Catherine the Great or Richard the Lion-Hearted, your ancestor's name was Francesco the Malicious?"

A smile lightened her voice, and his heart thrilled to hear it. He imagined her sunny, beautiful smile like he'd seen so often in Paris. "Just so. All Grimaldi have a streak of evil running through their souls."

"I should have suspected that."

More smile in her voice. Maxence felt an answering smile lift his mouth. "Anyway, Francesco Grimaldi disguised himself as a Franciscan friar. He wore the coarse brown robe and a crucifix, no shoes, the whole deal. He went to the gate and told them that he was a simple monk and needed someplace to shelter for the night. The guards tried to turn him away because they knew that there was an army out there trying to take the castle. Finally, he convinced them that if they opened the gate just a little bit, he could slip in sideways really quick, and the invading army wouldn't even know the gates had ever been opened at all."

"Uh-oh."

"Yes, cue the ominous music. As soon as

Francesco Grimaldi was inside the gates, he pulled out a long knife that he had hidden in his monk's robes and slaughtered the guards with it."

She gasped, "Oh my God."

"Once he had killed the guards, he opened the gates, and his army poured in and took the fortress."

"Holy cow!"

"The way they tell the story, he fought and killed four guards who were wearing armor and held swords with just his one knife, but the victors do write the history books. There's even a statue of him in the courtyard of our castle, which is still the fortress above the harbor of Monagasquay, and he's dressed as a Franciscan friar holding a long knife."

"Wow," Dree said, her voice happier. "That is quite a story."

Maxence felt himself smile, captivated by the lightness in her voice. "I have lots of them. Maybe next time, I'll tell you about my evil Uncle Jules and what an asshole he is. We should start calling him Prince Jules the Malicious."

A few days later, one of the towns that they were assessing for a NICU micro-clinic was large enough to support a three-room inn with a tiny restaurant run out of the owning family's kitchen in the apartment where they lived behind the tiny hotel.

Again, the innkeepers were thrilled to have guests during the off-season and rapidly kitted up the rooms for guests. The wife of the family asked, through Batsa, what they would want for dinner because she would make anything they had supplies for.

When the six of them asked for whatever was convenient for her, she assured them she would make a superb supper for them and they would love her dessert.

Maxence had no doubt they would. They were hungry and tired from the road, and the inn had showers in the adjoining bathrooms. Maxence had lived in third-world countries for much of the last several years, but he still appreciated a warm shower wherever he found one.

Supper was indeed a magnificent feast, and Alfonso seemed thrilled to be eating food he hadn't cooked. Through Batsa's translation, he praised the woman's cooking to the point where she was blushing and giggling.

Because this small town was nearer to a major city, medical care was more accessible for the villagers. Dree got a day off, and Maxence made sure that she rested and had some time to look around during it. She was still tired after supper, and she excused herself to turn in early while the rest of the guys sat around the table and enjoyed a Nepali beer.

Maxence watched as Dree walked up the stairs, her hourglass figure swaying as she ascended. He could watch the way she moved forever, feeling something between the aesthetic appreciation for a dancer's grace and a deep male desire to touch and caress every inch of her skin.

After she disappeared up the staircase, Maxence looked back at his beer and noticed that Alfonso was also just looking down at his drink.

Maxence was not jealous. His plans to be a priest would not be derailed by mere carnal lust nor inappropriate jealousy.

Alfonso caught Maxence's eye and grinned ruefully. "Andrea Catherine is an extraordinary woman, yes?"

Maxence felt safe agreeing with that.

Alfonso said, "She is very beautiful, and her dedication to helping other people is commendable."

Maxence also agreed with that, though discomfort rose in him at the effusiveness of Alfonso's praise.

Alfonso said, "I have great admiration for her. I think perhaps that you admire her, too, Deacon Father Maxence."

The world and all he believed crushed Maxence. "Dree is an excellent medical professional, and her dedication to helping people is without limits. She is a truly good human being."

Alfonso said, "This mission is not an appropriate place and time to express my feelings, but I have a growing attraction to her. When we are finished with this survey and return to our normal lives, I would like very much to see her, to see if something could work out between us."

Maxence quietly said, "It's only been a week. How can you know if you like somebody in a week?"

Alfonso's green eyes went dreamy. "Sometimes, you just know, or sometimes, someone is so special that a week is enough."

For Maxence, even four days with her had been enough.

He planned to become a priest, as he had for years. He had worked for long years to earn a doctorate in theology to become a Jesuit, and so he spread his large hands on the table and refrained from either discouraging Alfonso or throwing him up against a wall and demanding he never speak to Dree again.

Maxence had no claim on Dree.

He could never have a claim on Dree.

It didn't matter that Maxence thought she was beautiful, kind, intelligent, and perhaps the most incredible person he'd ever met.

Maxence was going to become a priest for so very many reasons, and that meant Dree would date and marry some other man and not him.

He said, "Alfonso, she's an absolutely wonderful woman. You would be lucky to have her."

CHAPTER 8
ONE HIGH-TECH PREEMIE MONO-TASKER

DREE

Hundreds of small villages dotted the foothills of the Himalayas in the Jumla district of Nepal. The settlements had sprouted up around rivers in the sharp valleys cut by snowmelt water flowing down the mountains.

Dree's days followed the same pattern: rising early to evaluate possible sites for the NICU micro-clinics, and then riding her motorcycle with the five guys to another village that was desperately in need of healthcare, where Dree would once again work herself to exhaustion. She didn't complain because there was no use whining about it. She'd been raised to be stronger than that and not to bleat about doing a job that had to be done.

She was dimly aware that she could have just not done it. She could have denied being a nurse practitioner and not mentioned the dwindling medical supplies in her motorcycle's saddlebags and her backpack, but not giving these people her time and supplies felt cowardly, weak, and simply evil.

As they drove farther into the mountains and away from the larger towns, the children seemed increasingly small for their ages.

When Dree had rotated through the peds wards, she'd been introduced to the racially corrected growth charts. Growth averages were different for children whose ancestors were from different parts of the world. Children of Asian descent were often on the lower end of the overall bell curve in both birth weight and eventual height and weight, and one needed to know that when evaluating whether to suspect a problem or not. A child of Asian descent might be growing perfectly naturally and be in excellent health, but a Black child with the same initial weight and growth curve should be evaluated further for health conditions that were inhibiting their growth. It made sense that Nepali children in Southeast Asia would be smaller than she was used to seeing in the southwestern United States.

Her nurse's eyes needed to adjust.

This was Dree's hypothesis until they arrived in a small village where they passed very few farm fields as they rode into town on their motorcycles.

A mother brought a small female child of perhaps six years old into the clinic, complaining that the child would not stop crossing her eyes. Two of the mother's friends, whom Batsa said were her cousin and sister-in-law, hovered behind the mother, nodding whenever she said anything to Batsa.

When Dree examined the small girl, she found the child had almost all her adult teeth, which meant she had to be at least twelve or thirteen.

When Dree asked the mother how old the girl was, the mother agreed that the child had been born thirteen winters before, a number Batsa confirmed several times before relaying it to Dree.

Dree knew all the reasons why a child might have such stunted growth. She examined the child for other nutritional deficiencies, including rickets and lack of protein.

She found just about everything she looked for.

Dree pulled Maxence over to one side and told him what she thought.

He squeezed his eyes shut and nodded. "I could tell by her eyes and the way she was walking that malnutrition was probably an issue. When we were setting up, it looked like all the children here show signs of it."

That was *ridiculous.* "Why are we building ten-thousand-dollar brick and cement neonatal intensive care units for premature babies instead of preventing malnutrition in these children for a few bucks?"

He sighed. "They need everything; all of them do. It's not their fault, and it is our responsibility to help them. I don't think we should be building NICU units at all."

Her chest hurt like a cramp. "That's not what I meant. Of course, we should be trying to save the lives of preemies. Last week when we got to the village too late to save that baby... That still upsets me."

"That's not what I meant. I mean that the basic plan here seems wrong. The Catholic Charities organizers are usually better about things like this. I'm worried that this is one of those projects where they didn't consult anybody on the ground before they decided to do it."

That wasn't what she meant. "But surely, there are no bad charity projects," she said.

Maxence said, "I was in Somalia and the Central African Republic a few years ago with a different group that I'm not working with anymore. They brought in a bunch of upper-middle-class white teenagers to dig wells for the village. Their parents wanted to 'turn them around' because they were mouthing off or failing classes in their private schools, so they spent thousands of dollars for their spoiled offspring to go dig a well in Africa so they would appreciate their privilege."

Dree's parents could not have afforded to send her off to Africa. If she'd been sassy, they would have made her muck out the barn alone for a month. "Slackers."

"That was a doomed project from the start. The project coordinators chased off the local people instead of including them in the project. They wanted the little white kids to dig the wells and feel accomplishment at helping the poor people. Instead, they dug wells, and nobody who lived there helped build them, had any emotional investment in them, or knew how to maintain them. Those wells broke within a year, and nobody who was there could repair them because they hadn't been included in the project from the start. This feels like that project. No one in these villages will be able to run the NICU incubators or maintain them. At this point, I'm here to gather information on what we *should* do."

Dree tried not to have a freaking fit at the stupid rich people who thought these things up. "These people need access to *all* medical care. They do *not* need one high-tech preemie mono-tasker. It's like they have an empty kitchen with no refrigerator, no stove, no food, and these guys are like, 'Here, have an avocado slicer.'"

Maxence nodded. "The problem is that Alfonso is donating a bunch of these micro-NICU units that he's designing. The charity wants to use the units because they are getting them. If they weren't getting these specific devices, this project would never have been conceived."

That, Dree understood. *"Ah.* Got it. When you've got a hammer, every problem looks like a nail."

"Exactly. It's why you can't trust billionaires when they 'do philanthropy.' Alfonso is designing and testing these units in the field here in Nepal. He'll get a tax write-off for the donations, which will reduce or eliminate the cost of design and production. Then, he'll take the design with a track record and sell them to small hospitals at a profit."

"It's a scam," Dree said, already pissed.

"It's a smart business strategy, but it's not quite a scam. You should see some of the scams that real estate investors figure out." Maxence rolled his eyes. "Half the real estate transactions in New York are money laundering for the Russian mafia, and the other half are intended to screw working people. The real estate tycoons are doing both at the same time."

"Oh, come on. No real estate guy is going to admit that."

Maxence laughed. "I went to boarding school with Russian mafia kids, the Butorins. They'll tell you all about their family's money-laundering deals. That one guy who runs around putting his name on all his real estate, Michael Funk, is a half-billion dollars in debt to the Russian bratvas, so he launders money for them. Every time I see a new Funk Tower somewhere in the world, I just roll my eyes because I know the Butorin bratva just cleaned another couple hundred million dollars."

"Okay," Dree said. She hadn't meant to get him going on what was obviously a pet peeve of his. "But what are we going to do about this little girl, here?"

Maxence sighed. "Sorry. I have to remind myself that I can't change the world. We can give her mother some of our supplies, but we can't do that for every family in every village. We're going to have to go back to the town we flew into or some other larger city to resupply soon since we're accepting as little as we can from the communities we help because they can't afford it."

"Surely the Church should open their coffers to do something for these people. I mean, even our little parish church in New Mexico was *opulent,* and my people there were dirt poor. The parish had gold chalices that the priests drank out of and precious metals and treasure all over the place. Even the airport that we flew into in Kathmandu had so many riches compared to the poverty that we're seeing here, where the children are severely malnourished. How are we letting this happen?"

Maxence shrugged, and his strong jaw set. "Good question."

That night at the campfire, Dree was still seething over the fact that she'd seen seven pediatric patients with a primary diagnosis of severe malnutrition and that expensive preemie incubators weren't going to solve the problem.

Alfonso tried to dish her up extra of his nightly

lentil stew and flatbread, which was tasty, though it could use a bit more heat. The soil of her childhood sheep farm grew chili peppers with the same heat level as a blast furnace, and she was just used to scorching New Mexican food.

She also kept picturing the handsome Spaniard pouring over balance sheets and figuring out how to deduct his design and experimental costs by donating stuff to charities that they didn't need and might actually hurt the communities where they ended up.

Finally, Alfonso said, "Dree, you are so sad today. What can we do to cheer you up?"

There was a moment when Dree seriously considered letting go on him, but that wasn't the point.

Alfonso hadn't started the game. He was just another player.

Instead, Dree said, "Several of the children in this village that I treated today show signs of severe malnutrition. I'm angry that the world seems to have forgotten them."

Alfonso nodded. "But we haven't forgotten them. That's why we're here. We are here to save the lives of premature infants. If we had already built these NICU micro-clinics, the child of that woman you saw last week might have been saved. Don't you think that is a worthy goal?"

"Of course, it is, but there's just so much that these people need."

Alfonso waved his hand. "There's so much that *so many* people need. Right now, we're doing this. Next year, we may be able to address other things."

Dree sighed. "A lot of these kids aren't going to

make it to next year. Even if they do, severe malnutrition like this confers lifelong problems. Their growth will be stunted forever. They're not going to catch up. Their bones will be softer and more easily broken for the rest of their lives. Their brains will not have gotten the nutrition they need, and they're going to have lifelong cognitive deficits."

"But we are doing what we can, yes?"

"Are we? Why can't we do more? If that were my kid, I'd move Heaven and Earth to get them more food. Why can't *we* get them more food?"

"You said that if you were the parent, you would do this. Why do the parents not get them more food?" Alfonso asked.

"Well, I—" Dree said, still mad but not knowing. "Because—but there's—they *can't.*"

"Correct," Maxence said, holding a bite of food in his fingers but not eating it yet. *"They can't.* There is no place that they could go to get enough food for their children. Even if they left their ancestral villages and moved to Kathmandu, they couldn't. If you divide the wealth and available income of Nepal by the number of people, *it's not enough.* On a population level, there is *nothing* all these parents can do to feed all these children."

"Available wealth and income?" Isaak asked from where he sat on the other side of Alfonso. Dree watched him talk. "What would you have Nepal do? Melt down all the idols in the Hindu temples for their gold and sell it to help the poor for one season? And then, there would be less tourism forever because there are no golden idols to look at, and the poor would be worse off next year."

Dree looked between the guys over the campfire. This was an intense discussion, but not a fight.

Maxence said. "A society can be judged by the way it treats its poorest citizens."

Across the fire, Father Booker cleared his throat and went back to eating his supper.

Max used a piece of bread to sop up some of the lentil stew on his plate and ate it, chewing as he stared at the plate and not looking up again.

Dree was ready to sink into the ground. She hadn't wanted to start an argument, but she didn't know what else to do for the kids who were on the verge of starving to death.

She managed to change the topic to a meteor streaking across the sky, leaving a trail of fire in the star-strewn heavens for a brief moment before it burned out.

Isaak had also seen the meteor streak overhead. "It's probably one of the Ursids. The peak of the Ursid meteor shower started on December nineteenth. Since the nineteenth was a few days ago, we should be at the peak for another day or two."

Dree had lost track of time other than the daily schedule of deciding which particular sites would not be ideal for a NICU micro-clinic, riding her motorcycle to the next village, and then trying to help the endless, *endless* patients. On a few days, Father Booker had celebrated a Mass, but she hadn't asked whether it was yet another Sunday or a different day that they should do Mass. "What day is it?"

"December twenty-second," Maxence said. He looked up at Dree, and her expression must've been puzzled because he added, "Father Booker and I have daily prayers that we are obliged to say, the

Divine Office. Every day, there are different prayers that have to be said. I keep track of the date with a downloaded file on my phone."

Dree managed to stay awake only about another fifteen minutes before she crawled into her tent for another quick sponge bath with a pan of warm water and wiggled into her sleeping bag, where her anger at the plight of her patients warred with her exhaustion.

Maxence crawled into the tent just a few minutes after she turned her flashlight off.

As always, he undressed as silently as humanly possible, and Dree resolutely stared at the fabric wall of the tent as he peeled the black leather off his body until he was nearly naked.

As the motorcycle leathers left Maxence's body, the subtle scent of his cologne, which was cinnamon, vanilla, and the secrets that happened in an orange grove at night where no one could see, filled the tent. She had no idea how he managed to smell so good when they were riding the motorcycles for days between the few overnight stops at inns where they could shower, but he did.

She clutched the fabric of her sleeping bag in her fists. If anything could distract her from the simultaneous rage and exhaustion that ran through her mind, it was the thought of Maxence sitting right behind her, his broad, strong shoulders and muscular biceps and triceps of his arms bared to the chilly night. His tight white undershirt would cling to his narrow waist, the lumps of his abdominal six-pack, and the strong sinews around his waist that pointed to the sexy line of coarse masculine hair that led from his navel, downward. Only a few weeks ago, she had run her tongue down his happy trail, and his sharp intake of breath had contracted his abs into a stack of bricks under his skin.

If she didn't hang onto that side of her sleeping bag for all she was worth, Dree might accidentally turn around and pounce on that ripped hunk who was just inches away from her, getting naked.

Or, nearly naked. In the morning sunlight, she'd seen the white rim of a tee-shirt collar above his sleeping bag.

But hey, a girl could dream.

Indeed, her dreams were turning increasingly erotic as their time in Paris receded into their history.

His flashlight clicked off, and absolute darkness smothered her sight.

In the dark, she could barely hear his faint whisper. "You awake?"

"Yeah. I might've dropped a bomb into the campfire tonight," she said.

"It's fine. No one was offended. The folly of these NICU micro-clinics is an important point that we're going to need to discuss sooner or later. Father Booker and Batsa have both made comments about the unsuitability of high-tech clinics for villages that have barely changed since the medieval era."

"So, what's going on between you and Father Booker? Out there at the campfire, the two of you were giving each other the hairy eyeball."

Silence blended with the darkness in the tent until Maxence said slowly, "No, he's not my type."

"No, silly. The hairy eyeball means that you two were shooting daggers at each other with your eyes."

"I haven't heard that expression, either, but I think I can guess what that one means. Father

Booker and I are not adversaries. I am quite sure that he and I both believe something we can never admit, even to each other."

"About God?"

"About the Church, but it's an obscure theology that is probably only of interest to Jesuits studying the difference between orthodoxy and orthopraxis."

"Maybe you should tell me that. Sounds like it would put me straight to sleep."

"Or, I can tell you about my uncle, Prince Jules the Malicious of Monagasquay."

Dree snuggled farther down into her sleeping bag in the dark because cold air leaked down her neck. As they had been ascending in elevation to more distant villages, the temperature had dropped, especially at night. "Do you really call him that?"

"We will as soon as I get back to a cellular signal and can text people. I have some cousins that are going to *love* that. No, Prince Jules the Malicious is the fourth son of my grandfather, Prince Rainier III. The current prince is his oldest son, Rainier IV, but he didn't father any legitimate children. Thus, the next person in line would've been my father, but he died when my brother and I were teenagers. So after that, it's my older brother Pierre, then me, then two of my cousins, and then Prince Jules."

Dree said, "Wait, I thought there was that Council of Nobles thing, and there was an election that isn't an election and stuff."

"Excellent memory, but previously, the Council has always offered the throne to the next person in the theoretical line of succession. That could change, of course, and my brother worried that it might. Like I said, he's definitely a psychopath, though he would have ordered the assassination of any psychologist who'd made that diagnosis. Finally, somehow, he figured out that he had screwed over enough people on the Council that they might want revenge. The last few years, he's been engaging in damage control, so I think they're going to give it to him. But if he hadn't done that, or if something had happened to Pierre, me, and my two cousins, Jules would have been the next person in line. The Council probably would've offered it to him, even though he's more psychopathic and delights even more in cruelty and evil than my brother. He is, however, better at politics with the other nobles than Pierre is."

"Well, if Pierre is going to be the prince, at least you know Prince Jules the Malicious is never going to get the throne."

"I hope not. It would be bad for the *world* if he did, not just Monagasquay. He's a racist. I would call him a fascist, except that the principality is essentially a fascist dictatorship, in that all power does rest with the sovereign prince. Monagasquay is barely a constitutional monarchy. For the last couple of centuries, the princes who have ruled have been relatively benevolent, so no one has made an effort to change the fact that a hereditary sovereign rules with an iron hand. Plus, everyone likes the lack of income tax."

"No income tax?" Dree asked as her body relaxed in the warmth of her mummy bag. "How the heck do y'all get away with that?"

"That casino that I mentioned brings in all the country's revenue. Monegasque citizens are not allowed to go in and gamble. We only take money from other people because the house always wins. Wealthy Monegasques are expected to contribute in significant ways, such as sponsoring the ballet or Grand Prix race. Plus, there's tourism and investments."

Dree laughed. "So, tell me the story about Prince Jules the Malicious."

"Prince Jules the Malicious is so awful that he got fired from one of the government ministry positions in Monagasquay. It's difficult to get fired from whatever government job you want if you're in the royal family. It was thought to be impossible before Jules managed it."

Dree listened from her warm spot, snuggled in her sleeping bag. "What did he do?"

Her voice sounded a little too gleeful, even in her own ears. But hey, if Maxence was spinning these stories and talking to her, she'd go with it. It was kind of like being read a bedtime story and kind of like flirting with a scorching guy who was nearly naked and only inches away.

Maxence said, "Jules started revoking citizenships for people who had been naturalized as Monegasque citizens unless they were billionaires. He threw dozens of people who owned small restaurants and shops or worked in the casino or hotels out of the country, the ones who keep Monagasquay going. There are fewer than forty thousand Monegasque citizens, so when you throw out a couple hundred people, that's a lot of people we lost within two years. And the worst thing is that there definitely was a racial component. Jules was throwing out people who had immigrated to Monagasquay and worked hard to become citizens and build a life there, and he just stamped some paperwork and destroyed their lives."

"That's reprehensible," Dree said.

"It's malicious. He blackmailed the billionaires who had immigrated and been naturalized as citizens. He forced them to pay him exorbitant bribes or else he would revoke their citizenship, which would have meant that they would have had to go back to their previous countries and pay all those years of income tax in arrears, plus penalties. It would have financially devastated them, and they knew it. And *he* knew it. Thus, he demanded bribes, and they paid. Eventually, a few years ago, he tried to blackmail a French woman who was the head of a Paris fashion house, but she had been good friends with Prince Rainier the Third's wife before she passed away. She told him and brought him proof of what Jules had been doing. Prince Rainier was *furious*. I mean, his rage against Prince Jules has become a legend in our family. Nobody is exactly sure what happened in the throne room that day, but there was blood on the floor, and Prince Jules needed minor reconstructive surgery afterward."

Dree couldn't help herself and giggled at the thought of royal princes duking it out in a playground scrap. She clapped her hand over her mouth, lest Father Booker and the other guys outside hear her and think that something was going on that wasn't.

Not that she didn't want it to, but *he* had made *vows*.

She said, "It's ridiculous how much I love these stories about Monagasquay that you come up with."

Maxence's baritone chuckle in the dark sounded

too much like any one of the times when he'd taken her to the panting edge of an orgasm and then deliberately stopped, which was infuriating and sexy as hell at the same time. It had been like he was so secure in his ability to make her come that he could waste all the opportunities he wanted to.

It was a good thing her ex-boyfriend had never tried something like that. He'd maybe had a five percent success rate, and if he'd have wasted any of those, she might've slugged him.

Maxence, though, was a different story. His confidence in his prowess was deserved, which made the revelation that he wanted to be a priest all the more unbelievable.

Absolutely unbelievable.

Just as she was working up the courage to ask Max again why he wanted to devote himself so completely to the Church that he would try to give up something he was obviously incapable of letting go, his breathing smoothed to the deep, even rhythm of sleep.

Well, Dree would just have to ask him the next time she got her courage up.

Which meant never.

CHAPTER 9
THE IMPORTANCE OF MILK
MAXENCE

Maxence sat on a rough-hewn kitchen table in a house in a hill village of Nepal, holding a small child in his arms while Dree examined the child's teeth. She was frowning slightly, just a tightening of the smooth skin between her blond eyebrows, as she peered into the boy's mouth.

Dree worked harder and longer hours in each village they rode into. She was kind to everyone and smiled gently at them, tended to their needs quietly, and cried when she thought no one was looking.

But Maxence was always looking.

The child sitting on his legs was terribly light, much too light for his age, and profoundly unhealthy. Not to put too fine a point on it, but this child *smelled*. His breath was sulfurous, and foul body odor wafted from his clothes every time he moved.

The odd thing was that he didn't appear dirty or oily at all. He looked recently bathed, and yet he *reeked*.

The child's mother was young, maybe still a teenager, and thin but not as sickly as the child. Three other women and one man surrounded the mother, petting her and discussing the child and the doctor with her. Batsa had said they were cousins, a sister, and her mother-in-law.

Again, Maxence considered the effect on this tight-knit community of outsiders walking in, announcing they would build a thing that the community could not understand, and then leaving them without the information and skills to use or maintain it. This project was so ill-planned, and he needed to bring it to a halt.

The mother and other family members had been struggling to hold the child, who was a willful little guy, so Max had stepped in. The child watched him from under his drooping eyelids, a baleful and suffering stare. Much of the child's petulance was probably because he was sick, but kids always behave better for people who aren't their parents.

Dree glanced up at Max, her blue eyes worried, and turned the child's head to look in his ears. Evidently, the child's ears were normal because she rapidly returned to holding the child's hand and gently rotating the boy's arms to inspect his skin.

Purplish bruises blossomed under the child's mahogany skin, concentrated near the joints. The child flinched when Dree barely prodded him, and a thin film of blood smeared the fingertip of her protective glove. Her bright blue eyes became more worried.

She asked Batsa, who was sitting in a chair beside the table, "How's his appetite?"

Batsa relayed the question to the mother and

then came back with the answer, "He is very pious and will not eat milk or yogurt because it comes from a cow, which is sacred, and he will not eat yak yogurt or milk because they are too much like a cow's. The family is vegetarian, and he eats all the subjis, which are cooked vegetables. His mother believes he will be a holy man."

"Eating both lentil and bread or rice?"

Quick chat. "Yes."

"So, he's getting all the amino acids, at least in theory." Dree asked, "Does he eat eggs?"

A quick chat in the Nepali language, and Batsa said, "She feeds him three eggs a week for strength, but he will not grow stronger."

"It's definitely not protein deficiency," Dree muttered under her breath. And louder, "Does he eat the egg yolks?"

Batsa conferred. "Yes, he eats the yellow parts very much. She gives hers to him."

"Probably not fats or cobalamin." Dree looked up at Max. "I thought it was going to be a lack of vitamin B12, but if he's eating eggs, then it's probably not. Any ideas?"

Maxence shook his head. "Absorption? Maybe celiac disease?"

"His stomach isn't distended, though." Dree asked Batsa, "How about diarrhea?"

Batsa conferred and replied, "She says yes, for a month now."

Dree blinked and nodded. "Okay, then. Maybe it's celiac or some other malabsorption problem." She turned to Batsa. "Tell the mother not to feed him any wheat, wheat flour, rye, or barley. No more bread for him. Get him rice, and make sure she doesn't put flour in anything that he eats. I don't know if that's it, but at least it's something."

Batsa relayed the information to the child's family, who seemed very upset at first that their child would not be able to eat rotis or naan and other bread. After a few more minutes of explanation, the family seemed to get it.

The family thanked Dree and the two guys profusely, of course, as always. The male cousin who had arrived with them gathered the fussing, very ill child in his arms and carried him out of the house.

Dree shook her head. "The pinpoint bleeding around his hair follicles, the bruising, and the joint swelling just doesn't look like celiac disease, but I don't know what it is. Celiac disease can look like almost anything, though."

Max agreed with her. "It doesn't look like other vitamin deficiency diseases like beriberi or pellagra, which I've seen in children when working in remote villages in Western Africa. His hair was brittle. It was uneven and didn't look like it had been cut, just broken."

Dree sighed. "I'm not a doctor. I'm just doing my best. I've got thirty more patients to see, and the sun goes down in three hours. I'll have to put him in the back of my mind while I try to help these other people."

Maxence watched Dree and helped where he could as she whipped through the next couple dozen cases. Many of them were easy. Some needed a few sutures. Others needed reassurance that it wasn't anything serious. A man needed one of Dree's precious tetanus vaccines that she slept with to keep them from freezing, which would inactivate them.

Dree was fluttering around her last few patients, dressing a wound on a little boy and explaining to a different young mother through Batsa that cradle cap is not life-threatening and just to scrub it off. She passed by Maxence and whispered, "I still can't figure out what that boy had."

He shrugged. "I haven't seen anything like it."

"Right," she said. "Me, either. It didn't look infectious. There were skin discolorations, but it wasn't a rash. There wasn't a wound that it stemmed from. It didn't look like a parasite or a bacteria or a virus. A month is too long for most infectious diseases to slowly progress unless it was leprosy or tuberculosis, which it wasn't. This was disseminated and progressive and weird."

"Why were you looking in his mouth?" Maxence asked.

"His gums were puffy and swollen. His teeth were loose. He was just a little boy, and his adult front teeth shouldn't have been loose at all. It wasn't like he'd gotten hit or something, though. All his teeth were the same degree of loose."

"It's odd," Max said. He felt like he should know what this was.

Dree shook her head and cared for her other patients, but Max could see she was fretting about the little boy.

As soon as they closed the door on her clinic and began to pack up the supplies for the motorcycle ride back out to the campsite, Dree said, "It's got to be something. He was around six years old. He wouldn't have lived this long if he had some inborn error of metabolism. I mean, they're all skinny, but they don't seem malnourished like some other villages we've seen." She ran her hand down the side of her waist and over her hip, emphasizing her hourglass figure. "I wouldn't call any of the people here curvy, though."

Maxence's mouth had gone dry, and he stared down at his motorcycle boots because his hands wanted to follow hers over her lush body. "No, I wouldn't call any of these villagers curvy."

When he looked up, Dree was staring at him. "What'd you say?"

Maxence muttered, "I just said I didn't think that anyone here has your curves."

"No," she said. *"Scurvy.* You said *scurvy.* Oh my word, that's it. I would never have thought that that little boy might have *scurvy.* An eighteenth-century British sailor trying to sail to the Maldives would get scurvy, not a little boy, now. *But that's it.* It explains the gums, and the loose teeth, and the bleeding under the skin and into his joints. He needs vitamin C. If we give him some vitamin C, he'll be fine in a week."

"I've read about it in history books, but never seen it before." Max sighed. "And that explains the child's abominable body odor and breath. Scurvy causes both as the body rots away from the inside, out."

Dree nodded, her eyes wide. "I know, *right?* That poor kid. That poor *mom.*"

Maxence had thought it might be a symptom, and it was.

She was already digging through their supplies, discarding multivitamins and other supplements until she found packages of drink mixes with large doses of vitamin C. She held them up. "The sisters thought of everything. I thought they threw these in so we'd have something to put in our water bottles for taste. *We have vitamin C.*"

"Excellent," Maxence said, smiling. She was just so adorable when her eyes flashed with excitement like that.

One of her eyebrows dipped. "But why would he be so affected when none of the other kids are?"

Batsa had been helping them pack up, and he said, "Vitamin C is found in fresh fruits and greens."

"Right," Dree said, but her voice was low like she already knew that.

Batsa continued, "No fresh food has grown around here for two months. None of the kids have been eating anything fresh since early October. Why was this kid the only one to get scurvy?"

Dree was scooping their supplies into their backpacks so they could leave. "Most other mammals, like cows and pigs and dogs, make vitamin C in their bodies. Humans and primates are one of the very few animals that don't make vitamin C and have to get it from our food. That's why it's an *essential* vitamin, because we can't build it."

"It's heat-inactivated," Max said, musing. "She said he was eating cooked food, but not milk."

"—Right," Dree said, thinking about it. "The mother said that he wasn't drinking milk. But milk doesn't have vitamin C—" She snapped her fingers. "*American* milk doesn't have vitamin C because it's *pasteurized.* These guys are drinking raw milk, straight from the ewe, *um,* the cow or yak. *Raw* milk has vitamin C in it because other animals make it, and especially powdered milk does. If all the other kids are drinking milk or eating yogurt and this kid isn't, then that explains it."

Maxence zipped the backpacks up and slung one over each arm. "Batsa, do you know where that kid lives?"

Batsa hoisted a heavy cardboard box and balanced it on his shoulder. "I can talk to people and find out."

With Batsa engaging every person they saw, it took only a few minutes for them to figure out which house the little boy lived in. Everyone knew how sickly he was and had been praying their kids didn't get whatever he had.

At the house, Batsa translated as Dree emphasized that the little boy must start drinking milk, especially powdered milk from the tiny store but also fresh milk. They mixed the vitamin C powder into water, and luckily, it made a refreshing orange drink that the boy guzzled right down.

They left seven more packets with the family, instructing them to make one drink per day for the boy, and then they returned to the campsite for the night.

The mother-in-law who had attended the appointment assured Batsa that she would mix the powder for the boy every day, and after this week, the boy *would* eat several servings of milk and yogurt every day, and there would be no disagreement.

Maxence smiled at her and bent to touch the mother-in-law's feet, and she said a blessing over him. With his family and a strong matriarch around him, that child was going to be okay.

Because Maxence had lived in Africa and Latin America for so long, the crucial importance of families and communities had become apparent to him. Europe and the United States seemed to have lost that cohesion and strong sense of belonging in the hustle to advance technologically. Social media seemed to be a woefully inadequate substitute.

Out in the countryside beyond the small town, the wind had picked up and bit through even Maxence's leather motorcycle pants and jacket that he wore. They'd been gaining in elevation with the last few villages that they had visited, and the air had grown increasingly frigid. The sun didn't seem to warm the black leather on his back and legs at all as they rode.

Earlier, when they'd ridden the motorcycles into town around noon, Dree had the shivers, but she'd seemed to warm up as soon as they'd gotten inside and started the clinic. The ski suit she wore had been sufficient to keep her warm for a while, but Maxence was becoming worried about her as the daily temperatures dropped.

At their campsite, Father Booker and the two engineers were tending to the fire and the food as they drove up. Alfonso had already made a main dish for dinner, and Batsa had arranged for delivery of bread, rice, and some side dishes, overpaying the lady handsomely.

The guys had built the night's campfire larger than previous ones because the freezing wind had turned biting.

Dree's teeth were chattering when she got off the motorcycle, and she stuck her gloved hands under her armpits as she surveyed the night's campsite.

Maxence ushered her over to one of the best spots around the campfire, not downwind where the smoke would choke her, but just off to the side where she would get the most radiant heat without the smoke coming right at her.

After a few minutes, her posture relaxed, and she took her hands out from under her armpits when Alfonso passed her a plate of warm food.

Around the campfire, Maxence ate and tried not to think about Dree's curvy body as he prepared to sleep beside her and keep his hands off of her for yet another night.

Dree received her plate from Alfonso and piped up, "You would not believe the day we had, guys. Father Maxence solved a medical mystery."

Maxence chuckled.

Isaak grinned at him. "Oh? Considering Maxence's proclivities in school, did he recognize the symptoms of a rare venereal disease known only in Turkish prisons and Brazilian brothels?"

Maxence stared down at his plate and refused to rise to the bait.

Dree said to Isaak, "No, *silly,* and I would really hope that something like that hadn't made its way to remote villages in Nepal. Nope, we had a kid with advanced *scurvy.* I've never seen a case, and I think you haven't either, right, Max?"

Max shook his head. "No, I'd never seen it. I've done most of my fieldwork in eastern Africa or Latin and South America, where fresh food is available the vast majority of the year, if not all year-round. I'd never seen scurvy before. It's hideous."

Dree nodded. "It's a terrible disease. When England was trying to explore and exploit the Poly-nesian and Indian Ocean islands, those ships would lose half their crews or more to scurvy. It's deadly."

Alfonso asked, frowning, "But, how do you know it was a vitamin C deficiency?"

Dree turned to him. "Once we figured out that's what it was, it was obvious. The symptoms matched. The kid wasn't drinking milk, and raw milk is a minor source of vitamin C. It must be pretty important here during the winter, though. All the other kids were getting at least some vitamin C from milk and maybe some from preserved foods like these hot pickled chutneys that the lady delivered, so they didn't get scurvy. This particular kid, though, wasn't drinking the milk. I didn't even think about *milk* being a source of vitamin C because, you know, it's not orange juice. He didn't have symptoms of calcium or protein deficiencies, so I think it's the vitamin C."

"But you didn't assay for it," Alfonso said. "You don't have a definitive diagnosis until you take blood and assay for ascorbic acid levels."

Dree laughed, and Maxence saw where this was going. She said, "We can't draw blood and send it off to the lab for a vitamin C concentration assay."

"No," Alfonso said. "But you can't treat a deficiency unless you are certain that the nutritional deficiency is the cause of the disorder. Otherwise, you may miss the true cause."

She said, "We don't have a gas chromatograph and trained technicians at our beck and call in this hill village. If it's not scurvy, then it's something that I don't know how to diagnose. I told his parents that if he doesn't get better to take him to the nearest city, but I don't think they can."

Alfonso was scowling. "These hill villages need medical laboratories, too, in addition to the NICU micro-clinics. How are we supposed to treat premature babies without access to modern medical techniques?"

Maxence smiled, sensing an opening. "That's an excellent question, Alfonso. If we build these NICU micro-clinics all over the mountains of Nepal, how will the staff perform routine procedures on these premature babies?"

Alfonso glared at his plate. "We'll just have to build medical laboratories, too."

Maxence kept his voice quiet. "Trucks don't come up here during the winter. How will we get supplies to them?"

"We'll mail them."

"There's no mail up here, Alfie. The store doesn't even get supplies for months. The clinics will need oxygen canisters and pharmaceuticals."

"We can get it to them," Alfonso growled.

"And where will we find medical technicians to work in these medical laboratories? Or pediatricians with neonatal specialties to work in the micro-clinics and send the tests to the medical laboratories staffed with technicians?"

Alfonso glared at Maxence with more anger than Max had seen from him since they were on the playground at boarding school. "Then what do you suggest we do? Are we just supposed to let these premature babies keep dying just because we can't do *everything?*"

Maxence wasn't a lawyer, but he'd been trained in rhetoric by the Jesuits when he got his doctorate in theology. He knew the answer to his question before he asked it. "Has a study been performed that shows highly technological micro-clinics will reduce premature infant mortality in far-rural areas *anywhere?*"

Alfonso sputtered, "Surely, there has to be. If a premature baby is born near a NICU and placed in an incubator, the baby has a better chance of survival. Incubators save premature babies."

"If a premature baby has access to an incubator and trained medical personnel in a hospital setting, yes, their chances of survival increase. But that's an entirely different situation than we are confronted with here." Maxence flung his arm sideways, indicating the vast, dark expanse of the Himalayan mountain range at night. "There are no doctors here. Dree is the first trained medical professional some of these people have seen in decades or their whole lives. Who is going to staff these NICU micro-clinics?"

Alfonso said, "We haven't reached that part of the project yet."

Maxence said, "I wasn't aware that the project had a budget for ongoing, long-term medical professionals to staff these micro-clinics. How many physicians or surgeons do you think are going to move to these remote stations and stand ready for the one infant who is born prematurely in this area per year?"

Alfonso said, "Once the micro-clinics are built, we can raise money to staff them. In the meantime, at least they will *exist.*"

Maxence caught Dree's gaze. She was watching their exchange with wide eyes and eating without pause. If she'd been sitting in a movie theater, she would have been shoveling popcorn into her mouth.

Father Booker and Batsa were casually chewing

their food. Booker shrugged when he saw that Maxence had looked over at him.

They had known that staffing and resupplying would be problems.

Isaak was staring down at his plate and frowning, using his fork to stab a rehydrated carrot. This argument may have been a revelation for him.

Later that night, Maxence waited while Dree went back to her tent for her nightly sponge bath and self-care. Luckily for all of them, she'd turned the flashlight away from herself while she was washing up, thus avoiding putting Maxence and the other men in a moral dilemma that they had passed last time, but barely.

There had been no more discussion about the establishment of the NICU micro-clinics. Indeed, everybody seemed to be stringently avoiding the conversation. Instead, they discussed the probable schedule for the rest of the trip.

Batsa pulled out a map and shone his flashlight on it as they traced the meandering path that they would take through the Himalayas.

He mentioned, "If we need to buy more supplies, there are alternate roads from these mountain communities that would be a straight shot down into the larger town where the airport was, Chandannath. We could stay at that inn again that had the delightful hot showers."

Alfonso added, "Chandannath has a medical college that trains doctors, nurses, and technicians. Since they have one of the larger medical schools in Nepal right here, why aren't there more doctors and technicians out in these hill villages?"

Batsa raised his head from the map and stared at

Alfonso. "Because maybe they prefer running water and better medical support services in Chandannath and the other larger towns."

Maxence kept his mouth closed and stole a glance back at Dree's tent, which was dark except for a tiny pinprick of light in one corner. "Looks like it's safe. I'll see you guys in the morning."

After his quick crawl into the pup tent and undressing as silently as possible, he slipped into his mummy bag and zipped it up to his face.

The tent was significantly colder than it had been on previous days, and even the few minutes of being underdressed in the icy air had chilled him.

Luckily, Maxence was mostly muscle, and he warmed up within a minute or two of zipping up the bag.

The frosty air snapped at his exposed cheekbones and nose.

Dree asked, "You okay?"

"Yeah, I warmed up as soon as I zipped up my sleeping bag."

"Yeah, it's getting colder as we climb in altitude. I had to break out one of the hand-warmer packs that Father Moses packed for me in Paris to warm up tonight. But I meant about arguing with Alfonso about the micro-clinics."

"Oh, that. Alfonso and I have known each other for years. We went to school together. That wasn't an argument. That was just a discussion about what's best. We both want what is best for the people who live up here. We just have differing opinions about what to do about it. He's not going to throw a rock at my motorcycle or anything."

Dree laughed. "I don't know, man. He looked

pretty pissed when everybody wasn't going along with exactly what he said."

"Alfonso wouldn't try to murder me over this. Now, stuff that happened in high school, *that's* where a motive for murder might come from."

She giggled prettily, and Maxence had a hard time not falling into the rabbit hole of his memory of her sunny smile, her flashing eyes, and her jiggling tits. She said, "It always surprises me when the motive for murder isn't something that happened in high school."

"Indeed, and boarding school is ten times worse than day school, I assure you."

"Did any murders happen at your boarding school?"

Maxence chuckled, his stomach bouncing under his fingers. "None that we know of. Anybody who went there was probably smart enough to hide the body or had security henchmen to bury it for them."

"Okay, fine. Did any murders ever happen in Monagasquay?"

Ah, she wanted a Monagasquay story.

Maxence considered what to tell her. Lots of murders had happened in the history of his small country, and he was quite sure his cousin had murdered a man. He wasn't entirely sure about the whole story, however.

Instead of telling Dree a highly conjectured version of what might have happened with Alexandre, Maxence said, "There's a rumor that floats around Monagasquay that one of the princes was kidnapped when he was a small child."

In the dark, her sweet little voice rose in excitement. "Oh, a kidnapping story. That sounds good.

I'm in the mood for a thriller. Wait, was the little prince rescued? Or is it like the little princes in the tower in England, where they never found their bodies? Because I can't handle it if he doesn't make it."

A shiver ran through Maxence. "He survived."

"Okay, then tell me the story," she said.

Maxence breathed in a deep breath, feeling the cold air all the way down into the base of his lungs.

The problem was the dark. He couldn't see, and he couldn't ground himself with his sight.

Instead, he concentrated on the warmth of the sleeping bag around his arms and legs. A scent like a peach and citrus-flavored alcoholic drink on a cypress dock over the Mediterranean Sea puffed out of his sleeping bag as his body warmed the remnants of his cologne.

Curls of his hair traced lines on his forehead and near his ears as he breathed.

His riding gear piled at the base of his sleeping bag emitted a leathery whiff into the air.

As Dree breathed, her breath whirred in the dark, and the nylon of her sleeping bag creaked.

His abdominals were lumps under the soft cotton of his shirt where he rested his fingertips. His mouth still tasted like mint from his toothpaste.

The ground was hard under his back and heels.

The very apex of the tent was a faint, yellow-gray smear of a line against the blackness surrounding him.

Maxence stared at the yellow-gray smear. His ears filled with the tiny whoosh of Dree's breath and the rustle of her bedroll.

Breathe.

He could breathe.

If he could breathe, he could speak.

Maxence said, "Once upon a time, there was a little prince of Monagasquay. He wasn't a very handsome little prince and he was second in line to the throne after his older brother, so nobody cared about him very much. He was just the spare in case something happened to the older prince, and he expected to have a very quiet life, which was just fine with him. As his older brother was not particularly kind to him about his extraneous status, the young prince made himself scarce as often as possible, which was probably why no one noticed for a week when he went missing."

"Wait," Dree said. "How old was the kid?"

"Nine years old," he said.

"And how long ago was this?"

"Years and years ago. Lifetimes," Maxence sighed.

"And nobody just went, 'Hey, where's the other kid?'"

"Evidently not."

"Who kidnapped him? Does Monagasquay have a rival, an ancestral enemy, like England and France were always fighting with each other back in historical times?"

Maxence chuckled. "Monagasquay is too small to have any real enemies. If we had an enemy, they would simply squash us. Back in medieval times, the nobles who ruled the Italian cities squabbled with each other with their tiny little armies. Whenever France got pissed off at us, they just overran us and stole all the art and jewelry from the fortress-turned-castle."

"That doesn't seem fair. That sounds like a big ol' bully picking on a little kid."

"It was a long time ago, a much longer time ago than the kidnapping."

"Oh, that's right, the kidnapping. Let's get back to the kidnapping."

Maxence said, "Monagasquay is right on the Mediterranean Sea, and we are a seagoing people. Boating and sailing are very important in our culture. One day, the little prince was out sailing his small sailboat when a larger motorboat pulled up alongside, snatched the little prince off his boat, and spirited him away to a tanker ship anchored farther off the coast."

"Does the little prince have a name?" she asked.

Maybe Max should call the kid Augustine.

Too obvious.

Maxence said, "His name has been lost in history."

She argued, "And yet, with motorboats and tanker ships, it doesn't sound like this happened a long time ago."

"I'm not that good of a writer. I'm just making stuff up as I go along. If there are historical anachronisms, I'll try to do better next time."

"Fine, fine. Tell me about the little prince whose name has been lost in ancient history who was kidnapped by guys on a motorboat."

The boat which had sped up alongside him and then carried him away had been long and narrow, and the sparkling red hull had splashed through the wavelets as he'd fought.

Max said, "The tanker ship had been moored

off the coast for weeks, as they had been looking for their chance to kidnap the prince."

"What did the kidnappers want? Money? Publicity? For Monagasquay to have some other political prisoners released from some other country?"

"It appeared to be money at first, but they didn't seem to know how much they wanted or where they wanted it deposited. This was all during a time of great upheaval in the history of Monagasquay, when an old sovereign prince was dying and an election was imminent in the Council of Nobles, which is also known as the Crown Council of Monagasquay."

"But you said that a prince election was happening right now."

"It happens every time a new sovereign prince needs to be crowned."

"That seems to happen a lot in Monagasquay."

"Or maybe I'm just a terrible writer, and you should find someone else to tell you stories to help you fall asleep at night."

Maxence immediately regretted saying that in case she did.

Dree sighed. "Okay, I won't quibble. Go on."

"So, the little prince was missing for a week. The kidnappers kept trying to tell people they wanted to be paid a ransom, but nobody would talk to them because they didn't know the prince was missing. Eventually, they realized they couldn't find the little prince, and then the negotiations began in earnest."

"Finally."

"That's what the little prince thought, too. On the tanker ship, the men who had kidnapped the little prince threw him in a squalid, unused storeroom. They only brought him water once during the first couple of days. They finally started feeding him after another few days, when it became apparent there would not be a quick resolution to the kidnapping."

"That's awful!" she said.

"Yes, it was."

Within days, the empty storeroom with peeling, rusty walls reeked, and so did he. As a child, he'd never been overly fastidious about cleanliness, as little boys often aren't.

That experience, however, had given him a new appreciation for hygiene. Out on these rustic charity missions, Maxence was careful to wash himself every day and sometimes two or three times a day, even if all he could muster was a sponge bath. Sweat and body odor drove him simply insane.

Maxence said, "Eventually, the kidnappers, who seemed to be pirates rather than professional kidnappers, began to berate the young prince for being so unimportant that the current sovereign prince, the heir apparent to the throne, and his own parents didn't seem to care that he was missing. They terrorized him. They beat him. They asked why he was so unimportant. They asked why their demands were not being met.

"The little prince did not know.

"Eventually, he began to tell himself stories about how unimportant he was.

"Eventually, he told his kidnappers the same stories, about how he had never felt like he was part of the royal family, about how he thought he was destined for other things.

"Eventually, the kidnappers believed him.

"And eventually, the kidnappers thought he was one of them."

"One of *them?*" Dree breathed. "The little prince became a *pirate?*"

Maxence nodded in the dark. "The little prince believed their revolutionary furor with all his heart. He believed so much that he was one of the pirates, a revolutionary, that he convinced himself, and he convinced them.

"By the end of the second week, they allowed him to leave the smelly storeroom for a few hours at a time.

"Within another day or two, he had a bunk with the other sailors and was eating their communal meals with them.

"He worked hard on the ship, mopping the deck and carrying anything that needed to be moved. He was sunburned. He was seasick.

"In another two weeks, he'd convinced them that he didn't want to go home because he was truly one of them."

Dree gasped. "But his family finally paid the ransom and got him back, right?"

Maxence breathed slowly, deep down into his stomach, keeping himself calm as he lay in a sleeping bag in the dark freezing tent in the highlands of Nepal near Mount Everest in December, which was about as far away from the summertime Mediterranean Sea as one could get, vertically and along the land. The Earth was even on the opposite side of the sun from that June day, which meant Maxence was vertically fifteen thousand feet, twenty-one and a half years of time, and a hundred eighty-six million miles of dead and empty space away from that rusting hulk of a tanker ship.

Breathe, he told himself. *Breathe.*

The scents of his leather motorcycle gear and his cologne, the feel of his hair around his face and his abdominals and shirt under his fingertips, the sound of Dree's breathing in the night, and that faint smear of moonlight glowing through the top of the dark, dark tent.

He had practiced for many years to be able to control his breathing. While his friend Casimir had been learning to not trust girls because they toyed with him, while Arthur had been learning to become an Englishman because that was all he could hold onto in the world, Maxence had been learning to disguise the fact that in some way, he was still a little boy locked in a filthy, utterly dark steel storage room of the tanker ship, knowing that no one was coming to save him and he would have to rescue himself.

Maxence said, "Just over a month had passed when the little prince convinced his kidnappers—by believing it hard enough and telling them what he believed with all the love in his heart—that he would go and tell the world their story and recite their manifesto. He told them that he could convince the world they were right and that they should be welcomed back from the sea as heroes. They believed he could convince the world because he had convinced them that he could."

"So, did he?" Dree asked breathlessly. "Did he become their spokesman and tell the world?"

Max stared into the darkness. The lightless obsidian of the cloud-covered Nepali countryside was not very different than the darkness of a windowless steel room with a sealed door. "He tried. The pirates set him adrift in a tiny tender, which is a small boat used to go from a bigger boat to the shore, like a rowboat. Even in just the few weeks that he had been helping on the ship, his muscles had grown stronger. He rowed the tiny vessel the few hundred yards to shore and walked out of the sea to freedom."

"His family must've been so relieved to see him!" Dree exclaimed, and then she laughed. "I'm ridiculous. Getting all caught up in the stories. You're a better storyteller than you give yourself credit for."

Yes, Maxence could make anyone believe any story that he wanted to. He still wasn't sure how. He'd been born with an uncanny charisma, but his ability to persuade people was a skill honed in fire.

"Some of them were," Maxence said. "But whoever was and whoever wasn't glad to see him was immaterial because the little prince was whisked away and returned to his boarding school as quickly as possible, to restore a sense of normality, they said. The odd thing was, whenever the little prince tried to tell his story, no one believed him. His family had not only been reluctant to negotiate a deal with the pirates, but they had also made sure that no one else knew he had been missing. If he told people, he was branded a liar."

Her gasp echoed against the fabric walls of the tent in the darkness. "Why would they do such a thing? If my kid were ever kidnapped, I'd be all over the news, trying to find them and bring them home. Their face would be on every telephone pole, milk carton, and local news channel in the world."

Ah, if only.

Maxence said, "The little prince's family decided against publicity for a number of reasons. First, if it became common knowledge that they had negotiated with and paid off kidnappers, even though they hadn't, no member of their family would ever be safe again. Every single one of them would have a dollar amount associated with their names."

"Hire some security men. That's what they're for." Dree's voice sounded disgusted that she had to tell him that.

He chuckled, and his abs shuddered against his fingertips. "They have security. Not that it matters. The other reason was that if the little prince became notorious for having been kidnapped and abused, he would become even more of a target. A few years earlier, another little prince of another country, although not a relative, had been the subject of a tragedy when he was about the same age. His name was Wulfram."

"Oh, so *his* name hasn't been lost to posterity."

"Right. Wulfram had an older twin, so he was also the spare to his older brother's heir. When Wulf was nine years old, just a few years before the main character of our story, his older brother was horrifically assassinated, shot with a high-caliber rifle in front of his twin and dozens of other kids from their school. Wulfram was wounded but survived. He became notorious, and he has lived with a target on his back ever since, even as an adult. It is better to be anonymous, our young prince's family decided. It was better if no one knew the tragedy and the horror, and thus be tempted to repeat it."

Dree said, "I hate people."

Maxence laughed. "That is the best reaction to that story I've ever heard."

A tiny sound scratched at the side of his sleeping bag. It sounded a bit like a mouse had gotten into the tent, but the mice should have been hibernating in Nepal at that time of year. Maxence unzipped his sleeping bag just a little bit and explored with his fingertips to where the sound was coming from.

Small, warm fingers were plucking at the nylon of his sleeping bag and, as he touched them, twined in his.

Dree whispered, "I don't know what that story is a symbol for, but the loneliness and desperation are breaking my heart."

Maxence held onto her hand. "It's just a story. You wanted a story about Monagasquay, and it's just a story."

The darkness stayed unbroken within and above the tent, and Max slowly, fitfully, fell into sleep.

The next morning when he woke, Dree was still holding his hand.

He held his breath, clinging to the moment of their palms touching and fingers intertwined.

The beige sides of the tent glowing with sunlight, the boxes at the back of the tent, her burgundy sleeping bag, the rattle of wood and crunch of tinder as some of the guys were building the morning fire outside, the feminine scent of her filling the air and his nose and his mouth and touching his skin.

He held on.

CHAPTER 10
PASHMINA
DREE

When Dree awoke the next morning, Maxence's eyes were closed, his eyelashes dark against his tanned skin. His hand under hers was limp, except his fingers twitched. His breathing was more ragged and high in his lungs than the deep rhythm of sleep.

Maybe he had allergies or was dreaming or something.

Her arm was cold, but her hand was warm where she held his palm.

Just as Dree was slipping her fingers out of his, his eyelids fluttered, and Maxence rolled over and stretched. "G'morning."

He didn't say anything about their hands, so neither did she. "Morning! I guess we've got to go look at the possible sites that Isaak and Alfonso found for their NICU micro-clinic, huh?"

Maxence groaned. "I really should not have started that argument around the campfire last night."

"It needed to be said. Those NICU clinics are going to be a waste of money and time that could go to help people."

They packed up the camp quickly and were just mounting the motorcycles when an older woman approached them from the direction of the village. They always made their camp close to the village, maybe a hundred yards away, for their privacy and to give the town the illusion that they weren't invading.

The woman walked carefully on the thin crust of ice that had grown on the rocky ground overnight. She wore the trailing end of her dupatta draped over her head like a hood.

When she was quite close, she yelled something in the Nepali language.

Batsa, who was holding his helmet under his arm and watching her, said, "She says she is looking for Lady Doctor Dree."

Dree supposed she looked different when she was wearing her bright red-and-white ski suit for riding the motorcycle. She lifted her arm and waved at the woman. "Here I am."

The woman walked over to Dree, and she recognized the woman as the mother-in-law of the child with scurvy the day before. "How is he?" Dree asked because Alfonso's words that the vitamin C deficiency should be diagnosed in a lab still rang in her ears. "Is he doing better?"

The woman held out a small, pale blue bundle that looked as soft as a cloud, and said something that Batsa translated as, "My sickly grandson is alive and doing much better today. He is better than he has been in weeks. His body is not bleeding from his skin anymore. His elbows and knees are less bad. He smiles. I thank you for saving the life of my grandson. I would like to give you this as my thanks and to give you my blessings."

Dree took off her gloves and took the bundle from the woman's hands, which turned out to be a shawl of the softest yarn Dree had ever felt. "It's *beautiful.*"

Maxence was standing beside her. "It's a pashmina. It's cashmere, but the *pashm* wool is the softest kind of wool the goat produces. This is probably one of the finest things she owns."

Dree glanced up at him, nervous about what was going on. "If it's so valuable, should I accept it? I don't want payment. I'm not doing this for payment."

"Yes, you should accept it," he said. "You saved her grandson's life. She'll probably pray for your health and happiness for the rest of her days. Community and family are the most important things to them. This is how humans have always lived, in groups of two to three hundred people. People are happiest when they form and live in highly interconnected communities. It doesn't matter if it's your birth family or a family unit you form, but it's essential. Even serious introverts like my friend Arthur live their best lives when they have people around them, for when they need them. You should accept the shawl and receive her blessing because she's giving it in the spirit of the ties that bind a community, not as payment."

"Oh," Dree said. She thanked the woman.

Batsa translated, and the woman did the classic blinking, head-shaking, and holding up a hand to say *it's-nothing-it's-nothing.*

Maxence touched her arm, which she felt through the puffy layers of her ski suit. "You touch her feet to receive her blessing." He bent and spread both his hands toward the woman's boots.

The older woman smiled and bobbled her head from side to side, grinning and saying something as she touched his shoulders and raised him up.

Dree handed him the scarf and whispered to him, "It's okay to do this even though we're Catholic, right?"

The cold wind whipped his black curls around his face. "It's fine. It's a community and cultural thing."

Father Booker leaned toward her. "Yes, it's all right, not that anyone asked the ordained Catholic priest for his opinion."

"Thank you, Father Booker," Dree said and performed the same bow and hand reach as Maxence had.

The woman raised Dree up by her shoulders and then smacked her hand to the middle of Dree's forehead, holding it there and chanting something to the sky.

Dree went cross-eyed, looking at the woman's hand on her face. Her palm smelled like baked bread and fresh butter.

She asked Max from under the woman's hand. "This is okay, too, right?"

Max nodded. "You should be honored."

"Okay."

The woman's hand on her face did not move,

and the woman said something serious to Dree in Nepali.

If this had happened back in New Mexico, the woman would have been spraying spittle and screaming while she called on the power of Her Savior Jesus Christ to expel the demons from Dree's soul, so this was a much nicer experience. Dree was all for less screaming and spittle.

The woman removed her hand and said something else, then pressed her hands together like she was praying and bowed.

Batsa told Dree, "She thanks you again for the life of her grandson. Do the namaste back to her, just like that, palms together and bow."

So, she did.

They said their goodbyes, and Dree kept an eye on the older woman as she went back to the village. The six of them shoved their helmets on their heads, mounted the motorcycles, and carefully pulled out onto the dirt road that led away from the village.

That day's ride was uneventful, and the next few days passed with little novelty.

In the next couple of villages, many people came to Dree's makeshift clinic to be treated, but there were no medical mysteries. There were the usual stitches, listening to chests and backs and dispensing antibiotics for pneumonia, wound cleaning and instructions, a few vaccinations she had, a frantic digging through the supplies for a tube of ocular antibiotic gel for a woman with a frightening eye infection, setting a few bones and plastering on a cast, rehydrating salt solution for a few children with diarrhea and probable food poisoning, just the usual.

One clinic was so busy that she couldn't stop for

lunch. Maxence handed her a bite of bread with yak butter every time she breezed by him. Yak butter was really good. It was almost as good as sheep butter, which was saying something.

And as usual, she worked as fast as she could while Batsa translated, and she worked until Maxence quietly told her that it was enough, she had done enough, and she must stop for food and rest.

Nights around the campfire weren't particularly tense. They stopped talking about the advisability of the NICU clinics. Discussion on the morning survey missions was limited to the suitability of the actual site, whether the ground was level, how much direct sunlight the plot of land would get per day due to the mountains, and the availability of water due to river proximity in the village.

Dree sensed a confrontation was coming, though. The air was thick with arguments left unsaid.

At one village, a woman who seemed to be in her forties slowly walked in, obviously in pain.

Maxence and Batsa had been creating makeshift curtains out of bedsheets from the house that they commandeered at each stop, so they had some semblance of privacy from the dozen or more people in the waiting room. That day's curtains were printed with a crimson and orange mandala.

The woman explained to Dree what was wrong, and Batsa translated it as, "She has a wound on her chest that will not heal. It has been there for a year or more. She apologizes for the smell, but she says that she cannot make it better."

Her eyes remained downcast on the souls of her boots as she unlatched her coat and blouse, and Dree reached over and touched her arm, saying, "It's all right. Just show me, and I'll do what I can."

As she unbuttoned her clothes, a foul odor rose from her body. The rotting smell was not sweat or common body odor, but something else entirely.

Dree caught a glimpse of Maxence's expression, which had become carefully neutral. He turned away, and Batsa also pivoted as the woman opened her clothes, giving her a little bit of privacy.

As her blouse opened, the woman's left breast was entirely rotted away by cancer, and the ulcer had infiltrated her torso and ripped open her skin over her ribs.

Dree did not react.

After a quick examination to make sure that the gaping, oozing wound was indeed cancer and not something that Dree could cure or even treat, Dree sat on the table beside the woman.

The woman did not pull away, so Dree opened her hand next to her leg. The woman took her hand and held on.

Dree told Batsa to say, "I am sorry. I am so sorry. This is very bad, indeed. I am sorry there is nothing I can do to help this, and you should do whatever you need to before the end of your life."

She wasn't sure how to say that the woman should put her affairs in order, and that was the best she could come up with.

After digging through the bag, Dree found some strong painkillers, which she gave to the woman to take home with instructions through Batsa.

The rest of the clinic that day was subdued, even though Dree evaluated three perfectly healthy, chubby, and robust babies, whom she inoculated against several deadly childhood diseases that they would now never experience. Usually, even one well-baby patient was enough to make her day, but nothing seemed to lift the soggy weight around her head and heart.

She did manage to sleep after that day, and the next morning was the usual discussion of a possible construction site for a NICU micro-clinic that should never be built. Then, they headed out on another frigid motorcycle ride to yet another small community desperately in need of far more help than she could give them.

The dirt roads they traveled clung to the steep faces of the Himalayan mountains, a craggy rock wall on one side of the road, and a sheer cliff that dropped straight toward a dry riverbed on the other.

Rocks, gravel, and small boulders littered the road in shades of silver, pale umber, tawny yellow, and white.

The valleys were slashes between the towering mountains, knifed into the earth by water. No trees and few bushes grew on this moonscape that reminded her more of the white gypsum sand dunes in the northern Chihuahuan Desert of New Mexico than any mountain range she'd ever seen.

One rockfall from the stony heights far above was still so loose that they dismounted and carefully walked their bikes over the least obstructed part. The fallen rocks were limestone, sandstone, and marble, which were more easily eroded than some of the slate and granite farther up the mountain.

Maybe the prevalence of fallen rocks should have

warned them, but they rode on along the road that clung to the side of the cliff, hoping and praying that no large rocks would fall into their path or hit them, until their luck ran out.

CHAPTER 11
CRASH AND BURN
MAXENCE

Maxence didn't see the jagged stone falling down the side of the mountain until it slammed into the front tire of his motorcycle.

As usual, he had crowded Dree up in front of him so that she was in the second position behind Batsa. It was just bad luck that Father Booker, Alfonso, and Isaak had also motored ahead of him, and Maxence was in the very last position when a rock bigger than his motorcycle helmet slipped off the cliff face and hit him.

Before he could swivel or dodge or even change the angle of impact, the black and ivory stone smashed the motorcycle's front wheel out from under him.

He skidded sideways.

The hard fall onto his side slammed through him, and he skidded over the ground.

The padded black leather of his riding suit shredded on the limestone sand and gravel.

The bike tumbled behind him, breaking apart.

One tire went over the edge of the road.

The rest of the motorcycles disappeared around the next bend in a puff of gasoline-scented exhaust.

Maxence rolled, the sharp stones and dirt banging on his elbows and knees and hips.

He tumbled to the edge of the sharp precipice, the upper half of his body dangling precariously over the long drop down to the river at the bottom of the gorge.

Through the visor of his heavy helmet that pulled him down toward the yellow-gray, barren abyss, he watched his front tire spin, bounce, plummet, and plunge down-down-*down* the cliff, until it rolled to a stop behind a large rock, still only a third of the way to the bottom far below.

Maxence scrambled away from the edge and crawled to the other side of the road, collapsing next to the wall.

His abdomen didn't feel like anything major had ruptured inside, though he was already sore from deep bruises. He didn't feel ripped apart, though.

No sharp pains of broken bones lanced through him, which was astonishing. Father Booker could commend Maxence to the Vatican for sainthood on the strength of that miracle, alone.

Yeah, no one was going to mistake Maxence for a saint.

His mind was simultaneously traveling through an emotional fog and making razor-sharp evaluations of his current state, which he concluded must be due to shock and adrenaline racing through his body.

He gingerly pulled himself into a seated position,

resting his back against the granite cliff on that side of the road, although he kept glancing up to make sure no more rocks were falling that might smash him in the head. He wrenched his motorcycle helmet off and unthreaded his arms from the straps of his backpack.

His helmet appeared undented, though long scratches cut parallel lines into its glittery finish.

The rear wheel of his motorcycle, still attached to what remained of the body, spun lazily in the late morning sunshine. Other parts lay strewn across the asphalt. A dark gold stain spread under the engine, and gasoline trickled from behind the bike and down the mountain road.

The faint roar of the other motorcycles echoing off the mountains toward the other end of the valley faded away.

His choices were to stay where he was and wait for rescue or to walk to the next village, which should be about forty miles farther down the road. The previous town was farther away.

The road stretched away from him in both directions.

He wondered how often trucks traveled on this road during the winter. Hours or weeks might pass before the next delivery truck rumbled by on its way to supply the small village stores with flour, sugar, rice, and other staples.

The rear part of the motorcycle hadn't gone over the edge of the cliff. His saddlebags contained a few essentials like energy bars that might keep him alive for days. Water was going to be a problem. Very little precipitation fell in Nepal during this time of the year, if any. The villages drew their water either from running rivers or from enormous ice-wells, an evaporation-cooled technology that grew a massive stalagmite of ice during the rainy season that could then be harvested during the dry parts of the year. But he knew there wouldn't be any ice wells near such a remote stretch of highway.

Upon further consideration, Maxence believed that he was not gravely injured, and his best option was to walk to the next town, even though he expected it to take at least two days.

Carefully, he held onto the rock wall and drew himself to his feet, noting that one of his motorcycle boots had taken the brunt of the skid over the rocks and dirt. The part that covered his ankle was shredded, and his boot flapped against the bottom of his foot when he cautiously took a step.

Maxence was far enough away from a bend on the road that he would have time to make it back to the wall if a truck lumbered around one of the far turns, so he limped across the few feet of dirt road to his decapitated motorcycle.

The medical and food supplies in the steel boxes over the back tire were mostly unscathed. A few of the protein bars bent at odd angles, and some of the boxes of bandages were banged up. He started moving everything in his saddlebags to his backpack, triaging what supplies were the most important, like vaccines, and which could be purchased again in Chandannath, like dry rice.

He ripped open a protein bar and ate it because it was easier than stuffing it in his backpack with everything else.

His teeth all seem to be firmly planted in his mouth.

That was a good sign.

He patted his helmet in thanks.

He considered his most serious challenges to his survival. The temperature was going to be a problem.

The nights had been well below freezing for the last week, and even the tent with Dree had gotten quite chilly. His bedroll was strapped to the base of his backpack and seemed to have survived the crash without rips.

In the saddlebags of the motorcycle, he also found one mirror-shiny thermal blanket, which he could put underneath and around the mummy bag, and several of the chemical hand-warmer packs that Father Moses had sent for Dree.

Since his alpine-rated mummy-style sleeping bag was intact and he had the other supplies, he stood a decent chance of not freezing to death.

Not that freezing to death was a bad way to go. You were cold, and then you weren't, and then you went to sleep.

Drowning was worse.

So was starvation.

Well, if he froze to death in the sleeping bag, then that's how it was.

But in the meantime, he could start walking to the next village where he would find supplies and, hopefully, Dree and the guys.

He replaced his superficially damaged helmet on his head because it would keep both his scalp and face warmer, and it would protect him from any small rocks that fell off the side of the mountain.

With the most precious of their medical supplies safely stowed in his backpack, Maxence hitched it up around his shoulders and began his forty-mile hike. He didn't think he had six hours of sunlight left. Most likely, he would need to make camp at least one night, alone, out in the hinterlands of Nepal.

He had shoved his gloved hands into his pockets for warmth, so he couldn't pull out his phone to read one of the daytime prayers of the Holy Office. Since he thought that he was probably in mortal danger from hypothermia, the Jewish law of *Pikuach Nefesh*, which is the principle that saving a specific human life overrides every other tenant of the Torah, applied to his situation. God would probably forgive that he had replaced saying specific Psalms ascribed to the day with ardent prayer because he suspected that even moving his hands from his pocket to hold his phone might cause a drop in his body temperature that might lead to his death.

He kept to the side of the road with the rock wall. If a supply truck came, there was a good chance he could leap on some rocks to signal them to stop and rescue him, or he could at least keep a large rock between himself and the truck so it wouldn't run him over.

If he'd walked on the cliff-side of the road, his choice would have been allowing the truck to run him over or leaping to his probable death down the sheer, rocky face of the mountain.

He had walked for about five minutes, hiking steadily, when in the far distance, he heard the distinct rumble of an engine.

Excellent. He'd heard it coming from far enough away that he could find a safe place from which to signal them or to avoid being run over.

Within a minute, he reached a small pile of fallen

rubble, and he climbed upon it to use as a vantage perch.

The truck's roar amplified as it neared. The grumbly wail of the engine suggested that it was probably large and diesel, so there was a chance he would be riding in the cab of a delivery truck rather than the bed of a pickup. The wind in a pickup bed might have chilled him too much.

The truck's sound intensified. The vehicle must be directly around the corner.

Maxence readied himself to raise his arms and yell.

Instead of a truck, five Royal Enfield motorcycles raced around the corner, spraying gravel over the edge of the road into the canyon on the other side.

A red-and-white-clad figure drove the motorcycle in the lead, her body clinging tightly to the bike for speed.

As Maxence raised his arms, the lead motorcycle braked hard, nearly laying the bike down. The tiny rider flailed one foot at the kickstand, managing to hook it with her ankle, and then leaped off the motorcycle and barreled into him.

Her helmet slammed into Maxence's stomach, knocking the wind out of him.

He stumbled backward, gasping, and slipped down the back of his rubble pile.

Dree's voice sounded tinny from inside her helmet. "Maxence, Maxence! What happened to you? I looked back, and you weren't there. When I looked in my rearview mirror, I saw three bikes instead of four, and I freaked out and I turned around to come find you."

Maxence managed to suck a tiny bit of air into his lungs, and he coughed.

"I rode as fast as I could, but the stupid dirt roads are so slippery. I almost went over the side one time, but I didn't slow down. I came to find you as soon as I could. I'm so sorry. I'm so sorry we lost you. Oh my God, what happened to you?"

At that point, Maxence had managed to suck in half a lungful of air, and he told Dree, "I'm all right."

Dree yanked off her helmet and dropped it at their feet. She grabbed him around the midsection, hugging him so hard that drawing another breath seemed impossible. "I'm so sorry! What happened?"

Maxence patted her arm. "I'm okay. Let me breathe."

"I looked back and you were gone!" She burst into tears.

He untangled her arms from around his waist and bent down to eye-level with her. "Dree, *chérie*. I'm all right."

"Tell me what happened to you!"

"A rock rolled down the side of the mountain and onto the road. It hit my front tire and knocked me over."

"Where's your motorcycle? I kept imagining you at the bottom of that stupid ravine, dead."

"The motorcycle is a few minutes down the road, in several pieces. The front tire is in the ravine."

She grabbed him with both arms around his chest and buried her face in his shoulder.

Maxence wrapped his arms around her, cradling her against his chest. Her body was shaking, and he murmured anything he could think of near the pink shell of her ear, assuring her that he was fine, telling her that nothing could ever happen to him or her, and just trying to make it all right.

Dree stepped back, wiping the tears off her face with her palms.

Maxence stooped and asked her, "Are you okay now?"

She nodded. "I should be asking *you* that. Are you *hurt?* Do you need medical attention? I'm a frickin' *nurse* and I'm supposed to render *medical aid,* not be a ninny!" She grabbed his collar and began tugging at his coat's zipper.

He laughed at her. "I'm fine. I'll have some bruises, but I don't think I even broke a rib. I'm just sore."

She sighed and braced herself with her hands on her knees, her chest still heaving.

Maxence looked over her head, where Father Booker was still sitting astride his motorcycle, both his boots planted firmly on the ground. He'd removed his helmet and was watching them with a pensive solemnity in his eyes.

Priests should not have women throwing themselves at them like this.

Max took a step backward and settled one hand on Dree's shoulder, a solidly platonic gesture that also kept her away from him.

Dree drew one last sigh and looked up at him with her clear blue eyes still swimming with tears. "Your bike is back there somewhere? Why did you leave it?"

"It's totaled. Some pieces might be salvaged for parts. The oil and petrol had leaked out of the engine and gas tank. I got most of the important stuff out of the saddlebags, but some rice and other dry goods that I couldn't carry in my backpack are still in the storage containers."

"But you're *okay?*" she asked again.

Maxence showed her the scrape on his helmet and the shredded leather on his thigh. "I had good gear."

"Well, thank heavens for that." She turned to the other guys and spread her arms. "Okay, guys. We have five motorcycles and six people. Who's going to double up? It seems most efficient if the two lightest people ride on one bike together, which I assume would be me and Batsa."

Batsa's dark eyes widened, and he looked at each one of the other guys as if he needed someone to defend him. "I am a married man. I do not think my wife would like me to ride on a motorcycle with a young woman. That is not what I signed up for."

Isaak and Alfonso began scrutinizing each other, but neither one wanted to be the horny jerk who insisted they *wanted* to ride with the pretty young woman they'd been eyeballing for weeks.

Isaak said, "Alfonso, I do not feel comfortable with you lying against my back, as I have said time and time again in our tent."

Alfonso sputtered, "I would be driving. You would be against my back, and I'm not comfortable with that, either, for you have smacked me in the face while sleeping more times than I can count."

Isaak turned back to Max and Dree. "Maxence should have to double up with someone because he's the one who crashed his motorcycle. If Maxence and I were on the same bike, it would slow down a great deal. He should ride with someone else."

Alfonso said, "Max should not ride with me, either. It would slow us down just as much."

Father Booker grumbled, "Don't look at me. I'm definitely the heaviest one of us." He patted his slightly thick midsection. "It would make no sense for me to double up with anyone."

Batsa said, "I have a wife and children. I do not want anyone lying on top of me."

Dree braced her gloved fists on her hips. "Well, he has to ride with one of us. We're in the middle of nowhere."

Alfonso shifted to one foot and looked at the sky. "I guess he could ride on the back of my bike."

"This is nonsense." Dree rolled her eyes. "If you guys are too insecure in your masculinity to snuggle up with another dude on a bike, Max can ride with me. Besides, I'm the lightest, so it makes sense that I should be one of the two people on a bike."

Maxence shrugged. "It makes sense."

It made more than good sense to him, and his heart double-timed in his chest.

Alfonso scowled and stomped back to his bike.

As they walked back to her motorcycle, Maxence said to Dree, "You can ride on the back. I can drive the motorcycle."

She scoffed, "Evidently, *no, you can't.* I'll drive."

Luckily, all the motorcycles they'd rented had extended seats that allowed for a second rider.

Dree swung her leg over the back of her motor-cycle and scooted forward. She patted the seat behind her curvy bottom in what she probably meant to be a perfunctory manner but was alto-gether too enticing. She said, "Saddle up, partner."

Behind Max, Father Booker cleared his throat.

Maxence was not going to survive this.

He faked a casual demeanor and strode over to the motorcycle. He planted his left foot firmly on the ground and swung his right leg over the back of the bike, settling onto the extended seat behind Dree.

His hands found the curve of her waspish waist and settled on her round, womanly hips. The warmth of her skin emanated through the puffy insulation of her ski outfit and filled his palms and fingers even through his gloves.

Max's fingers wanted to flex his hands and dig his fingertips into her hips just the slightest bit, because the last time he'd been holding her waist and hips from behind like this, she'd been on her hands and knees and he'd been watching his hard cock ram into her. She'd thrown her head back and screamed when she'd come, strands of her short, blond hair clinging to the sweat on the back of her neck. He'd grabbed the back of her neck there, forced her face down to the soft bed, and fucked her harder.

He did not tighten his fingers on her hips.

Refraining was one of the most difficult things he'd ever had to do.

At the touch of his hands on her waist, Dree stilled.

The other guys were struggling to pull their helmets over their heads while sitting on their bikes. The helmets were properly fitted, which meant they were tight.

Dree leaned her head back closer to his, reclining against his chest, and whispered, "Don't do anything that's going to make me drive off the side of the road, okay?"

Maxence said, in a voice lower than he had anticipated, "I wouldn't."

"Then it's a good thing you're riding in back instead of me, because I would." She yanked on her helmet and buckled the chinstrap.

Yeah, he was not going to survive this.

Max shoved his helmet onto his head.

Dree slowly guided the bike back onto the road.

As always, Batsa took point because he was also the navigator, but Dree and Maxence were in the second position with the other three guys surrounding them.

Father Booker, wearing brown leather motorcycle pants and jacket and a sapphire blue helmet, rode on Maxence's left, a constant reminder of priestly behavior.

Every inch of his body oriented on Dree's luscious form pressed against him, separated from his exquisitely sensitive skin by her ski suit's insulation and the half-shredded leather of his motorcycle gear.

After they retrieved the few remaining items from the storage bins on Maxence's wrecked motorcycle and pushed it over to the side of the road, they proceeded to the town Batsa had identified as their next stop.

The ride to the next town took two hours and forever and was over far too soon.

When they arrived in the small town, Maxence dismounted the motorcycle and surveyed the stone huts as if his dick wasn't standing at half-mast. His black leather motorcycle pants might strangle his balls if he popped a full erection.

Dree gripped his arm, and it felt like his motorcycle pants had grabbed onto his nuts just a little tighter. She said, "Why didn't you stay with the motorcycle after you crashed?"

He shrugged. "It was obviously totaled."

"You should've stayed with the bike."

"Why would I stay with a broken motorcycle? It was going to get cold when night fell, and I couldn't wait out there for days or a week until a truck came by and I could hitchhike a ride to the next town. So I started walking. I think I had enough gear to survive a night or two. I didn't think I'd have to walk for more than two days."

"We turned around as soon as we noticed you were missing. It's just that you were in the back, the last motorcycle. It was only ten minutes or so before I looked in my rearview mirror and noticed you were gone."

"It was fine. I was getting myself out of the situation. I calculated how far the next town was and how long it would take me to get there at three and a half miles per hour, which is around my normal walking speed. I figured I would find you guys there."

"In the next town? But that was forty miles away! Of course, we turned around and came to find you as soon as I noticed you were missing."

Dree's mouth dropped open just the slightest amount, and she blinked.

She said, "Maxence, I'm not sure what-all that story about the pirates *really* meant, but *of course*, I *noticed* you were missing within a few minutes. *Of course*, I came to *find* you. I would *never* leave you *lost* somewhere and *not* come and *find* you."

Maxence flipped his fingers in the air. "I was fine

on my own. I would've made it to the next town eventually."

"Maxence." She stared straight into his eyes, and he blinked at the intensity of her blue gaze. "I would *never* fail to notice that you were missing for more than a few minutes, and I will *always* come to find you."

Maxence's heart quivered, and he looked away. The blue-gray mountains in the horizon looked like towering waves that would batter a rusted-out hulk of a cargo ship to pieces. "It's okay. I'm fine."

She touched his hand. The pressure of her fingers on his motorcycle glove grabbed his attention. "You deserve to have people around you who love you and who will notice if you are *missing.*"

He said, his voice lowering, *"I'm fine."*

"Did you—" She took a deep breath, and her red-and-white ski suit expanded with her breathing. "Did you—panic?"

"Oh, no." He flipped his hand in the air again, dismissing that. "I was a little disoriented from crashing the bike and landing on my ass for a few minutes, but that's not a kidnapping-claustrophobia thing. Kind of a dark places-thing. I don't like boats very much. But it's not every situation. I'm pretty reliable in a lot of emergencies, and it only hits me afterward, anyway. And, this just didn't apply. This was a vehicle accident, outside, under a very open, sunny sky, and no one was grabbing at me. It's a different situation."

"Okay," she sighed. "When I realized you weren't with us, I freaked. I slammed on my brakes. Alfonso and Father Booker nearly ran over me as I skidded like I was motocross racing and flipped my bike around on the road. Thinking that you might be dead freaked me out. Thinking that you might be alive, hurt, and panicking *really* threw me."

His eyes were full of the mountains because they did not move. "Like I said, it might have taken me a day or two, but I would have walked into the village and caught up with you guys."

Dree went on to set up her clinic, and Maxence stared at the jagged, slate-blue horizon until the blood stopped rushing through his veins and he could breathe again. That wasn't due to the motor-cycle accident or finding himself alone, he knew. Dree's insistence that she would always come and find him if he were lost cracked something inside him, and he didn't know how to fix it.

After Father Booker and Batsa procured a suit-able house for the day's clinic, Maxence stole Batsa away for a few minutes during the set-up phase to find a seamstress who could repair the tears in his motorcycle gear and a cobbler for his boots. A woman assured him that she and her daughters could do a first-rate job on everything, and consid-ering the delicate embroidery on their clothes, he believed them.

When they delivered his outfit back to him a few hours later, he had to tilt the leather in the sunlight to find the tiny black thread of the repairs. The boots were more comfortable than before, so he paid them ten times their original negotiated price. He'd planned to do something like that, anyway, but their stitching was excellent work. He was keeping these repairs as a souvenir and wouldn't buy a new kit when he got home.

Maxence walked back to the house where Dree had her clinic so he could help.

After the woman with cancer yesterday, the way Dree had tossed and turned in her sleeping bag all night, and then his motorcycle accident, Maxence prayed to every saint he could think of to intercede and give Dree a calm and easy clinic that day.

The saints did not listen.

A middle-aged woman was led into the house they had appropriated as clinic space by her adult daughter while two small children ran around their feet. Dree inspected the woman's eyes with an ophthalmoscope and then squeezed her own eyes shut, sighing. She told Batsa, "Please tell her that she has exudative macular degeneration, or 'wet' MD. I'm sorry, but her eyesight will continue to worsen until it is gone."

After they left, Max sat beside Dree as she gathered herself.

A mother and her sisters brought in a young boy who they said was twelve years old. Two of the aunties half-carried him by slinging his arms over their shoulders. He was light enough for them to carry because his arms and legs were severely wasted. When Dree inspected him, his muscle tone was diminished. Between that and other signs, she had to tell the mother, "I'm so sorry, but I believe he has muscular dystrophy, most likely Duchenne Muscular Dystrophy."

Dree went on to explain the terrible course of the genetic disease to the mother, how her son would become weaker and weaker during the progression of the fatal disease, and that if she had any more sons, half of them would also be afflicted with it.

As the sobbing family was leaving, Dree asked Maxence, "Should I tell her that half of her daughters are also carriers, and half of their sons will also have it?"

"No," Maxence said. "They don't have access to genetic testing facilities up here, anyway. Half of the girls are not carriers, and the family would be ostracized."

As darkness was falling, Dree laid her head on her arms on the table and sighed.

The waiting area had only two more people, both of whom Father Booker and Maxence had triaged.

One had a minor rash that Batsa had translated as having been on his arm and unchanged for six months. Maxence thought that it looked like a second-degree burn, and Batsa discovered that the man leaned against his family home's heating stove at least once a week, burning himself in that spot. Max put a bandage on it and told the guy to wear sleeves around the stove or move his chair.

The other was a little girl with a slightly inflamed scratch that looked like the family cat had gotten mildly peeved at the child. He and Father Booker dressed the scratch with antibiotic ointment and sent her home.

Maxence crouched beside Dree. "*Chérie*, come back to the campsite. You need to rest."

She rolled her forehead back and forth on her arms, shaking her head no. "There's more. I can't leave them."

"You are all done. You saw them all and helped them. You need food and sleep now."

When she rolled her head back and forth to

signify no again, Maxence helped her into her ski suit, gathered her up in his arms, and walked out of the small house. She was nothing but blond fluff against his chest, and her arms reached around his neck.

Father Booker held the door for them and helped Maxence situate her on the back of the motorcycle.

As Father Booker removed the gray veil over her hair and pressed her helmet onto her head, Max heard him tell her, "'Well done, good and faithful servant.' Your work is done here, Sister Andrea Catherine, and it is time for you to rest tonight. Hold on tight."

Her arms cinched around Maxence's waist, and she leaned against his back.

Maxence followed Batsa slowly back to the campsite, which was only a few minutes' slow ride beyond the village.

When they arrived, supper was ready and waiting for them. Maxence led her over to the fire, and again made sure she sat in the warmest spot but where the wind would not blow smoke in her face. She perked up enough to eat a little food, and then she dejectedly murmured her good nights and staggered into the tent Isaak pointed to.

Maxence was going to stay behind to allow Dree her customary few minutes of privacy to wash up, but her flashlight clicked off moments after she had crawled inside her tent.

Father Booker exchanged a worried glance with him, and Max stood to follow her.

Just after he turned and walked away, Father Booker jogged after him and caught his arm. "Minister to her as a priest. Do not succumb to your temptations for this woman."

Max's longing for her must be as apparent to everyone else as it was to him. He said, "I do not have a sin against chastity on my conscience."

Father Booker nodded gravely, but he didn't look like he'd gotten the answer he wanted yet. "She is grieving, and she is wounded. Don't take advantage of her."

It was Maxence's turn to nod solemnly. "I won't."

Father Booker whispered to him, "You have the soul of a priest, Deacon Father Maxence, but I do not know if you have the heart of one."

Father Booker left him, and Maxence crawled into the tent after Dree. As he entered the tent, he whispered, *"Chérie."*

"I'm awake. I feel like I won't ever sleep again," she said in the dark.

He zipped the tent flap behind himself and lay on his sleeping bag, facing her.

Dree had zipped herself up into her mummy bag, and just her face was visible as an oval in the crimson fabric in the lowest beam of his flashlight, hardly any more glow than a votive candle.

Her red-and-white ski suit was a crumpled lump near the rapidly dwindling boxes of vaccine at the back of the tent.

Maxence said, "On my first project for Catholic charities into South America, I felt like I didn't sleep for weeks. Every time I was so exhausted that I passed out, the dreams of what had happened that day would wake me up again."

She said, "All these people, and they're all so sick.

I can't work fast enough. I can't work *hard* enough. There's always still more of them and they're always still coming."

"We'll go back to Jumla city tomorrow. We'll stay out for a few days. You can't keep doing this."

"But if I *don't,* no one else *will.* There's no one else *out* here. No one will help them."

She cried tiny hiccupping sobs like the saddest little hamster weeping.

Maxence flinched forward to take her into his arms, but he knew he shouldn't.

She asked him, "How do you do it? Do you just harden your heart to it and not care anymore? How do you *survive* this?"

"I don't think I hardened my heart. It's more like I surrendered. Even if I were the Prince of Monagasquay and had a billion dollars, although I think it's a bit more than that now, I still couldn't make a dent in this. I could help a few people here and there, but I couldn't change it. The Prince's power is mostly through influence anyway, making deals behind the scenes with meetings and conferences. No matter what we do, we can't solve everything. We just do what we can. We can be kind when we can. But we can't change every person's life. We're lucky if we can change *any* person's life. You vaccinated two babies today against common childhood diseases that might have killed or injured them for life. Ninety percent of people here have had rubella. Congenital rubella infections cause most cases of deafness here. Who knows how much suffering you prevented today? It's just harder to see that. "

"That seems so little in the face of a woman who has a few weeks to live at the most, another woman who is going blind, and a teenage boy who is going to waste away and die."

"You're right."

Her voice was a quiet wail. "Why does God allow this? Why would God allow any of this? If He is all-powerful—" She trailed off.

Maxence said, "I studied theodicy during my graduate work, the study of what and why evil is. It's the old paradox. 'If God can prevent such suffering and evil and does not, then He is not good. If He cannot prevent it, then He is not God.'"

"*Yes,*" Dree said. "If you could prevent this, wouldn't you?"

"You did today."

"But I didn't do enough."

"The only way I can reconcile it is to think that evil *just is.* It's not from or of God, and prevention of it doesn't seem to be God's job. But some people make more of it, and they are evil to their core and deserve to be damned to Hell on Earth and in the world to come. I could go on and on about who they are and what the Church should be doing about them, too. And some people love and heal the world, who try to make the world have less evil in it. They're good. They're wonderful. They're God on Earth. They're angels."

"Why the Hell aren't there any of *them* around?" Dree hiccupped.

"You're an angel, Dree. You made the world so much better today. That woman with cancer knew she was dying. You talked to her with kindness and grace. The woman whose son had Duchenne Muscular Dystrophy doubtlessly had a brother or two who died of it because she must be a carrier. She knew what she was seeing. You told her the truth, but you did it with love and empathy. There is evil in the world, but the world is what we make it."

And we could be making the world so much better, if only the Church and good people dared to do it, he thought.

A tiny sound like a rip squeaked in the small tent.

When he glanced over, he saw that Dree had unzipped her sleeping bag near her neck, and her fingers extruded from the small opening.

Her eyes were closed.

Asking, but not demanding.

Surely, this wasn't a sin. She was an angel in need of comfort because she'd seen too much of the world's evil.

Maxence extended his hand and tangled his fingers in hers.

She gripped his hand, and her eyes creased.

He held on.

He held on for hours, until her breathing smoothed and her eyes and mouth relaxed into sleep.

And still, he held on.

CHAPTER 12
TATTOO
DREE

Dree didn't know how long she'd slept before she realized her hand was freezing and water was splashing inside the tent.

She did the most obvious thing first. She pulled her hand inside her sleeping bag, zipped it up, and crammed her cold fingers under her armpit, thus solving that problem.

But, for the other, it was too cold for rain.

Any rain would be snow.

Snow and ice.

And she wasn't wet.

So, it couldn't be some kind of a snowmelt flood, and if the tent were leaking rain, she would be wet.

Also, the air inside the tent didn't have the wet-dirt scent of petrichor.

Citrus, balsam, and lavender hung in the air.

It smelled really good.

Really good.

So, the splashing could not be rain.

Why was good-smell splashing waking her up? she grumbled inside her head.

Her eyelids were mostly dark, so there was not much light.

It wasn't going to be too bright when she opened her eyes to figure out the splashing.

She cracked one eyelid open, squinting because even the flashlight on the dim setting was brighter than the Nepali night.

Deacon Father Maxence was stripped to the waist, half-naked, wearing nothing but black, tight boxer-briefs and a smile.

Well, she couldn't tell whether he was smiling or not because he was facing away from her as he rubbed a small cloth down his arm, scrubbing his elbow and armpit.

A shiny thermal blanket lay over his sleeping bag and under his bare legs, where he kneeled on top of it. Sharp-cut crevices ran between the massive muscles of his thighs. His toes peeked out from under his muscular butt, a pale shade of tan under the black cotton of his underwear. His black hair was damp and curled in loose spirals near the nape of his neck and the tops of his broad shoulders.

His tawny skin was the color of a lion's coat, but blue and burgundy bruises were beginning to rise on his ribs and above his underwear's waistband.

He twisted, causing the thick muscles on his back and around his waist to bulge, and soaked the wash-cloth in a small steel pot beside his sleeping bag. He didn't wring it out but merely gathered the small cloth in his fist and squeezed with one hand, shaking the droplets off his knuckles. His forearm muscles tensed and stood out under the tanned skin of his arm.

When he turned to rinse out the washrag, his back turned away from her, so she only got a glimpse of the black tattoo ink staining his skin. Again, her only impression was of delicate, shaded vertical lines running over the bulk of his muscles and the indentation of his spine down the center.

She asked, "What's that tattoo on your back?"

Maxence didn't startle at her sudden question. He just looked down at her and raised one black eyebrow as water ran over his knuckles and dripped back into the pot. "I thought you were asleep."

"I woke up."

Maxence blinked and shook his head before he continued to run the washrag over the heavy rounded pectorals of his chest, getting himself glistening and wet.

And her, too.

Not that they could, *you know,* because he was a *what-he-was* and she wasn't going to do anything about it because she wasn't like that.

Really, she wasn't.

Like *that.*

Fine masculine hair lay thicker down the center of his chest and formed a darker line all the way down to the waistband of his underwear.

She wanted to pet him.

Instead, she said, "So, that tattoo. What is it?"

Maxence leaned back as he stroked the washcloth down over the ripples of his abdominals, which forced the muscles of his torso to contract and made them stand out more.

Jeez, that was like one of those sexy dance moves

the male strippers did when they were on their knees, and he looked just like one of them.

Dree's fingers, now warmed, wandered down her sternum and stomach to the waistband of her underwear.

She couldn't.

He would *know*.

Hey, she was inside a completely enclosed mummy bag. Nothing except her face showed. If she could keep control over her facial expression and, to some extent, her breathing, he *couldn't* know.

Her fingers dipped inside her panties.

Maxence was still looking down at the wet washcloth that stroked down the crevice between his abs and over the transverse lines that crossed his abdomen, and he said like he was just noting the weather and nothing sexy was going on, "My friend Arthur designed all our tattoos after we graduated from high school."

He stroked the washcloth across the lowest lumps of his abdominal muscles, rubbing away the sweat and salt and faint male musk of his skin that she remembered on her tongue. Her face had been right where that rough washcloth was, breathing and tasting him as he shoved his cock down her throat with wild exultation in his dark eyes.

Her fingers stroked across her folds, and one fingertip slipped inside to graze her clit. The dirty pleasure of it spiraled through her. "So, are your tattoos the same as your friends'?"

Maxence said, "No, the ones on our back don't match. These do, sort of." He extended his arm where the three shields were tattooed around a triangular design. "The ones on our backs are all different, but Arthur designed all of them."

Her finger circled her clit just like his tongue had when they'd been in Paris. "You said Arthur was the —introvert? And the one who left the suits in Paris that you wore?"

Maxence smiled and looked up at the ceiling, emitting a sexy chuckle. He flung the washcloth across his back and stroked the cloth over his heavy flesh and ink. "He pretends not to be, but I've seen him walk into his computer office and not come out for eighteen hours without talking to anybody, and then do that for weeks on end. And yes, he designed them. I told him what I wanted, but he made some adjustments before he gave the design to the artist."

"What did you—want?"

"I wanted an illustrated cross, a monochrome outline of a cross filled with Celtic knots or some other patterns. Sort of a graphic illustration. Arthur told me that he had altered the design substantially, and part of the project for the three of us was to have his art with us wherever we went. I keep thinking about finding a design of a Celtic-knot cross for my pectoral."

He smoothed his hand over his heavy chest, presumably where he would allow someone to touch and carve the design into him.

As his fingers brushed over the round part of his pec, the memory of his hands on her breast, grasping and pinching her, filled her mind, and her finger grazed her clit again. She rolled her fingertip around the sensitive spot.

Maxence continued, "The tattoo looks like falling lines of water at first glance, like a waterfall, but it's not. The surfaces of Arthur's designs always hide his true intentions, which may be the best description of Arthur himself that I've ever thought of. He said that the overall pattern that you recognize at first glance was water rolling down my back as I emerged from the sea."

He turned, showing her his entire back.

Trails of real water trickled over his thick muscles and down his spine like she wanted to do with her fingers and tongue. With him turned away, she rubbed deeper between her folds. Pleasure awoke in her, and her body began to tighten.

"But that's not what the real design is," he said.

He rinsed out the washrag again in the little pot of water beside his bedroll, squeezing it again in his strong fist. Rivulets of water trailed from between his fingers and across his knuckles, falling back into the pot.

The tension in the knot between her legs was tightening, almost at a peak, but she couldn't move her hand enough to finish herself because he would see.

The water ran down his fist.

His underwear was a dark line around his tight, rippled waist, and his skin glistened because he was wet.

"Aren't you going to," she gasped a little, "wash anything else?"

His head turned, and he stared at her.

She pressed her lips together and barely inhaled through her nose, but her heart was racing, and she felt her eyes flutter, rolling just a bit.

Maxence's voice was deep, almost hoarse, as he whispered, *"Harder."*

"Wha-*what?*" she whispered.

His voice was a growl, and he didn't look away from her eyes. He moved forward so that he was close, nearly hovering over her, and he whispered, "Don't come yet. Rub your fingers harder against your clit and roll them. Feel how slick you are. Slip one finger inside yourself and press forward, pinching your clit from the inside."

She did, and she couldn't look away from his dark, knowing eyes as he watched her.

"Harder," he said, his whisper and breath sliding over her lips and throat. "Now two fingers inside yourself, and stroke yourself deep and hard, the way I want to bury my cock in you. Don't come. Don't let yourself. Fuck yourself like it's me taking all of you, like my cock is rubbing inside and fucking you until your clit is so raw that it hurts not to come."

She rubbed her fingers inside herself and brushed her knotted clit more lightly and to the side because he didn't want her to come yet, and she wanted his deep voice to tell her what to do. The tension was unbearable, and the tent spun.

"Are you ready?" he asked.

She nodded, and her teeth biting her lip was delicious pain that kept her from dying.

"Do you want my cock?"

She nodded harder.

"Now," he said. "Pinch your clit and let yourself come."

His permission was all she needed to fall over the edge, and the tight pressure around her clit and her fingers inside made the waves keep rolling through her like he was pushing her down on a bed and taking her hard.

As she let up, the tiny tent around them drifted into her view. She whispered, "Did I make noise?"

He was leaning forward, his fists braced on his knees, and his eyes were ablaze with dark fire like anger. "No. You were utterly silent."

"Oh, good. I thought—well, I was worried. Because I wouldn't want to cause questions for you."

He settled back on his heels, but his muscles wrapping his body were still taut as steel cables. "It won't be a problem."

The ripples of her orgasm ebbed.

Inside her mummy bag, she was stifling hot and sweating.

Maxence dried himself roughly with a towel like he was angry at his skin. He tossed it up by her ski suit at the rear of the tent and slipped inside his sleeping bag. He grabbed at the flashlight and clicked it off, filling the tent with darkness.

Questions ran through her head, whether he was mad at her or whether she shouldn't have done that, but she didn't ask them.

There was, however, one thing she did want to know.

"If it's not a waterfall, what's the real design of your tattoo?"

His voice was rough like he had been shouting. "It's wings. Long feathers and strong hollow bones, but the feathers are black, and the bones have been snapped. Arthur's design is of the broken wings of a fallen angel."

Dree woke up the next morning after a long deep sleep that was truly refreshing. She was kind of embarrassed about how she had managed to get that deep sleep, but she felt a lot better that morning that she had for several days.

Hey, Paris had been *weeks* ago, and she'd had no privacy since.

Maxence was thoroughly casual toward her when she finally crawled out of the tent. If anything, he seemed to be a rerun of the kind gentleman he'd been acting like for the last few weeks.

There was just no deviation in his demeanor.

It was pretty impressive.

She almost wondered if she'd dreamed it.

As she sat on a warm rock holding her plate of eggs and fresh flatbread and began eating, Isaak looked up at her with a grin and said, "Happy Christmas."

Dree forced herself to swallow the large bite of eggs in her mouth and said, "I lost track of what day it is. Is it Christmas?"

Alfonso said, "Christmas Eve. It's December twenty-fourth. Father Booker will offer a Mass for us tomorrow morning because it is a holy day of obligation." His voice was a little drier as he said, "It is fortunate for us that we have a priest along who can make sure none of us skip Mass, not even once, *not even a little.*"

Father Booker paused his eating with a spoon in his mouth to glare at Alfonso with one raised eyebrow.

Dree laughed at him. "Guess we're just lucky."

After breakfast, they struck the camp and rode to

the village's possible site for the construction of the NICU micro-clinic, which was again unsuitable in several ways.

Isaak said a sheet of shale was running under the surface soil of the village, so the earth was unlikely to pass a perc test for the septic system. He also glared at the shadows of the mountains and noted that the entire town seemed a bit too new, which may have something to do with watermarks high on the rocks that may have indicated a recent flood.

Alfonso said, "None of these sites are perfect, but are some of them good enough?"

"No," Isaak said. "All the sites have fatal flaws."

"Then what are we supposed to do? We are perfecting the design for specialized incubators for premature babies, and we have premature babies being born in every area of Nepal. Why can't we just save the lives of some premature babies by giving them access to incubators?"

Isaak said, "There's a good chance that every ten years, this village and your incubator and your micro-clinic are going to be swept away by a flood. There hasn't been a hundred-year flood in Nepal for a long time, so those high watermarks must mean that more common floods produce high-water marks in this region."

Dree stepped back. She was glad that Maxence hadn't been the one to start this argument with Alfonso. There seemed to be something *else* going on behind their debates.

Alfonso shook his hand, gesturing at the marks on the rocks. "How do you even know that those are flood marks? You can't correlate the age of the houses with that. There was a major earthquake in Nepal in 2015. Whole villages were leveled. That watermark, if it is a watermark, might have nothing to do with the fact that this village has a bunch of new houses. It might have been fifty years ago. It might not even *be* a watermark."

Isaak's voice rose. "We can't install a basic septic system in this location because of the shale. There isn't enough direct sunlight in this valley for *months* out of the year to run solar panels here, or in any of these villages due to those damn mountains. *Nepal* isn't the right country for your NICU micro-clinic project, Alfonso. *It's not going to work.*"

Dree caught Maxence's eye. He was watching the argument closely but didn't look like he wanted to jump in.

She sure as blazes didn't.

Alfonso said, "We can *make* it work. We've *made* other projects work."

Isaak rolled his eyes. "We've thrown money at other projects that never panned out. That doesn't mean the problems were solved. Throwing money at problems doesn't make them go away. It just makes the people keep coming back for more, and then other, more successful projects don't receive adequate funding. Back me up here, Maxence."

Alfonso raised his hand toward Maxence in a typical stay-out-of-this gesture as he said to Isaak, "But this is a problem we *know* exists. Premature babies in these rural villages stand an eighty percent chance of dying. If we saved *half* of them, it would be an enormous step. Back me up on this, Andrea Catherine."

Oh, crap. Dree said, "I'm not here for the technical specifications. I'm just here to be medical personnel feedback."

Beyond where Isaak and Alphonso were arguing, Dree saw Batsa elbow Father Booker. "Looks like nobody is asking our opinions about this."

Father Booker shook his head. "Enjoy it while it lasts."

Isaak told Alfonso, "The incubators have too many technical challenges. No one here will be able to run them. They will break, and no one will be able to fix them. Max, tell them I'm right."

Maxence stepped forward.

Dragging him backward probably wouldn't keep him out of the argument, so she didn't.

Max said, "I know you planned to involve the locals in the construction of the micro-clinics, Alfonso, and that is the best practice. However, that just means they're going to be able to fix the walls and roof. They aren't solar power technicians for when the panels go down. One good hailstorm can destroy an array."

Isaak nodded so hard that his blond hair flopped around his head.

Max continued, "And you don't just stuff a premature baby in an incubator like a Christmas fish into an oven for them to finish baking. Premature infants often need complex medical procedures to keep them alive and not cause further damage. Many of them must be intubated or need IV lines run. There are no doctors here. There are no nurses or nurse practitioners or other *basic* medical professionals, let alone NICU specialists, as Dree can tell you."

He gestured toward her, and she slouched.

The men were just determined to drag her into their catfight.

Dree sighed and said, "The people here need basic medical care. They will not be able to operate neonatal incubators."

"We're designing the incubators to be simple. They're essentially a turnkey operation. Take the preemie, walk into the micro-clinic, place the preemie in the incubator, and enter weight and vitals. The computer will calculate the oxygen saturation, temperature, and so on, and then the baby can be treated properly."

Dree's nursing bullshit detector was clanging with all its bells and whistles. There was something very *wrong* with Alfonso's plan.

She asked with a low voice, "Who's going to take the baby's vitals, Alfonso, and where are the tanks of oxygen going to come from?"

"Fine," Alfonso said. "So, when there's a premature baby born, they can call down to the Chandannath city, and the medical center there can send a doctor to take the vitals and treat the baby in the micro-clinic."

Isaak flung his hand at the sky. "We've been riding these roads for weeks on motorcycles. Have you *seen* any phone lines out here?"

"Fine, they'll use their mobile phones," Alfonso grumbled.

Dree recognized a classic let-them-eat-cake line and flinched.

Maxence asked him, "Have you seen any mobile phones out here? Or cellular towers? I haven't seen any cell-phone towers sticking up off the cliff faces of the Himalayan mountains."

Alfonso said, "Then we'll put satellite phones in the micro-clinics. When they have a premature baby being born, they can call down to the Chandannath city, and the medical clinic can helicopter a doctor up to them."

Dree was getting tired of all the fruitless arguing, and she was looking at the mountains. "If you're going to use a satellite phone to call for a helicopter, why doesn't the helicopter just pick up the baby and take it back to the hospital at Chandannath, where they have neonatal incubators, modern medical equipment, and hot and cold running doctors?"

All the guys stared at her for a minute, and then the real arguing started.

Isaak yelled at Alfonso, "You just want free field-testing for your NICU micro-clinics so you can get a tax write off."

"Calling for a helicopter would take too long," Alfonso yelled over the din. "With a NICU incubator on-site, you could place an infant in the incubator within minutes. Arranging helicopter transport might take hours, if one is available at all. I don't know that Chandannath hospital even has a medevac helicopter."

Maxence argued, "One medevac helicopter and a few dozen satellite phones would be a hell of a lot cheaper and more effective than scattering NICU micro-clinics all over the mountains."

Alfonso yelled, "If they don't have the education to fix a broken neonatal incubator, they can't maintain and fix *a helicopter!*"

Isaak pointed in the general direction of down the mountains and yelled, "There's an airport and a heliport at Chandannath! *We* flew in there! They must have trained airplane and helicopter mechanics in that much larger city that is several hours away by car!"

Alfonso turned to Maxence. "Paying local people for construction work on these micro-clinics would infuse needed capital into these villages, too. There are multiple levels of benefit to these communities for this project."

Maxence shook his head. "That's one and done, Alfonso. Yes, they know how to construct buildings here, and your charity will pay them a pittance to build one more. But they still can't maintain a NICU and a solar array."

Dree piped up. "The most important thing is that these villages don't need a NICU unit like they need a lot of other things. They probably have three pre-term infants born in a village this size per year. Maybe one of them would be so premature that their life would depend on an incubator." Like that baby a week or so ago when they'd arrived a day too late that Dree still couldn't get out of her mind. "But they have probably a dozen cases of cancer every year that, without detection and therapy, are invariably fatal. The people here have constant outbreaks of preventable, communicable diseases like measles, mumps, and rubella. Secondary pneumonia is one of the most common reasons people die in all of Nepal. If you want to save the most lives, instead of constructing a whole building for one premature infant, place a box of antibiotics in every village and send a nurse with a trunkful of vaccines to make a stop here twice a year. That would probably save fifty or more lives *every year* plus greatly reduce long-term disabilities like deafness from congenital rubella."

"But, the *babies,*" Alfonso said.

Dree lost her cool. "Saving the *babies* doesn't mean *shit* if you're going to let them die of the *measles* when they're two!"

Alfonso dismissed her concerns with a wave. "But by the time they're two, it is their parents' responsibility to get vaccines for them."

She wanted to wring his rich, stupid neck. "Their parents can't *afford* vaccines, and they don't have *access* to them if they could! That's why Sister Mariam and the Little Sisters of Charity raided their supplies and sent up boxes and boxes of vaccines with us because they knew it was their *one shot* to get vaccines up here!"

Alfonso's eyes widened at her rant, but Dree was not stopping now.

She said, "Rich people like you keep talking about the importance of personal responsibility when there is *no way* these people *can* take personal responsibility. That's like criticizing my parents for not having internet access for their kids' educational enrichment when there were no *cables* anywhere *near* our sheep ranch, and we couldn't afford satellite access or even computers, at all, *ever.* They struggled to keep food on the table, and we were all pretty skinny. These people are even skinnier! Half the kids I see have stunted growth, and half of those are *wasted* from malnutrition. How can you expect their parents to pay enormous amounts of money and travel for *weeks* to get somewhere there is a doctor and get a vaccine!"

Alfonso shrugged. "It's not my fault they aren't educated enough to understand the importance or make enough money to afford proper health care."

Dree was the veteran of a thousand schoolyard scraps, and the rage in her body did not notify her brain before she leaped at Alfonso to knock his stupid head into the ground. She was just suddenly flying through the air, fists outstretched and teeth bared.

Maxence caught her around the waist, and they spun around like they were square-dancing the Virginia Reel.

She yelled at Max, "That *asshole!* How dare he blame these people who are *just doing their best* about things that they have no control over!"

Maxence pushed her behind himself and held his arms back to contain her.

Dree tried to get around him, swinging wildly, but he was a concrete wall of muscle in front of her.

Beyond Maxence's waist, she saw Alfonso had stepped backward. Shock widened his eyes. From Alfonso's vantage point, Maxence must look like an eight-legged, writhing monster as Dree kicked and punched and tried to fight her way through Max to knock some sense into Alfonso.

She yelled, "How dare you look down on these good country people who are making a living by growing food for their families and doing the best they can. It's not their fault that they never had a chance. They never had a *Sister Annunciata* who told them they could go to college and be a nurse and helped them get financial aid so they could. They never had a *Father Moses* who gave them clothes so they wouldn't freeze to death. They had to do it all on their own, and they're doing the best they can. What's *the Church* doing to help *these* people, *huh?* What's your *stupid* charity and the *Church* and everybody else *who should be responsible* doing to help *these* people out?"

Batsa had walked over. "I admit, I have had concerns about the long-term commitment to these NICU micro-clinics. I have seen too many charity projects begun and abandoned. Would it not be better to run this project through the Nepali government rather than relying on the continued involvement of individual people and your small charitable organization, Alfonso?"

"That won't work!" Alfonso yelled at him.

Batsa raised one eyebrow and planted his right foot behind himself. Yeah, he'd gone to junior high in the States.

Dree dodged to go knock the hell out of Alfonso, but Maxence caught her.

"Don't," he whispered. "You've made your point. Watch what happens."

Father Booker had followed Batsa over. "Batsa was partly raised here and has visited relatives over the years in Nepal. He has strong cultural ties to the area and local knowledge that none of us have. Batsa, give us more of your thoughts on the ramifications of establishing these high-tech, single-use clinics in isolated, rural villages."

Alfonso spun and glared at Father Booker. "Asking the question that way isn't fair. Besides, the Nepali government and other governments have had their chance to lower the mortality rate of premature infants in Nepal. They didn't do it."

"They haven't had the money," Maxence said, his voice low. "The Nepali government has very, very little money for these far-flung regions."

"But the government has to have *money,*" Alfonso

said, his anger giving way to dismay. "How else will they buy the supplies that the clinics will need every six months or so?"

"Whoa!" Dree said. "They have to buy the *drugs? Who's* going to buy them?"

"The Nepali government will buy them, or the villages can," Alfonso said.

"There's no *way* these people can afford that!" she cried.

Isaak butted in, *"Wait.* I thought those were going to be *donated."*

"Of course not," Alfonso said. "Pharmaceuticals are routine expenses. The clinics will need to be resupplied when the drugs expire every six months or so."

Father Booker stepped up. "Hang on, so the perishable drugs aren't part of the charity deal?"

"Of course, they'll have to buy supplies. Supplies aren't free," Alfonso said as if this were obvious.

Dree said, "You can't expect these communities to cough up a couple of hundred dollars every six months. The combined wealth of these people is less than that!"

Alfonso shrugged. "It's a minor expense compared to the cost of the construction of these clinics. Surely, they can kick in some money to supply the clinics. They need to have some 'skin in the game.' That's what you call it, yes?"

"These people barely have *clothes* on their *backs,* and now you want their skin, too?" Dree demanded.

Maxence asked, his voice low and dangerous, "And where are they going to buy these perishable supplies from?"

Alfonso raised a shoulder. "They must buy the

supplies from my company. It is part of the contract to build them a NICU micro-clinic."

Dree stomped backward. *"Seriously?"*

Max asked, "And are you going to sell them the supplies at cost? Are you going to supplement the expense of these expensive pharmaceuticals and other supplies to far below cost?"

"Of course not. They can buy the supplies at the same rate as everybody else."

Dree clenched her fists. "You shouldn't be making a profit off these impoverished people by holding their premature babies hostage! You shouldn't be *making money* by making people *pay you* so they won't be sick or not *die. Ever, at all!"*

Alfonso sniffed. "That's not the way the world works, Andrea."

"But it *should,"* she said. "People used to come into my hospital with horrible complications of diabetes that had made them so sick they were disabled. If they'd had proper care, they could have been contributing, working citizens of society, but instead, some asshole decided to make money from the fact that they need insulin to stay alive. Rich assholes shouldn't be *making money* off of *medicine."*

Alfonso rolled his eyes. "We can't do *everything* for the poor. If we just hand these communities money, they'll waste it. They'll just spend it on frivolous things like stereos and soda pop and diamond-encrusted phones."

Isaak asked him, "Weren't you just deriding these people for not having cell phones so they could call for helicopter rides?"

"Common people are stupid," Alfonso said, scowling. "People like *us* have been bred to make decisions for them because they don't have the education or sophistication to know what they need. Look at them. They're idiots."

That statement splashed into the conversation, and everyone stepped back and raised their hands to avoid the moral mud splatter.

"What the—!"

"Hold on there, Alfie."

"That is not acceptable."

Maxence growled at Alfonso. "You weren't so smart and industrious that you built your corporation from nothing. Your father, the King of Spain, gave you two hundred million dollars to start your company."

What?

Dree stared at Alfonso, who had not mentioned she should be calling him Your Highness or curtsying or anything, not that she would've. *Heck, no.*

Alfonso glared at Maxence. "How about you? How dare you berate me for being from a royal family, considering who *you* are?"

What the hell was that? Dree twisted her head to look at Max.

Maxence's face was rigid with anger. "Me? I'm *nobody.* I am *nothing* but a man who wants to be a priest, and nothing more. I will be an anonymous priest in a black Jesuit cossack, and I will make it my personal mission to change the world for the better one shovel of dirt at a time. My place is to obey the Pope and the Catholic Church, not to *lead* anyone, not to *be* anyone, and that is all. When I take Holy Orders, I will *disappear* into the Church *forever."*

His conviction shocked Dree. She'd thought he was conflicted about entering the priesthood, or he *should* be considering how he "slipped" every chance he got, but the adamance in his voice sounded like he had firmly decided to be a priest.

"We can't all be so self-sacrificing, Maxence," Alfonso said, his tone deeply sarcastic. "Some of us are not running away from what we were born to be."

"We were *told* that's what we were born to be, but we do not have to succumb to what others tell us is our fate," Max answered.

"This is ridiculous," Isaak said. "Why are we even continuing this charade of a charity mission? Alfie has practically admitted this whole project is a tax haven and a scheme to sell overpriced pharmaceuticals to impoverished villages."

"*I* need to continue," Dree said.

Max's head whipped around to look at her, and the other guys stopped their argument to listen.

She said, "I am doing something *important* here. I mean, nursing in the inner city of Phoenix was important, but this feels like why I became a nurse. It's grueling. It's killing me. But I need to make it through the next few villages. We said it was a month, and we've only got a week left. I'm staying. I signed up for this."

"But what are you going to do when this trip is over?" Alfonso asked her, his voice laced with sarcasm. "Are you going to continue to travel the world, eating a few lentils for supper and not bathing for weeks? Or maybe this is just a roughing-it vacation for you to see how the impoverished world lives."

Maxence stepped forward, his fist beside his shoulder.

Dree grabbed him this time. She could probably bury a body out in the wilds of Nepal, but Isaak had said there was a layer of shale under the ground here, so it wouldn't be easy.

Maxence said, "She's a nurse, and she's been working herself to death. This isn't disaster tourism for her. She isn't out here as a publicity stunt or financial strategy for a company. Dree is helping people, one person at a time. If she's staying, I'm staying."

Alfonso mocked, "Of course you are staying. You're sleeping in her tent with her, and who knows what—"

Father Booker stepped closer. "Sister Andrea Catherine is an example of Christ in action to us all. I will not abandon *her* mission."

Alfonso said to Father Booker, "You know she's not a religious sister, right?"

"She is my sister in Christ, and I have nothing but the utmost respect for her."

Dree was not going to cry. She was *not.*

Batsa stepped up to stand beside Father Booker. "I agreed to serve as a translator for a month. I will be staying to help Sister Andrea Catherine."

Isaak told Alfonso, "If nothing else, I'm here as moral support. This mission may have begun as a strategic move for your company, but it's *her* mission now."

Dree hadn't meant this to be a mutiny, but it had turned into one.

The mountains turned to water in the morning sunshine. The tear that dripped down her face was hot, then turned cold in the freezing winter air.

Alfonso's expression hardened. "My company

will design and donate incubators and NICU micro-clinics to the country of Nepal. I will continue to survey and analyze sites for the clinics. I will not abandon this project. It will save the lives of premature infants, and I will not abandon them."

With that impasse, they left the site and went to their motorcycles to travel to the next town.

As Dree was ready to mount hers, Maxence squeezed her fingers before he settled onto the bike behind her. "You did well."

That day's clinic was moderately heartbreaking, not the worst Dree had seen, but certainly not the best.

The daytime and nighttime temperatures had continued to drop, and Dree worried that their precious vaccine stocks would freeze even inside the tent that night.

The house where they set up the clinic was frigid despite a fire burning in the fireplace and a wood stove glowing in the corner. As the afternoon progressed, her fingers became colder and began to lose sensation. Her nose ran constantly, and the tip was chilled.

The motorcycle ride back to the campsite was punishing. After she began shaking too badly, Maxence tapped her to pull over and insisted they trade places so that he would block the wind from hitting her. She had to admit that with his big body in front, she huddled down behind him, and the wind wasn't quite as cruel.

Though the campfire was large and blazing and the food that Alfonso had cooked was just as warm and tasty as every other night, she continued to lose body heat. She was chattering within minutes.

Maxence and Father Booker exchanged glances, and then Father Booker insisted that she sit in her tent to finish eating.

It didn't help. The shaking got worse.

Dree didn't take off her ski suit before she slipped into her sleeping bag, zipping all the way up to around her face.

The shaking of her muscles intensified.

Maxence crawled into the tent a few minutes later, saying, "What a day that was. Are you all right?"

"Y-Y-Y—"

"Mon Dieu, chérie. I can hear your teeth chattering. I thought Father Moses sent some of those hand-warmer packs with you."

"I have one. It warmed my hands for a few minutes, but I would need, like, fifty of them to warm my whole body up. Aren't you cold?"

Maxence said, "I am bigger than you are. Size matters."

Dree snorted. "I wish I were bigger. I'm freezing."

Her body seized with the cold, nearly flopping with trying to get warm.

Maxence sucked in a breath. "Dree, you're going into hypothermia."

CHAPTER 13

NECESSITY

MAXENCE

Maxence paused because he knew that he absolutely should not do this, and yet Dree's teeth were chattering so hard that they sounded like castanets.

He lowered his voice. "We could zip the sleeping bags together, and I could warm you up."

Dree didn't answer for a few of Maxence's stuttering heartbeats. He'd gone too far. She thought he was offering something he wasn't, even though it was something he so deeply desired.

She said, "I thought you weren't supposed to do that. You took vows or something."

"I'm not suggesting we have sex. I wouldn't," he lied. "I won't take advantage of you." That was true. "You're freezing. I don't want you to get sick. Just for practical matters, if you get severe hypothermia, I'm not sure what we would do. We only have motorcycles to get you into town, but riding a motorcycle is not good for someone with hypothermia."

Dree didn't answer for a few minutes, and

Maxence considered that she might be wrestling with her conscience.

He was undoubtedly wrestling with his.

Finally, she said, "I'm really cold. I would appreciate it if we could zip the sleeping bags together for a while."

"Don't unzip your sleeping bag yet. Let me think about how to do this." His mind mulled over various combinations of ways to unzip and re-zip the mummy bags together. "Okay, this is what we're going to do. Let me get mine completely unzipped and myself ready, and then we're going to unzip yours and re-zip them together as fast as possible. Wait just a minute. And, we're going to need some light to fit the zippers together. We should point the flashlight toward the back of the tent. Otherwise, our silhouettes will cast right on the sides of the tent, and it will be obvious what we are doing. I'm not ashamed, but we don't need those guys to talk about it."

Dree turned on her flashlight to a medium setting and aimed it toward the back of the tent, where the boxes of vaccines and other temperature-sensitive medical supplies were stored.

Max opened the zipper that wound around his sleeping bag and wrestled his bag into position next to hers. He stripped off his riding leathers and clothes down to his tee-shirt and underwear. The frigid air in the tent poured over his skin, instantly chilling him. "Okay."

"I'm wearing my ski suit," she said, still chattering.

"You should've taken that off."

"I'm *so cold.*"

"You'll warm up faster if we're"—he felt like he was choking because his throat closed—"skin to skin."

She looked up at him with her fathomless blue eyes and didn't say anything.

He cleared his throat. "Or at least without three inches of insulation between us. Can you take it off inside there and push it out the opening for your face?"

She lifted one eyebrow even though her jaw was vibrating, which was impressive. She wormed around inside her mummy bag, but in the end, he had to unzip it about halfway for her to move her arms and legs enough to strip off the ski suit and push it out. She said, "Jeez, the sleeping bag is cold inside."

He laid down in his unzipped bag and flipped the top over himself. "Okay, wiggle around in your sleeping bag until the zipper is over on this side so we can get the two of them zipped together as quickly. as we can."

Dree writhed in her sleeping bag, turning the bag sideways. The side of her head was visible through the face-hole at the top, and her blond hair flipped around as she undulated. "Okay. I think I got it."

The zipper scraped as she unzipped it, and Maxence stared at the top of the zipper, refusing to peep at what she must be wearing or not wearing inside the sleeping bag.

As soon as the end of the zipper came apart. Maxence grabbed the edges of her sleeping bag and fitted them against his, zipping the two sides of the bags together as fast as he could. Part of this was in self-preservation because the air flowing through the seams of the tent was sucking the heat out of him, but he also wanted Dree to get warm as soon as possible.

Part of his hurry was, indeed, practical concerns about hypothermia.

Part of his frantic pace was because he was starving to feel her soft form against his skin.

The zippers connected at the top, leaving only an oblong hole that had been their two face-openings. He reached through the hole into the chilly air and clicked the switch on the flashlight, leaving them in the bare, dimmest of light, just a glowing pinprick in the lamp. He aimed it at the back where the boxes were because the last thing he needed was his stupid silhouette splayed on the walls of the tent.

Maxence was wearing a cotton tee-shirt and form-fitting boxers, leaving his arms and legs bare.

Soft cotton touched his skin as Dree cuddled up to his chest, and her skin was as cold as porcelain against his and rattling with chill.

Maxence grabbed her and pressed her against his body, trying desperately to warm her up as quickly as possible.

Dree tucked her head under his chin and pulled her arms and legs in, and Maxence felt every inch of her soft pliable body twined around the hardness of his.

Dree said, "I'm sorry. I didn't mean to get this cold. I just didn't know how to stay any warmer."

"Have you been this cold since we left the town?"

"I warmed up a little bit by the fire, but I was kind of joking to myself that I didn't need to chew my supper because my teeth were chattering so much."

"You need to tell somebody when you get this cold."

"I was sitting as close to the campfire as I could without catching myself on fire. You put me in the warmest spot, and I was too cold to argue."

Maxence wrapped his arms more tightly around her with one arm around the back of her shoulders and the other around her waist. The softness of her breasts was pushing against his chest, and he rubbed her back with his hand down to her slender waist. "We have to find a way to keep you warmer than this."

Her breath brushed his throat as she sighed, relaxing against him.

All sorts of ways to warm her up occurred to Maxence, and he knew he couldn't take advantage of any of them.

Dree's hands slowly slid up his pectorals and rested on his collarbones, her arms folded against his sides.

Because the mummy bags were not meant to be zipped together the way ordinary, rectangular sleeping bags could be, the opening at the top was irregular. Half his head was sticking out into the darkness.

At the far end of the tent by their feet, the tent-flap door glowed orange from the still-lit campfire outside. Shadows occasionally moved across it as the other men walked around and finished up the evening chores.

At other times in his life, Maxence would have felt a thrill at the possibility of getting caught half-naked with a woman in his tent, their limbs intertwined.

Hell, at other times in his life, Maxence would have made sure to take advantage of the situation, although the women he liked probably would have zipped their sleeping bags together also fully intending to take advantage of it. He'd never been satisfied with mere consent from a woman. He liked sensual women who wanted him, too.

Dree shivered against his chest, and Maxence tightened his arms around her. His hand around her back trailed lower, over the cotton of her underwear to the lace at the top of her thigh. He ran his fingertips over the ruffle and tried not to think about the very thin, stretchy layers of cotton on her body that could be moved aside for his fingers, his tongue, and his cock.

She said, "Your skin is hot. You're like the surface of the sun. Like, it almost hurts to touch you. You don't have a fever, do you?"

Maxence chuckled. "No, Nurse Andrea Catherine, I don't have a fever. I am genuinely concerned you might have hypothermia, though."

"I'm f-f-f-f—"

He laughed a little more at her, and he wrapped his hand around her head to press her cheek more firmly against his shoulder. "You'll be f-f-fine in a minute. Now stop talking so your teeth will stop chattering."

He wasn't going to be fine in a minute. He was going to have the most advanced case of blue balls ever known to science.

As a matter of fact, his dick, which had been

constrained in his unyielding motorcycle gear all day, was becoming heavy.

Uh-oh.

He said, "Dree, I'm apologizing ahead of time. I'm not an animal who can't control my voluntary actions. I am not obligated to do anything about it, and neither are you."

"Wha-What are you talking about—*oh.*"

His dick hardened further and grew to a gallant half-mast. "It's not under my conscious control."

"I *know* that. I'm a *nurse.* I took anatomy and physiology."

Paris had been a long time ago, and he hadn't performed any act that would cause him to need to go to confession since then. "Excellent, as long as everyone is current on the science."

His skin was dragging against his tight underwear. He released Dree's back for just a second to adjust himself, and she rolled to the side to allow it a better range of movement, giggling while she did so.

He grumbled, "Yes, laugh at it. Maybe that'll make it go away."

"Has that ever worked before?"

It rose to a diamond-hard swollen staff held firmly against his stomach by his elastic underwear. "No woman has ever laughed at it before."

She chuckled louder at that. "Yeah, I'll bet. I thought about screaming and running away when I first saw it. I was kind of worried you were going to rip me into the four major pieces."

"Now you're just encouraging it."

"'Pride goeth before a fall,'" she quoted.

"That's Proverbs 16:18, and that *thing* doesn't feel like it's going to *fall* anytime soon."

"Maybe if you tried punishing that bad boy?" she said, and she sounded like she was purring.

Why, *oh why*, did she sound like she was purring? "I tried slapping it around when I was a teenager, but that only seemed to encourage it."

She snickered, and then her cool skin—because she was beginning to warm up—moved slowly over his stomach.

The head of his cock was sticking out of his underwear near his belly button, and the gentle glide of her skin over the top of it was a delicious friction that he enjoyed too much.

He drew in a breath and closed his eyes. His fingers tightened into a fist in her hair.

She whispered, "Should I stop?"

"No."

He regretted how quickly he said that. He hadn't even slowed down to consider it.

As her body slid over his stomach and cock again, his thoughts dissipated.

The silk of her skin filled his senses, from the silken threads of her hair in his fist and the plush satin of her body rubbing from her feet near his knees to her cheek on his shoulder.

And her soft stomach gliding over his cock, rubbing between their bodies like he was inside her.

He groaned, just a pulse of a sound.

Her breath hitched near his ear.

He pressed his forehead to hers and rolled her over, tasting her breath in his mouth. He didn't kiss her. If he kissed her, it would be all over, and he'd plunge inside her. They both wanted it. He craved it.

Instead, he parted her legs with his knee and pressed up.

Her body arched in his arms, rubbing harder against him. A tiny gasp escaped her lips, lighting desire in him.

They moved slowly in the sleeping bags, careful, tiny movements, each calculated to produce delicious friction and heat. She was panting in his arms, rubbing her body on his thigh, his skin becoming slick through her underwear.

She arched harder in his arms, her head thrown back and her eyes squeezed shut, and a squeak escaped her lips.

He watched her orgasm, a delicious, enticing sight, knowing that he had controlled her body's response to produce this.

As she relaxed, coming down from the high, he rubbed his cock on her stomach, feeling her skin against the head of it. He bit his lip.

"Wait," she whispered. "Let me turn around."

"Why—*ah.*"

She'd turned her back to him and snuggled her luscious ass against his groin. With a deft pull, his shorts were under his balls, and his cock was wedged between her thighs.

"Damn," he whispered, pushing forward.

She crossed her ankles, tightening the pressure, and Max bowed to rest his forehead on the back of her head.

He pushed through so that the head of his cock popped through her thighs.

That delicious woman *licked* her finger and drew circles on the head of it.

He slid through her thighs wet with her orgasm, and the pressure built.

Only a few more strokes, and his body was steel

bands contracting around his bones. "I'm almost there."

"Go," she whispered, wiggling her ass against him.

His desire to jam his cock inside her core or her ass almost overcame him, but he jerked himself off between her silken thighs, one hand around her breast and pinching her nipple until she gasped because he liked to do it to her.

Firecrackers ran up his spine, and the moment of nothing drew him in and consumed him.

CHAPTER 14
GRACE
DREE

That night, Dree and Maxence slept in each other's arms in the zipped-together sleeping bags, their arms and legs and fingers intertwined. Dree slept well again because she was so warm.

The next morning, she started to get up, but Maxence pulled her back down and wrapped himself around her, nuzzling his nose in her hair. "Don't go."

She whispered, "They're going to figure us out."

"Just one more minute. If Alfonso stomps off in a huff today, I'll have to go sleep in Isaak's tent, or there *will* be questions. Let me have one more minute of you."

Maxence was sleepy and smiling a blissed-out look like a kid, his dark eyes barely slit open. Black stubble covered the angular planes of his jaw, and even his thick, black eyelashes turned up at the corners of his eyes like a smile.

She laid down in his arms again, and he tucked

her head under his chin. He hummed with happiness, and this moment was just perfect in her mind. His body expanded and contracted in her arms as he breathed and was warm all around her.

Every breath was heaven.

And yet, people were moving around outside the tent, near the campfire. They were surely making breakfast, and the camp would be struck soon.

She whispered, drawing out each syllable, "We should go."

"No," he whispered back, also elongating the word as he breathed.

She giggled as quietly as she could and started to untangle herself. From the strong sunlight and their warmth, the air inside the tent wasn't as biting cold as the night before. She changed her clothes quickly and laid out her ski suit.

"Oh, come on," Max said, grasping the air where she'd been. "Don't leave me. I have something for you."

"Yeah, you sure gave me something last night," she said, struggling with the little buckles and straps and Velcro on the ski suit. "We've got to get going this morning, buster. I'll bet you've never had a girl screw you and leave you before."

He chuckled while staring at the top of the tent with his bare arms folded behind his head. His thick biceps and shoulder muscles bulged under the pale gold of his skin. "All of them, actually."

The buckle finally slipped open. "Nah. A guy who looks like you?"

"Looks have little to do with it, I'm told."

She looked up. He almost sounded like he was joking, but not quite. "But, you're exquisite. I mean, you're the most beautiful human being I've ever seen up close."

He shifted a little in the sleeping bag, frowning a bit, maybe in embarrassment. "Let's not discuss this. Vanity is one of the seven deadly sins."

"Well, not vanity. Pride, because it's PEWSLAG, right?"

"Pewslag?" he asked, frowning but silly.

"Yeah, the initials of the seven deadly sins spell PEWSLAG: pride, envy, wrath, sloth, lust, avarice, and gluttony."

He chuckled. "I guess they do. Father Booker was right to have adopted you as an honorary religious sister."

"Lots of my aunts and cousins did a couple of years with one of the sisters' institutes. I could've."

"You don't see many women religious standing up in a bar and announcing they are going to fuck every man in the place."

She shrugged. "I was going to feel guilty about it."

"I suppose it's all right, then."

She dropped one of her boots. "I can't believe any woman *ever* left you. You seriously look like a movie star." He had that otherworldly male beauty that didn't seem to happen to ordinary people.

He shook his head, and the black curls of his hair danced. "I'm not. I've never acted or modeled."

"You could."

He shook his head, his nose wrinkling. "I don't have the temperament for it."

"There isn't a temperament for acting, unless it's just being weird and a little crazy."

He turned on his side, holding his head up with

one spectacular arm. "There is. It's a willingness to please, and patience for endless retakes are essential. I have been assured I'm entirely unsuited for it."

"You don't seem impatient to me. Who told you that?"

"My grandmother. Her name was Grace. She did some modeling and a bit of acting before she married my grandfather."

"Oh, a friend of mine's grandmother did that. She modeled in New York City for a year before she got married. She was a secretary for a big law office there and could type over a hundred words a minute. No one in my family ever did anything interesting like that. I'm the first person to have been east of the Mississippi River in over a hundred years. Some of my cousins went to Disneyland in California, but I've never even done that."

Maxence was still smiling at her. "We should have gone to Disneyland in Paris."

She cracked up. "I can't even imagine telling my family, 'I went to Disneyland, *in Paris.*' They probably wouldn't believe me. Some of them would be mad at me for putting on airs."

"Maybe next time we're in Paris," he said, rolling up and contracting all those amazing abs of his while he grabbed a tee-shirt from the end of the bedroll and sniffed it.

"Yeah," Dree scoffed while she stuffed her legs into her ski bib. *"Maybe next time we're in Paris."*

He twisted in his sleeping bag and looked at her, meeting her eyes with absolute seriousness. "We could go to Disneyland in Paris sometime."

She dragged her ski jacket over her arms and shook her head. "Max, I'm the last person who should be talking because I don't know what I'm doing with my life next *week*. I think half the reason I'm so adamant that this mission needs to continue is because I need the time to think about what to do."

He was smiling at her. "You could stay in a hotel in Kathmandu for a week, or Sister Mariam would take you in as a roommate in a heartbeat. That's not the reason."

"Yeah, okay. Anyway, after this week, I don't know if I should beg Sister Annunciata to find me another trip into the far outback or go back to Phoenix to face the music of my dead, idiot, ex-boyfriend's drug dealers, or maybe go hide on my parents' sheep farm in New Mexico. But you, my friend, *you* need to make some decisions about your life."

"I can't," Maxence said, wrestling his tee-shirt over his head. He rested his arms on his bent knees that were still in the sleeping bag and stared at the back of the tent.

"Oh my God, you *can't*," she mocked him. "Can't died when he was a pup,"

"I beg your pardon?"

Fine, the Jesuit with a doctorate didn't know old country proverbs. She explained, "A momma dog had two pups: Can and Can't. Whenever Can encountered a problem, he hopped up and said, 'I Can!' and he tried it. He didn't always succeed, but he tried and he learned. Whenever Can't was faced with a problem, he laid down and whined, *'I Can't.'* So he never learned how to run, escape, hunt, or eat. Thus, Can't died when he was a pup."

"Ah," Maxence said, laughing. "I am schooled."

"Yeah, you are. The problem is that you 'slip' a

263

lot. Like, every chance you get. I mean, I totally shouldn't be so easily led down the garden path or the happy trail—"

Maxence lifted his shirt and frowned at his lower belly, where a fine trail of hair was forming between his abs. "I should have made time for waxing in Paris, too."

"—because I'm going to get my heart broken at some point, but you're an ordained deacon. You *really* should not. I mean, deacons aren't supposed to have relations unless they're already married, and if they aren't, they aren't allowed to get married."

He shrugged. "My Holy Orders to be a deacon were a little different than the usual rite."

She rolled her eyes. "There are no 'different' Holy Orders. It's a sacrament. Sacraments are, like, set in stone by God or something. If the priest screws up and says the wrong words during your baptism, it doesn't count and you have to get it done again. You can't get kind-of married or just a little baptized, or sort-of some Last Rites. Either they were done right, or they weren't."

Maxence cocked his head to the side and shrugged. "I'm not a priest yet, they assure me. Pope Vincent de Paul assured me that if I want or need to marry, he'll do it himself."

"You can't do tha—*Wait*, you've met *the Pope?*"

He nodded, still staring at the back of the tent. "We met ten years ago when he was a cardinal, and we've kept in touch. He's a nice guy."

"Wow."

Maxence shrugged.

"Okay, *did he*—*was he*—okay, that's beside the point. The point is that you keep saying you're an ordained deacon, which is a degree of Holy Orders. Father Booker and your school friends seem to believe it. You're not even supposed to be bopping your tallywhacker. I mean, we all aren't, but *you*, especially."

Maxence snorted. "All my friends who are priests express less remorse about their 'solitary sins against chastity' than their solitary sins against pasta. You can be absolved after sawing one off." He slapped his flat, muscular stomach. "Carbs are forever."

She pulled on her gloves and motioned between the two of them with one puffy finger. "This isn't solitary."

"I know," he sighed. He struggled out of the double-wide sleeping bag and grabbed his pants.

"What are we going to do?"

He shook his head. "I don't know. I've never had this problem before. I've always had this life," he gestured toward the side of the tent where he'd inserted a silver crucifix suspended on a chain of black rosary beads between the tent wall's fabric and the tension-sprung rib holding it up, "and then I've had, that life." He gestured between the two of them like she had. "They've never crossed before. For months or years at a time, I do this." His open hands encompassed the mission and the crucifix. "And then, if there is a week or a weekend that is unaccounted for between assignments, sometimes, I *slip*."

"So, I'm just a 'slip,'" Dree said, knowing it was true in her heart. "And that's okay, but you need not to *slip* anymore. You shouldn't play with my heart like that, and you shouldn't do it to other people, either."

"No," he said quietly. "You were never a slip."

"Then, what am I, Deacon Father Maxence?" she asked, staring straight at him.

He regarded her for a long time, examining her eyes, her mouth, and the curls of her hair, until he said, "I don't know."

"Great, you don't know whether I'm 'just a slip' or not." She half-stood as much as she could in the pup tent. "In any case, it's only for a few more days. Then you'll go wherever the Church sends you, and I'll decide what to do after my little sojourn here. I'm hungry. I'm going to see if those boys have rustled up breakfast yet."

She stomped out of the tent as much as she could, but she ended up stomp-crawling the last few steps to get through the flap.

She let him get a good view of her ass when she was shimmying out of the tent, though. She should've told him to kiss it.

Dree wiggled out of the tent and found the other guys standing around the brightly blazing campfire, but no breakfast cooking.

Dang.

Father Booker had set up an altar on the back of his motorcycle seat as he'd done every Sunday since they'd started the mission. "Is it Sunday again already?" she asked.

"Happy Christmas!" Isaak told her, and he handed her a piece of cloth sewn into a small pouch.

Lumps filled the bag. She asked, "What's this? Some mini-bottles of your family's vodka?"

He laughed, his blue eyes sparkling in the morning cold. "A Christmas present. It isn't much because I didn't know we were going to spend Christmas out here—"

"You got me a Christmas present?" She was stupidly thrilled. "I'm so sorry. I didn't get you anything."

He shrugged. "You can buy me a coffee in Paris someday."

"I can't imagine I'm going to be able to go to Paris anytime soon," she said.

His smile widened. "Then I'll fly you there."

Okay, that was odd. "Can I open it?"

He sat beside her. "Please do."

Inside the bag were a bunch of yellow crystalline rocks with white crystals on them.

She smiled brightly at him. "Rocks?"

He laughed. "Ginger candy. I bought them from one of the ladies a few towns ago."

"Oh!" She popped one in her mouth and sucked on it. After weeks of eating no cookies or candy and only the barest minimum sugar in her coffee to conserve their supplies, the ginger candy was a burst of super-sweet spiciness on her tongue. "Oh, *wow*. It's so *good!*"

He laughed.

Uh oh, she was being a candy hog, so she held out the bag to the men standing around her. "Everybody should try one."

Father Booker waved her off. "We all got a few, too. You got the big bag, though."

"Okay, then." She popped another one in her mouth. *Spicy and sweet, and OMG, she loved it.*

Maxence crawled out of her pup tent behind her, ruffling his hair like he'd just woken up. "Happy Christmas?"

"Happy Christmas, sleepyhead," Isaak said and tossed a tiny bag to him.

He looked inside. "I heard it was ginger candy?"

"It is."

"Thanks, Isaak. That's cool of you." Max ate one, and a surprised look rose on his face. "These are good. Hey, here's something for you. Happy Christmas." He pulled little things wrapped in foil out of his pocket and tossed one to each person, including Dree.

When she caught it, the dark brown-covered nuts seemed to be candied almonds. "Thank you!"

And, oh yeah, they were good, too. Crunchy and brown-sugary in her mouth. Europe made better candy than the US.

He said, "Aha, and the other thing approaches."

A woman wearing a bright red-and-brown coat and pants was approaching their camp. She'd brought her daughter to the clinic the previous day with a broken arm, which Dree had set and cast. Dree waved, and the woman smiled.

She was holding a small bundle, which she gave to Maxence, who accepted it with much bowing and smiles, and she went back on her way.

"Good God, Maxence," Alfonso said. "What's that?"

"*Pan de Natale,*" Max said, handing it to Father Booker. "It needs to be blessed at the Mass before we can eat it. It's a tradition from home, a sweet bread made with almonds and hazelnuts in it. There's supposed to be an olive branch on top, but I lost it when the motorcycle crashed. At least I found the nuts. It's still warm."

"Hey, we can wrap it in the pashmina to keep it warm." Dree crawled back into her tent and retrieved the baby-blue pashmina.

As she was bundling the warm bread in paper and then in the cloud-like shawl, Alfonso tilted his head and looked at the cross made from almonds on the top of it. "Is that from—"

"Monagasquay," Maxence told him. "Yes, it's an old *Monegasque* tradition."

Alfonso looked up at him, paused, and then asked, "What?"

"An old *Monegasque* tradition."

"Right, but what did you say—"

"Nothing," Maxence said. "I said nothing."

After the Mass, they ate the bread, and it tasted like a particularly good donut.

When they were striking the camp, Maxence drew Dree away for a few minutes and held out his fist. "I have one more thing for you."

Dree held her hands under his, and when he opened his fingers, a small silver cross on a thin chain fell into her palm.

She asked, "Isn't this the one you wear under your shirt?"

Maxence touched the larger, blackened-silver cross he wore around his neck. "I have this one. Angels should have a cross to wear."

Dree asked him, "This isn't a family heirloom or anything, is it?"

He shook his head. "I bought it in Rome because I liked it, but now I want you to have it."

He helped Dree with the clasp, his fingers brushing the skin on the back of her neck. She didn't have a mirror to look at it, but the cross seemed delicate over her black wool turtleneck. "Thank you. It's beautiful. Is it silver?" She would have to make sure she kept it polished so that tarnish didn't eat it away.

"Platinum."

She started to take it off. "That's too expensive."

He laughed and waved at her. "I wish I'd had time to buy something for you in Paris, but I didn't think we'd ever meet again. I'm glad we did. I want you to have this."

"Okay," she said dubiously. "I do like it."

He grinned. "Good. Now let's get this tent down so that we can ride our motorcycles through that icy, *icy* air to the next village."

The next village wasn't all that far away, and even though they'd had Mass, breakfast, and struck the camp, they managed to get there before noon. Everyone went their separate ways for the usual arrangements, though Alfonso and Isaak were bickering because Isaak thought the NICU micro-clinic project was over, and Alfonso didn't.

Nepal is a primarily Hindu country, so Christmas was not celebrated. Dree supposed she could have insisted on taking the day off, but tending to people's needs seemed more in keeping with the spirit of the holiday.

After they arrived, they performed their usual routine of commandeering one of the better houses in the middle of the village and stringing up bed sheets on a cord to make a curtain for some semblance of privacy. That day's sheets were a gorgeous sunny yellow with an orange paisley pattern.

Dree had been seeing patients for about two hours, a usual mix of babies and kids who needed vaccines, people with pneumonia or intestinal ailments who needed antibiotics, and assorted other communicable and non-communicable diseases.

Maxence and Father Booker triaged the patients while Batsa translated.

Isaak had followed them into the clinic today instead of going with Alfonso, and he was doing whatever the others told him to. Alfonso had gone on to evaluate NICU sites even though Isaak had told him again that it was a waste of time. Father Booker tagged along with Alfonso because going off on one's own seemed like a bad idea, and Father Booker was the only one with whom Alfonso was not having an active argument.

Dree was bandaging a little girl's arm and telling Batsa to translate to the mother that she needed to apply the anti-fungal ointment twice per day and keep it covered, and the ringworm would go away. She stripped off her gloves and chucked them in their med waste bag.

Shouting rang outside the door.

Batsa said, "I heard the words for 'woman' and 'bleeding.'" He ran to the door, calling for Maxence and Isaak.

Two women were standing at the door, yelling and pointing.

Batsa talked to them for a minute, his voice rising as he understood more. He turned and said, "Dree, they said there's a woman giving birth, but it's not her time yet. They said they didn't expect the baby until spring."

Dree grabbed her backpack and swept all the supplies she could grab back into it. She yelled to Batsa, "Take Isaak. Go on ahead and find out what's going on so you can tell me when I get there."

Maxence was beside her. "What can I do?"

"Carry this." She shoved her backpack in his

arms. "Do we have more antiseptic anywhere? We're running out of everything."

"I think Isaak has seventy-percent alcohol in that flask of his."

"Good. I didn't think of vodka as being seventy percent alcohol, but you're absolutely right. That should sterilize instruments for when we need them. Come on, let's go find those guys."

As they ran out of the makeshift clinic, Isaak was roaring up on his motorcycle and sprayed gravel as he stopped. He flipped up the visor of his helmet, and his blue eyes were wild. "I came back to get you. The house isn't far. She's in labor, and I think it's any minute!"

They mounted Dree's motorcycle and followed Isaak. The house was just a little way down the dirt street, but riding the bikes was faster than running.

Isaak halted his bike in front of a small, neatly kept cottage. Dree shoved her heel against the motorcycle's kickstand and waited for just a second for Maxence to get off the bike first because he was behind her. As she started to swing her leg over, Max already had his gloved hand out to steady her, and she grabbed hold of his hand with hers.

An older woman was gesturing at the door, motioning for them to hurry, and they all ran inside.

Batsa was sitting beside the bed. "Thank God you're here. I think this is happening now."

Dree dropped her backpack on the floor and snagged two sterile gloves out of the packet in the front pocket. "How do you know it's time? Did you examine her?"

"I have five children. I don't need to look. The mother is nearing the end of stage two, transitional labor. She is beginning to push instinctively. The child's head should crown any moment now."

Behind her, Maxence said, "I can find clean towels."

Dree said, "Good. Yes." She took a peek between the woman's legs, but she didn't see the crown of the baby's head.

Batsa asked her, "Have you delivered a baby before?"

"Twice. How about you?"

"I delivered the last two of mine. I did the last one just eight months ago."

"You left your wife home alone with an eight-month-old baby and four other little kids for a *month?*"

"Nepali families are very close." He gestured to the women standing beside the new mother's bed. "With each of our children, my wife's parents came and did all the cooking and cleaning for the first six months, and my parents came and did it for the second six months. It has been eight months since the birth, so I think my wife is all right to go to the grocery store and drive them to church once a week now."

With a deal like that, no wonder they kept having kids. "Do you want to catch this one?" she asked.

The mother yelled something at Batsa and waved at him, and then the two other women beside the bed began haranguing him in Nepali.

Batsa said, "They are concerned for her modesty. If I stay up here near her head, they might let me stay in the room. You'll have to catch the baby."

The woman strained and screamed, her teeth bared and her face turning dark red.

The two other women started speaking again, and Batsa retreated up by the woman's head, grabbing hold of her hand.

The younger of the two women clambered over the bed and grabbed the new mother's other hand, encouraging her.

When Dree caught a glimpse of the other woman's eyes, the woman was plainly terrified.

Batsa told Dree, "Her mother-in-law, who is the older woman on that side of the bed, said she fell while trying to reach something in an upper cabinet this morning, and that brought on the labor."

Maxence came back. "The stove has a fire in it, so I put water on to boil. I should have sterilized towels in a few minutes."

Dree dug through her backpack and handed him her few rudimentary surgical instruments, including two clamps and a pair of medical scissors. "Boil these, too. Keep them in a sterile towel."

Dree counted between the mother's contractions, and they were about a minute apart. She and Batsa caught a glance at each other over the woman's heaving abdomen, and he had obviously been timing them too. He held the woman's hand in both of his and murmured to her.

Maxence came back, holding steaming towels. "I twisted them out as well as I could. They're still pretty hot."

Dree asked him, "You didn't burn yourself, did you?"

"No, I have about an inch of calluses on my palms and fingers."

Dree shoved her sleeve up her arm and checked the temperature of the towels. Warmth rose from the thin cloths, but in just a few minutes they wouldn't be too hot if the baby landed on them, not that Dree intended to drop it. She spread the towels on the bed beneath the woman, just as she screamed and strained again.

Batsa murmured soothingly to her again, but he muttered to Dree, "She's calling me curse words in Nepali I've never heard before."

The top of the baby's head appeared.

Dree said, "Crowning."

Batsa said, "Hopefully, the baby will be face up. Support the head, and then you'll get one shoulder and then the other. Just tilt the baby up, and the rest of it will come right out. It's best to lay a baby directly on the mother's abdomen, but I'm not sure what to do with a preemie."

Dree nodded. "That's what we did at the hospital."

Batsa said, "My cousin was our OB. She said that women have been giving birth for all of time. She's against medical intervention."

Dree chanted what they had been told in nursing school and doctors had told her when she worked in the hospital. "Before 1900, almost all babies were born at home. It's only been since 1969 that most babies have been born in hospitals. We can do this. She can do this."

Dree prayed they could do this. She also knew the statistics of women and babies dying before 1900, and they were wretched.

With the woman's next push, the baby's head became visible, and the rest of the birth proceeded as Batsa had described within a few minutes.

The baby was tiny, though, so very tiny, where

she lay on her mother's stomach. She was hardly longer than Dree's hand. Her pitiful cry was too soft, not the lusty wail of a full-term newborn. A fine layer of down covered her dark red skin.

Dree used one of the cloths Max had sterilized to wipe blood and mucus off the baby's face and then covered the child with another cloth that felt just the slightest bit warmer than her body temperature, leaving room around her face for her to breathe. "You're okay," she whispered to the mewling infant. "You're okay, baby girl."

The baby wasn't okay. She was far, *far* too small to survive.

Eighty percent died, Alfonso had said.

Batsa shook his head. "She is smaller than my third-born, who was just under four pounds and in an isolette in the NICU for a month."

"There isn't a NICU here." Dree's eyes stung with tears.

Maxence growled, "We need one of Alfonso's damned micro-clinics right here, right now, not a year from now."

The older woman said something else.

Batsa, the baby's mother, and the other woman at the bedside said something harsh back to her. The woman looked angry instead of chastised.

Batsa said, "The mother-in-law has asked why the baby has fur. I've explained that it's because she was born too early and it will disappear, but she said something superstitious. I am concerned about the child's safety."

Dree asked him, "Where's the nearest larger town with a hospital?"

"It's still Chandannath, I would think. Where are

my maps?" He started digging through his backpack on the floor, throwing paper with notes and clothes onto the cement floor.

Isaak was plastered against the front door of the house, his hands spread on the thick wood like he was keeping the monsters of the afternoon out. "We've been riding the motorcycles for weeks. It has to be twelve or fourteen hours away."

Batsa said, "We've been making a loop around Chandannath. There might be a road straight back down. I just need to find—"

He retrieved a folded paper from his backpack and pressed the wide sheet onto the floor. Thick black and blue marker streaks colored the roads on the map.

Using one finger, he traced lines until he found what he was looking for. "There's a direct route. We could be back in Chandannath in less than three hours, but we don't have a car."

Isaak peeled himself off the door. "We can take the baby to the hospital on the motorcycles. Batsa and I can carry some of the baby's relatives on the backs of ours."

The mother cried out again, though not as loudly. She arched her back, and Dree caught the baby's placenta. She held the placenta aloft before clamping off the umbilical cord, cleaning the area with super-premium vodka from Isaak's flask, and cutting between the two clamps with the instruments Max had sterilized.

Dree stripped off her gloves. "The reason we put premature babies in incubators is to keep them warm. Premature babies lose heat, and they die of hypothermia in minutes. That's why I covered her with a warm towel on her mother's tummy. We're in the Himalayas in December. It's freaking freezing outside. There's no way any baby would survive a motorcycle ride of even two minutes in this weather, let alone over two hours."

Maxence said, "I can hold her. We can put her under my leather motorcycle jacket."

His skin was warm, as she'd discovered a few nights before. "We have those hand-warmer packs Father Moses sent from Paris, too. We can pack those around her. And he sent that shiny space blanket. That thing reflects heat, and it's waterproof. It must be windproof."

Dree started digging through her backpack, throwing materials on the floor. "And we can use the pashmina the lady gave me between the baby and the hand warmers. We can fashion an incubator around her and you."

Isaak walked over and crouched beside her. "That's ingenious."

Dree laid out the supplies. "That's how we country folk do it. If you don't have a thing you need, you make do. You wear it out, use it up, repurpose it, and make one out of spare parts. If we had time, I'd quilt all these things into a little isolette for her and make it pretty. I'm thinking some nice applique with a touch of turkey-trot red cotton for the home and hearth, and for luck."

Isaak smiled at her, a spark lighting in his blue eyes. "It's like a wearable incubator."

She twisted around from her work. "Batsa, explain to them what we want to try and how risky it is. Tell them it might not work, and the baby might not survive the trip."

Batsa explained to the family about their plan to get the baby to the hospital.

The mother was nodding and crying.

The mother-in-law must have said something negative because the other woman started berating her and then turned and said something insistent to Batsa.

Batsa translated, "This woman is our new mother's oldest sister, and thus she makes decisions for their family. She will go with the baby to the hospital until the mother can recover and arrive. They're very aware of how few tiny preemies survive."

Dree started ripping open hand-warmer packs and told Maxence, "Strip."

Maxence hadn't bothered to put on his leather pants before they'd made the emergency ride over to deliver the baby, so he did that, and then he stripped down to his tee-shirt. He laid down on the floor.

Dree scooped the baby up with the warm towel, dried her off, and wrapped her in the lovely pashmina like a tiny little burrito, careful to fold a tiny hood over the baby's head but not her face.

In the pashmina's outside layer, Dree inserted the hand-warmer packs, which were already getting toasty to the touch. She tied the space blanket around Maxence's waist and shoulder, fashioning it into a shiny baby sling.

Isaak watched her construction closely. "Insulation, warming gels, and then an outer protective layer. Got it."

Maxence carefully zipped his black leather motorcycle jacket around himself and the baby while Dree, Batsa, and Isaak yanked on their outerwear, and they started walking out to the bikes.

"I can't believe you fit her inside your jacket," Dree said to Max. "I didn't think there was room."

He whispered, "I'm not breathing much because I don't want to squish her. Let's get to the hospital as soon as we can."

The afternoon sun was wan but strong enough to warm Dree's ski suit. Shadows slithered from the mountains into the valley.

Batsa took point, as always, because he had memorized the map and could read the signs.

Isaak bundled the older sister onto the back of his bike and wrapped her arms around his waist, showing her how to lean with him when he turned. The woman's expanded eyes looked frightened, but she was nodding vehemently.

Maxence mounted up behind Dree. "This isn't safe. We should have a car seat or whatever they do for motorcycles."

"I know, but it's her only shot. If we find a truck going that way, we'll hijack them."

He nodded. "Excellent idea. I have an innate knack for piracy."

They jammed their helmets on and buckled them.

They left a note for Father Booker and Alfonso at the house where they had set up the clinic.

Dree gunned the motorcycle, riding as fast as she thought might be safe. She crouched low over the handlebars like she was riding a racehorse for speed, but she wanted to stay upright so her body could act as a windbreak for the baby between them.

Usually, while they were riding together, Maxence wrapped both his arms around her waist or braced them on either side of her, but that day he held onto her with one hand and the baby with his other arm.

The three motorcycles sped through the afternoon as the shadows lengthened, every turn feeling fraught with danger. Dree could have sworn she didn't breathe until they pulled up to the covered awning at the regional hospital.

The three motorcycles stopped in a row. Maxence dismounted the bike and walked directly toward the doors of the ER.

Dree started to follow him, but the older sister nearly fell off the back of Isaak's bike, grumbling something in Nepali. Dree caught her arm before she face-planted on the frozen asphalt.

Batsa translated to Isaak, "She says she will die a thousand deaths on the wheel of karma and Lord Shiva will dance and destroy the universe before she gets back on that motorcycle, but she is very grateful you brought her here."

Dree chased Maxence through the doors. Batsa, Isaak, and the baby's aunt were right on her heels.

Maxence was unzipping his coat and calling out, "Emergency! We have an emergency!"

Batsa caught up to him and began calling out in Nepali.

A woman wearing a dark blue sari and a long white lab coat ran up to them. "I am a doctor. What is your emergency?"

Maxence was having trouble getting the pashmina-wrapped bundle out of the knotted space blanket under his jacket.

Dree reached between his arms and retrieved the tiny infant. "Premature birth, perhaps twenty-eight weeks gestation. We're not sure. She seems to be more than a kilogram but less than two. She was born in one of the small villages, and it seemed better to try to get her here instead of treating her up there."

The doctor took the baby from Dree's arms and spread the folds of the pashmina away from her tiny face.

Dree saw the baby's mouth open in a yawn or an instinct to suckle and nearly collapsed with relief.

The doctor started walking, her long white coat fluttering in her wake, and their entire company followed. "Our neonatal unit is this way. What is this warm under the shawl?"

Batsa said, "Dree Clark, who is a registered nurse practitioner, put hand warmers in the pashmina to keep her warm."

The doctor nodded, flaring her already enormous eyes. "That is very good, yes. You did a good job, Nurse Dree."

Batsa said, "Your English is very good. Did you study in the United States or the UK?"

"I did a Masters in Molecular Biology at the University of Iowa."

Batsa said, "I am living in Iowa City for the past twenty years! Did you try India Café?"

Her head bobbled. "I thought it was excellent, but I went to Masala Cuisine more because I am pure vegetarian. Here we are at the NICU."

A NICU specialist bustled over. "What do we have?"

Dree talked medicine with them, explaining the circumstances of the baby's birth and the relationship of the baby's aunt, who stepped forward and took over the conversation while the neonatologist placed the baby in an incubator and took her vitals.

After a few moments that felt like forever, the doctor looked up at Dree and said, "You got her here in time, and she is warm. Her vitals are very good for a baby who is one and a half kilograms. We will do our best for her." She called out something in Nepali, and nurses bustled over to take charge.

The mother's oldest sister stayed with the baby, and Maxence guided Dree back into the hallway because she felt like she couldn't even breathe.

After they had walked away a good fifty feet, Dree's knees gave out, and she crumpled.

Maxence caught her before her knees banged on the ceramic tile and whisked her up in his arms. "You did it. She's alive, and she's in good condition for a preemie."

Dree tucked her face into Maxence's neck, and to her utter chagrin, began to sob. "I don't want her to die."

His strong arms cradled her. "You did all you could. If you hadn't been there, she wouldn't have any chance at all."

"I don't think I can head back to the village just yet. Maybe if we can find some tea, or maybe if you drove the motorcycle. I'm just exhausted, and I don't even know what I'm doing."

He whispered in his deep voice, "Let's stay here in Chandannath for the night. It's beginning to get dark out there. I don't want to drive a motorcycle on those twisty roads above the cliffs in the dark."

"But Father Booker and Alfonso—"

"We already had the campsite set up before we left. They've got two motorcycles, a fire pit ready to go, and three tents. They each have the opportunity to sleep alone in a tent tonight. I think if we go back, they'll be mad at us."

Dree nodded into his neck. His sandpaper stubble scraped her nose and forehead. She just wanted to sleep in his arms again.

CHAPTER 15
JUMLA, AGAIN
DREE

Maxence settled Dree on the motorcycle behind him. She held onto his muscular waist and leaned her helmet against his back. She wasn't trying to tempt him or herself, but holding onto his body with both arms comforted her. She rubbed her gloved palm over the black leather of his jacket, trying to distract herself from worry over the tiny baby they'd taken to the hospital.

When they got to the inn they'd stayed at their first night in Jumla and wrenched off their helmets, Maxence must have caught a glimpse of her tear-streaked face because he grabbed her hand and pressed it between both of his, saying, "You did the most anyone could have done."

"I should give you that cross necklace back. Angels can work miracles. I think I did something stupid that cost a baby her life today."

"That baby didn't stand a chance if we hadn't tried something. We'll check on her tomorrow morning before we head back to the village. But no matter what happens, you gave her a shot, even if it's only a slim chance. She was very small. Her little limbs were just skin-covered bird bones. She didn't have a twenty percent chance of surviving up there. She had no chance at all."

"When Batsa said that about the mother-in-law, all I could think was to get that baby out of the house."

"That's yet another reason, and you're right."

They went inside and found the same three available rooms and eager innkeepers who appreciated wintertime guests.

Isaak grinned and stretched his arms as they checked in. "A real bed all to myself with a warm shower? I have died and gone to Heaven."

Maxence swiped his credit card and paid for the rooms and meals, even though the innkeepers were willing to bargain again and let them have the rooms for only the price of supper.

When Dree asked Max about it, he said, "I'm unwilling to surrender to the relentlessness of poverty today. Perhaps saving one baby's life has inspired me to fight on, at least for tonight."

Dree didn't feel it.

The innkeeper's wife made supper for them. They sat at a table in the tiny lobby.

The plant in the corner was still dead.

The world was caving in on Dree. No matter how hard she worked, she couldn't save anyone. She'd come up with one harebrained scheme to wrap a few random items around a neonate and drive her for hours on a motorcycle.

Dree had probably killed the baby.

She hated herself. She was a stupid, undertrained nurse who thought she was MacGyver.

Maxence's knee and lower leg pressed against hers throughout the meal, though he didn't seem to notice it.

She did. The warmth and pressure reminded her that Max thought they hadn't done something lethally stupid, even though she suspected he was wrong.

Isaak and Batsa sat across from them in a booth and ate steadily. The hard, wooden seat was bruising her tailbone.

Batsa had stayed at the hospital a little longer to help if he could, and then he'd caught up with them.

He told them that yes, when he'd left, the baby was still alive. "They were pleased with her suckling response, and she had eaten two ounces of neonatal formula all by herself, not with a feeding tube. That is a very good sign. My premature daughter did not eat for herself for a week in the NICU."

Isaak said to Dree, "The travel incubator you put together really was a stroke of genius."

Dree shrugged and didn't look up from where she was sopping up chicken chunks in tomato gravy with a piece of bread. "It was a stupid idea."

Max said, "I don't think it was stupid, and she might be okay."

Batsa said, "The doctor seemed very pleased about her condition when I left. She doesn't have a name yet. The mother didn't tell her sister what she wanted to name her."

A NICU doctor might be "pleased" with a preemie's condition because half of their patients died or had significant brain damage. A nurse like Dree saw healthy babies all the time and could recognize a desperately endangered preemie when she saw one. That baby had a minuscule chance of survival.

Isaak said, "Whether this baby ultimately survives the ride or not, the *idea* of transporting a preemie in a warming cocoon is what's important. All prototypes can use some refinement."

"It wasn't a 'prototype,'" she said to him. "We weren't in a medical device engineering lab running mathematical models of wind resistance and thermal insulation. We wrapped a premature baby in a frickin' pashmina and drove her for hours on a motorcycle. I took a Hippocratic Oath, and today, I'm pretty sure I caused a *lot* of harm."

"She was alive," Batsa said again.

"Not just for that baby," Isaak said to her. "But like Alfonso was talking about, there are premature babies born in those villages all the time that probably would survive if they could be rushed to a hospital. If they are kept warm enough and got to a hospital in less than three hours, a heck of a lot more than twenty percent of them would survive."

"But I won't be there to do something so stupid and rash and take them on a damned motorcycle."

Isaak reached over and tapped the back of her hand. "I don't think you realize what you've invented. With the insulation, heat packs, and a wind-breaker outer shell, you can transport a preemie to a hospital instead of just letting them die."

"But they *can't*," Dree said. "Batsa knows. The reason that these people haven't had medical care is that they don't have transportation, and it's a three-day walk to Chandannath. We can't build a warmer that will last for *three days.*"

Isaak's bright blue eyes swiveled up, and he contemplated the water-stain on the ceiling. "We might be able to."

"That's it." Maxence held a piece of bread pinched in his fingers. "Alfonso kept asking what we could do with his NICU micro-clinics. That's not the right question. The right question to ask is, *why* are we doing this? That's the *real* question, the *why.* The reason *why* we wanted to build those NICU micro-clinics is to save more premature babies. Therefore, our correct question is, *how do we save more preemies?*"

Isaak pointed at Max as punctuation. *"That's* what I'm trying to say. That's what we need to ask, *why?* The way we save preemies is a transport capsule that's a refinement of what you put together today, paired with an ambulance."

"These villages can't afford an ambulance," Dree said. "It's the same problem as with Alfonzo's micro-clinics. The villages here couldn't maintain a half-million-dollar ambulance full of computers and electronics. No one could drive it. It would fall apart and rust away."

"But *a motorcycle,*" Maxence said. "Motorcycles are simple to maintain and drive. That's why the underdeveloped world has so many of them. It's not just that they're far cheaper and use a fraction of the petrol. It's that people can be taught to fix them in a few days."

Isaak nodded. "These villages could all use an ambulance motorcycle, anyway. There were so many of these cases that you treated over the last few weeks that should have been seen at a medical clinic.

Plus, if there's a disease outbreak or something, someone could travel to Chandannath to bring back help."

Max nodded. "So, if the real question is how do we drastically increase the health and medical care in these villages, the motorcycle ambulance is *also* the answer."

Dree blinked, but she just couldn't get as excited as the guys. "Well, I'm glad I didn't screw up too badly."

Isaak reached across the table and jostled her shoulder. "You made something amazing out of spare parts, imagination, and love. You should be proud of yourself today. You gave that kid a fighting chance."

Batsa nodded. "My parents told me about what life was like in their village before they left to go to America. The communities are strong, and they still miss their families and friends. That is one thing that we do not have in the United States, a strong community ethic."

Dree nodded. "Yeah, I noticed that. No one came to the clinic alone. Even for a kid with a mildly infected cut, the mom arrived with three or more relatives or friends as backup. In the States, you get pregnant women driving themselves to the ER while they're having contractions."

"That would never happen here," Batsa said. "There are always aunties and cousins and sisters around when a woman is in a family way. However, a motorcycle ambulance would be a blessing that would help everyone."

Maxence said to Isaak, "We can begin writing grants tomorrow."

Isaak said, "We can start delivery of ambulance motorcycles in a month or two. I can start working on schematics for Dree's preemie pod tomorrow, too. Finally, it's good to be an engineer. The heat pack will be tricky. I'm envisioning something that can be recharged in boiling water. I've got friends who are chemical engineers whom I can get in touch with when we get back to Kathmandu. We can have test models in production in a few weeks, and refined versions rolling out in a few months. This could change how premature babies are handled in all underdeveloped countries, not just Nepal."

Batsa said, "For the price of ten of Alfonso's micro-clinics, we can put a thousand ambulance motorcycles and five thousand preemie pods in the villages of Nepal, and we can do it in months instead of years."

Dree had stopped eating and was just listening to their grandiose plans. "But we don't even know if it worked."

Batsa frowned at her. "The baby was alive when we got her to the hospital, and her condition had not deteriorated much at all over several hours. *That's* a win. That's an *enormous* win."

Maxence said, "And such a project would be far more community-based than the construction of micro-clinics that nobody asked for. Several people from each town can be taught to ride and perform basic maintenance for a motorcycle. These motorcycles won't be computer-based technological marvels like the ones in Europe and America. We'll use Royal Enfields like we're riding, or something like that. Just having several people with the basic technical skills to change the oil and brake pads on those bikes will raise the technology level of this whole region. Other people will be able to get motorcycles because basic maintenance will be available."

Dree nodded. "There are gas stations about every five villages or so. Gasoline shouldn't be a problem." Maxence's strong arm was right beside hers. He'd taken off his black leather motorcycle jacket when they'd sat down for supper, and his coat was hanging over the end of the booth. His biceps and triceps curved around his arm, and his lower arm bulged with muscle. His ripped arm looked like an illustration from her anatomy textbook or maybe one of the models from the life drawing class she'd taken.

Maxence said, "Greater access to transportation means more trade. It means that villages that are close to Chandannath will have more opportunities for employment there, which means more money in those villages. Then, villages that are close enough to those places will have more opportunities for trade, employment, and wealth. This is a project with positive ripple effects."

Batsa nodded. "When I was a child, I often visited my extended family's village. We filled our suitcases with anything and everything we could find for them. A few motorcycles in nearby villages would have raised access to things they needed, from iodized salt to more diverse food in the winter."

Maxence said to Isaak, "This is the kind of planning that charities need. We don't need billionaires to exploit impoverished people for tax write-offs or to make money off of charity projects."

Maxence dropped his hands casually at his side while he spoke, but his fingers crossed the small space between his thigh and Dree's and laced with hers.

She could scarcely breathe, and she held on.

Isaak nodded. "Even I, whose family fled the Communists and used capitalism to build factories to produce alcohol, must agree with you. Creating a product to sell to people who have money and want it is right and proper. Indeed, my family has become very wealthy doing it." He smiled at Dree, and she was confused. "Sucking a profit out of a charity and exploiting people's children is grotesque."

Batsa said, "Exploiting poor people should be a grievous sin, right, *Deacon Father Maxence?*"

Deacon Father Maxence.

Dree loosened her grip on Max's fingers, but he didn't let go. He *wouldn't* let go, even when she made her hand go limp. He held on, and if anything, tightened his grip.

It was easy to forget the vows he'd made to the Church when his arms were around her.

Too easy.

Maxence nodded. "As Dree mentioned a month ago, in the Gospel of Matthew, chapter twenty-five, Jesus Christ himself said it was a mortal sin."

What on Earth was he talking about? He couldn't have known that she was thinking about mortal sins and his hands, his body, his lips on her neck.

Right?

"I didn't say anything," she mumbled.

"Oh, yes, I remember," Isaak said to her. "It was around the campfire when Father Booker got nervous about the personal responsibility mandate. I was listening to you."

Maxence continued, "Matthew is the first book of the Gospels for a reason. That entire chapter is the key to understanding Christ. The key to all three parables, but especially the Sheep and the Goats, is right at the end. Christ talks about the people who were hungry or thirsty, or the strangers and the prisoners, and he says, 'I say to you, whatever you did for one of these least brothers of mine, you did for me. And what you did *not* do for one of these least ones, you did *not* do for me.' He points to the people who let the poor and prisoners die and says, 'And these will go off to eternal punishment, but the righteous to eternal life.' Letting poor people die and doing nothing about it is a mortal sin, straight from Christ's mouth."

Batsa nodded. "And thus, we have a personal responsibility, according to the Church."

Maxence shook his head and squeezed Dree's fingers. "But Christ doesn't gather *people* in that chapter. He gathers 'the nations.' *The nations.* We have *more* than personal responsibility. We have a mandate from Christ as a society, as a *civilization,* to not let the poor be lost, to protect those who are in danger, to feed those who are hungry, to bring justice to the world, and to not stop until we do. Most religions believe this. It's not unique to Christianity. That baby girl whom we transported to the hospital tonight, none of us asked whether her parents had the money to pay an ambulance. Nobody asked whether the baby's parents were rich enough to *deserve* their child's life to be saved. *You just do it.* You just wrap the baby up and get her to the hospital because it's the thing a decent person does."

"Personal responsibility," Batsa said.

"But you don't stop there," Maxence said. "Because we have seen the poor and the sick, because we have seen the preemies who die, *then* we make more preemie pods and make sure there are motorcycles for the next time, because *that's* the right and decent thing to do."

"Right," Isaak said, nodding. "Not just this baby, not just this one time."

Maxence went on, his words filling Dree's ears and eyes, "But it's not just us. It shouldn't be just us. It should be *everyone*, because if you have a few tough years, your kids shouldn't die. They shouldn't be physically stunted from not getting enough to eat because you lost your job or the harvest failed. Your kids shouldn't be blind because you couldn't get them testing or treatment. That's unchristian. It's evil. And Jesus Christ himself said you would go to Hell if you allowed that to happen to other people's kids. We need to practice Christianity as Christ preached it."

The words he said filled her lungs and her soul like air.

Dree squeezed his hand. "You're doing it again."

Max released her fingers and sat back in his seat. "I am. You're right. *Dammit*, I don't know it sometimes, but it's important. It's important to talk about and to know. I can't stand by and watch people who have billions of dollars swindle other people who work hard for their money. Alfonso is still out there, looking for places to build his NICU micro-clinics and overcharge impoverished people for the drugs to keep them running. He'll make Nepal poorer, not richer."

Isaak shook his head. His expression looked

pained. "He surprised me. We were friends in school. I didn't think he'd do something like that."

Max nodded. "I didn't, either. It surprised me when this project was approved, and then it shocked me when he admitted that it was all to turn a profit for his company. This is a charitable organization we're working with. Everything is supposed to be not-for-profit, and there shouldn't be forced-sales gimmicks hidden inside charitable donations. We have to get billionaires out of charities because they use them to strip regular people of their money."

"But you've been working with charities ever since I've known you," Isaak said. "You and Flicka put together that extravaganza for her wedding to your brother. You did amazing things with that money."

Maxence shook his head. "For every amazing thing we did, some other psychopath used the charity system to suck more money out of the poor and people who work for a living. This is why I *need* to become a Jesuit," Maxence said. "I want to work from inside the Church and change everything. The Catholic Church can make our *practice* of Christianity line up with what we *say* about Christianity. Instead of saying that some people, somewhere, should help and then absolving them when they don't, we can *make* it happen. Everything we do should take the poorest people and the condition of the world into consideration when we decide what to do with missions and during sermons."

Isaak sat back. "The guys on the yachts will destroy you if you tell them that they cannot suck even more wealth from the working and lower classes. We both know people who will do it. We grew up with them at Le Rosey, and we've met them through our connections from there. They'll fight back. They'll fight *you.* They'll make sure you can't become a priest if that's what you want to do."

Maxence shook his head and frowned. "My uncle isn't long for this world. I sat by his bedside for a month. As soon as my brother Pierre takes over, he'll give the Vatican permission to give me the sacrament of Holy Orders, and I won't be stuck in this limbo of waiting and wanting. He'll do it because he wants me out of the picture. I will disappear into the Church, and then I'll change the world from within it."

Maxence was going to disappear into the Church.

Dree needed to remember that, even when his cologne wafted through the air like the musk of desire in front of a fire built from cinnamon and vanilla.

She asked him, "Why does your brother control your life that way? That's weird."

Maxence nodded. "Yes. Yes, it is. But it's the way my life works. But after I take Holy Orders, I will belong to the Church."

He would *belong* to the Church.

Not to *her.*

She'd never thought he belonged to her.

Really, she hadn't.

The screwing around in Paris meant nothing.

They'd both *agreed* to that. That was the *plan.* That was *her* plan.

And yet—

And yet the whole world was falling down around her.

"Right," Isaak said to Max, sitting back in his

seat. "Then you'll be a Jesuit and you'll belong to the Church."

Isaak looked straight at Dree.

Dree was sitting beside a man she was falling in love with, but whose heart already belonged to the Church.

Oh.

The rest of the supper passed in a blur. There was more food. A dessert made of milk, rose water, sugar, and something round and white was on the table, and she ate one. The sweetness was cloying in her mouth because she just wanted to leave.

Her room was the same one as before, with a wooden, double-sized bed. Last time she'd slept at this inn, she'd slept alone and dreamed of a man named Augustine, a man who'd given himself to her utterly for four beautiful days, and she'd thought she was miserable because she couldn't have him again.

This time, she was in love with a man who had given his heart to the world, and the world wouldn't give him back.

Even though exhaustion weighed on her body with every step, Dree paced.

She shouldn't go to Max's room. The time when they'd shared a pup tent in the Nepali countryside had been a fantasy, and she was stupid to have believed it.

Maybe he would come to her. Father Booker wasn't around to narc to whomever priests narced to about ordained deacons who screwed around.

Maybe there would be a knock on her door, and maybe it would be Maxence.

Maybe he would tell her that this last month and

his ordination were the real lies, and his name was Augustine, and they could go back to Paris forever.

Lord, grant me sobriety and chastity, but not yet.

She hadn't realized that he was praying to be a priest.

Her footsteps covered the floor as her body tried to believe what her mind was telling it.

She was pacing away from the door and had just passed the quilt-covered bed when a fist thudded on the wood of her door.

She ran.

She wasn't proud of it, but she *ran* to the door, twisted the lock and the knob, and opened it, expecting the dark-eyed, black-haired unearthly male beauty of Maxence, an angel who wanted to save the world with a tattoo of demon wings on his back.

The man standing outside Dree's door was blond and blue-eyed, a man Dree would have thought was the most handsome man she'd ever met, except that she had seen Maxence.

Isaak Yahontov was standing one step away from her door, his hands clasped behind his back. He said, "Perhaps this isn't the right time or the right place to say this, but we've spent a month together, and every day, my admiration for you has grown. You are a beautiful woman, an exceptional nurse, an excellent engineer, and the most wonderful human being I've ever met. I would like to see you again after this project is over, spend some time with you, and see if the future could hold anything for us."

Okay, that was *not* what Dree had expected.

Dree stammered, "I had no idea you felt like this."

Isaak shrugged. "My apologies. I'm bad at this. I've never had to tell a woman I'm interested in her before. Usually, they're climbing all over me. All I have to do is open my hands, and they fall into them."

Dree laughed. "I don't know what to say."

"From what I understand, you are in some unusual circumstances, and I don't know if you have a phone. Thus, I will leave you with my contact information. Send me a text or however you want to get in touch with me." He held out a business card to her, but he looked up. His bright blue eyes caught hers. "Or, I'm taking a helicopter back to Kathmandu tomorrow, where my plane will be waiting to take me back to Paris. Come with me. No strings attached. We'll just have some coffee and talk. If that works out, then a few meals, maybe a walk through the Tuileries. Nothing else."

The option of leaving Nepal and Maxence boiled through her.

Being near Maxence wasn't good for her. It was like walking around with forbidden fruit in her pocket. Eventually, she was going to bite it.

Her hand reached across the infinite space between them, and she took his card. "I'll think about it. Thank you, Isaak. I'm not sure what I'm going to do tomorrow, but I appreciate your offer."

"As I said, no strings attached. Wait, one string. I would like a cup of coffee with you. We can sit in a lovely Parisian café on the sidewalk, outside, and talk about ourselves and our lives. That's all. One cup of coffee, that's all I ask."

A smile pinched her cheeks. "And where would I be staying?"

He waved his hand in the air. "I will get you a hotel room, if that is what you would like. I will pay for it for as long as you would like to stay there. One cup of coffee, that's all. Other than that, consider it a free ride on an airplane that's going to Paris anyway."

"Okay," Dree said. "Okay. I'll think about it."

They said goodnight, and Dree closed her door and locked it again.

She leaned against the wood and bonked the back of her skull against the door.

Well, that was unexpected.

The world tipped and felt off-kilter after finding the wrong man outside her door.

Maybe Isaak wasn't the wrong man. Maybe Isaak or some other guy would be the right guy, because Maxence obviously wasn't the right guy for her.

She stood there until the world felt right on its axis, a world that wasn't centered around Maxence but was centered around other possibilities.

Getting on a plane out of Kathmandu with Isaak for the price of only a cup of coffee was a perfect idea. Even if she ended up back in Phoenix, even if she ended up back on the sheep ranch in New Mexico, even if she called Sister Annunciata and begged for another mission to Chile or The Congo, she needed to leave Nepal and *soon.*

Isaak might leave Chandannath by helicopter early the next morning to meet his private plane in Kathmandu for the flight back to Paris.

To a girl who grew up on a sheep farm in New Mexico, that thought sounded *so weird* in her head.

But if she wanted a ride on his plane, she should tell him *right then.*

Dree took a deep breath and decided that yes, she wanted to walk away while her mind and her heart weren't shredded, and she needed to go with Isaak on his plane to Paris the next day.

Dree turned, twisted the lock and knob of her bedroom door, and flung it open.

Maxence stood outside, his hands in the pockets of his leather jacket, and he looked at her with dark fire smoldering in his eyes.

Her hand reached out before she could stop herself, grabbed a fistful of his white tee-shirt just below his throat, and yanked him inside her bedroom.

His mouth found hers before the door slammed behind him, and he caught her waist with his hands to crush her against his chest.

She hadn't kissed him since Paris despite their furtive touches in their tent, and she was starving for him. His tongue pushed into her mouth, stroking hers, and his groan matched her hunger.

Maxence shoved her legs with his muscular thighs, walking her backward to the bed. If he had been anyone else, the insistence and the strength he used to compel her might have scared her, but they had denied themselves for a month. Her body hungered for him from the inside out, wanting to feel his silken curls in her hands, his skin pressing her body into the bed, his cock in her mouth and throat and filling her up inside.

All the reasons she should stop weighed on her, but she yanked the shoulders of his tee-shirt. He contracted his chest and ducked as she pulled it off over his head, baring his shoulders to her palms. His skin was satin and velvet over the iron of his muscles, and she dropped his shirt on the floor.

The backs of her legs hit the bed frame, and she climbed onto the mattress and kneeled on it, making her several inches taller.

His lips captured hers again, and he slipped his hands under the hem of her shirt and found her waistline.

His fingertips stroked her flesh, and she inhaled.

He kissed lower, sucking her skin under her jawline. She arched backward, curving her whole body to press her breasts against his chest but let him mouth her throat. His arm behind her back crushed her against him. His other hand roamed, grasping her breast and teasing the tight point of her nipple through her shirt, and then kneading the soft flesh of her ass.

With almost a snarl, he grabbed her clothes and pulled them away, dragging her shirt over her head and her jeans and panties down her legs. In seconds, she was naked in the cool room, and he grabbed her and squeezed her body against him. His head bowed to her shoulder. His hands were relentless as he explored her body, touching, squeezing, pinching her if it seemed she was paying too much attention to her explorations of his firm, rippled body.

She dragged her fingers over his broad shoulders and the flat ripples of his abs, and he hissed as he inhaled through his teeth. His next bite on her shoulder was more savage, so she wrapped her hand around his muscled ass and gripped the denim-over-steel of his backside.

That earned her a hard pinch of her nipple and

a strong push back onto the bed, where she almost bounced, but his hands on her thighs and his mouth between them held her down.

He parted her folds with his tongue and devoured her, sucking and rubbing as her back bowed. She reached behind her head to grab the quilt and hang on. She couldn't scream. The walls might be thin.

When she'd scooted on the bed too far for his famished attack, he grabbed her ankle and hauled her back to his mouth.

She whipped her head back and forth, trying so hard to be silent. Her body was tightening, the muscles of her hips straining. She couldn't restrain one soprano whimper.

Another hard yank on her leg pulled her entirely off the bed, and she landed on her knees on the cold floor.

Maxence grabbed a fistful of her hair and yanked her head back. His jeans were already open, and he shoved his massive cock into her mouth and down her throat. She grabbed the bottom of the bed behind her butt for balance.

He whispered, his voice gravelly, "Hands behind your back."

Dree did.

She clasped her hands behind her, pushing her breasts out, and complied with what he told her to do because she couldn't imagine doing anything else. If he couldn't give her his whole life, if he could only give her that night, she was going to *take* it.

He rocked his hips forward, shoving his cock into her mouth, pinning her back against the side of the bed and her head between his fist and his cock. Her nose neared the black mat of hair above his root, and the aroma of his clean male body, soap, and the spice and burning oak of his cologne filled her nose and mind.

He jerked, shoving it deeper down her throat, and a tear ran out of the corner of her eye. The rough denim of his jeans scraped her chin.

This wasn't a blow job. This was claiming every part of her. It wasn't for his pleasure but for his power.

And her gaping mouth was empty.

She coughed with the openness of her mouth and throat.

He hauled her up by her shoulders and shoved her backward on the bed. He pushed his jeans down his legs, stumbling and leaning on the bed, bending the mattress under her, but then his magnificent body was naked and gleaming in the light from the nightstand and crushing her beneath him.

His mouth grabbed hers again, and his fingers rubbed her clit that was raw from his mouth as he found her opening and guided himself into her.

She bit his shoulder, whispering, "Please, *please.*"

With one violent thrust, he shoved himself hard into her, and she almost flew off the bed from his invasion of her body. He had her by her shoulders, though, and she couldn't move. He had impaled her with his cock, slamming her hard, and her fingers found his shoulders. She shouldn't scream, *couldn't scream.*

Her hands curled on his skin and dug in.

His voice in her ear was a growl, "More, *more* or I'll fuck you harder."

"Yes." She was arching against him, desperate for

more of his skin and his body and the rich scent of his cologne like fire, crushed herbs, and natural musk overpowering her. *"God, yes. Do it."*

His rough body scraped her clit and inside her, pushing her harder as he shoved her back on the bed, climbed on with his knees, and forced himself deeper into her.

Her head was spinning, and she was breathing too fast, and she clung to him with her fingernails as he barreled into her, crashing his body into hers as she tightened and spiraled higher.

Her mind screamed because her throat couldn't.

She bucked under him, almost crying, and that last scrape of friction broke through. The orgasm crashed through her, a blast that ripped through the tension and broke her apart, and her hands dug deeper.

Maxence was gasping against her shoulder, a choke in his throat, as the last instinctive jerks ran through his body. His arms tightened around her shoulders.

Dree curled her arms and legs around him because this moment might be all she had.

He didn't move, but his breath was restless.

She held on.

After a few minutes, he pulled away, the sweat of their coupling running down her sides. She thought Max might just pull on his clothes and leave without a word because the conflict in him must be tremendous, but he held his hand out to her.

She took it.

He led her into the bathroom and washed her body, taking care of her like she was a doll he'd abused.

As he crouched to wash her legs, warm water from the shower rolled over the dark red parallel lines from her nails that crossed the tattooed feathers in his skin. The black silk of his hair clumped as water flowed through it.

She touched his shoulder, and he looked up at her, his dark eyes watching her. She let her fingers trail under his chin, and with just the gentlest pressure, guided him to stand.

He kissed her gently as water covered them, and then he dried her off and carried her to the bed, where he wrapped his body around hers.

Still, he didn't say anything.

And he left the light on, like he might need to see when he put on his clothes to leave her.

She let the silence drag on because she didn't want to drive him away with words, any words.

Finally, the pain of not speaking overpowered the fear of driving him away.

She said, "You want to save the world, not just every woman who's in danger, but everyone."

His skin moved under her palms as he shrugged.

"You want to be a priest," she said.

"A Jesuit."

"And so, there's no future for us," she said.

"There is," he said, and he took her hand, laying their clasped hands on the velvet skin of his chest. "I saw you working out there, pouring your spirit and your life into this project and this country and the people you cared for. You're an angel sent to Earth to save it. You belong out there with me."

"I'm not an angel," Dree said. "I'm a woman. I want a husband and a family. I want to be a wife and a mother to my own children, as well as to be a nurse. I want that love around me all my life, and I don't want to give that up."

Maxence's body tightened under her hands. "I see."

"You want to be a Jesuit. You want to dedicate yourself to something bigger than yourself, and you —" She sighed. "I saw you at the pulpit. That wasn't an accident. That's what you are meant to do. You and I have no future together. You have your future, and I know what I want in mine. They aren't the same."

He lifted her hand and kissed her fingers, then the back of her hand, then the inside of her wrist. "We could meet sometimes."

Dree shook her head. "You'll break my heart."

He pressed her hand to his chest between the rounds of his pecs. "You'll always have mine."

She wrestled the covers and her body around to push herself up on her elbows. "You don't seem to want to live the life of a priest."

"Of course I do," he said, his eyes drifting away from her.

She didn't have to confront him on that. It wasn't her place, or this wasn't the time. "I'm not going to be the woman you run to for an easy lay when you can't take it anymore. I'm not your temptation, and I'm not going to wait for the rest of our lives for you to change your mind."

He nodded, still looking away from her. "But we have the rest of this trip."

She shook her head. "Tomorrow, I'm going back to Kathmandu and then Paris."

His muscles tensed under her hands, not like he'd

almost jumped up, but like she'd landed a punch to his gut. "You're burned out."

"It's not burnout. I'm a nurse in an inner-city hospital. I work eighteen-hour shifts all the time. I've worked forty-hour shifts with a four-hour nap during crises, and I've done that for weeks on end when the need is great. I can't do this *with you*. I can barely stand the thought of leaving tomorrow. If we did this for two more weeks, I don't know what I'd do when we had to walk away. I know addiction when I see it, and that's what's happening to me. You would tear me apart. My mom always said that when you find yourself in a hole, the first thing you do is stop digging. I have to stop digging myself deeper into this whatever-it-is with you. I need to leave, and I need to leave tomorrow."

He didn't say anything for a few long minutes.

Instead, he kissed her slowly, his mouth taking its time to plunder hers, and then he did the same thing with his body.

And she held him in her arms, cradling him as he moved gently in her, their souls melding as their breath mingled in the night.

In the early morning, he dressed and kissed her, saying, "I'll meet you downstairs before you go to the airport. The first helicopter flight to Kathmandu isn't until ten."

Dree curled her arms and knees around a pillow after he left, crushing it so she wouldn't cry. If she let herself cry, if she allowed the gaping emptiness within her to coalesce into tears and flow through her, she might not leave.

And she had to leave.

Showering again and throwing herself and her

backpack together took just a few minutes, and she walked downstairs, feeling a little guilty, to see if Isaak was there yet to take her to the airport with him.

Before she made the last turn on the stairs, male voices from the lobby rose into the stairwell.

Maxence's voice said, *"No. I renounce. I renounce it all."*

Was Father Booker there, and was Maxence renouncing his deacon vows?

Horror at her influence and exultation warred in Dree—*Yes,* he was going to walk away from the priesthood, he was going to be *hers,* they had a *chance,* there was a path for them.

And then the timbre of his voice leaked through her hopes.

Anger harshened his voice in the way men express terror as outrage.

Dree ran down the stairs.

CHAPTER 16
RENUNCIATION
MAXENCE

Maxence's mind roiled as he stepped down the stairs, his motorcycle boots stomping on each tread.

God grant me sobriety and chastity, but not yet, St. Augustine had prayed.

Please, Lord my God, I beg you as I have begged you for many years, hollow me and let me become an empty shell. Let me have no desires, no senses, no future, and exist without time. Let me want nothing and feel absolutely nothing with all my heart. Allow me to move through the world, soulless and empty, and my husk will do Your work because I cannot stop. *My soul is shredded. I want to go with her more than I want to live, and my brother, Pierre, may kill us both if I walk away from the Church and become a threat to him.*

Max's backpack swung against his spine, and he walked into the lobby. His mind was so turned inward that his eyes did not see except to step around the table and benches where they had eaten supper the previous night.

Last night, Dree had been sitting beside him in

that booth. The side of his face had been bathed in her warmth, and the occasional brush of her soft clothes against his had drawn lines of sparks over his skin beneath.

And now she, too, would walk away from him.

As she should.

He was a target at the bottom of a pit, surrounded by enemies pointing weapons down at him. Dragging someone else down there was not an option for him. That's why all of his "slips" were during times when he had eluded his security detail and was free.

No wonder his "slips" were rare, and why evading palace security was one of his most highly developed skills.

The Jumla district of Nepal was so remote and Max was so confident he must not be under surveillance that he remained lost in thought as he approached the counter to check out of the little inn, and he missed the three men standing, motionless, near the door.

He shouldn't have overlooked them.

Their gray-blue military fatigues weren't the flashy hiker apparel of foreigners traipsing about the Nepali countryside in late December, and the odd bulges under their uniforms indicated they were armed.

A man near Max's shoulder said, "Prince Maxence, Your Highness, we're here to escort you to Monaco."

That voice was familiar, and Max's skin rippled under his tee-shirt and jeans from the impact of the man's voice.

Max didn't allow his body to jump, but he tensed.

He turned his head and looked down into the gray, nearly colorless eyes of Quentin Sault, the director of Monaco's security services who answered to Maxence's older brother, Prince Pierre, even though their uncle was the titular sovereign.

Two commandos wearing winter fatigues guarded the doorway.

This was it, then.

Max wasn't sure why or why *then*, but they had come for him.

Sault was thoroughly Pierre's creature. Pierre must have decided to execute Maxence, and he'd ordered Quentin Sault to do it because Sault followed Pierre's orders, *all* his orders, even the most vile.

That was why Sault and his soldiers were in Nepal. Pierre must have given Sault that final order.

There was no other possible explanation.

Sault stood at Max's side.

The other two commandos guarded the inn's front door, which was the only escape from the room other than a frantic sprint up the stairs and a probably futile attempt to leap through the glass of one of the second-story windows.

But if Max made it upstairs without being shot, which room would he choose to lead the assassins through? Because surely, these men would not leave witnesses alive.

Would the sacrifice be a father of five young children *and* his childhood friend from boarding school, or Dree?

It wouldn't be Dree.

But those were both unacceptable options, so Max wouldn't run.

That left the option of fighting his way out.

A fight would pit three highly trained, probably heavily armed, military men against one moderately trained unarmed man who did not practice his self-defense skills.

Thus, there was no way out.

The air evacuated the lobby of the inn.

Max pressed his palms on the cracked linoleum of the inn's check-in counter and tried not to show he was drowning in emptiness.

If Pierre had indeed finally ordered Max's execution, his only choice was how he behaved in these final minutes of his life.

Though *perhaps*, he could talk his way out of it.

Maxence turned back and stared, unblinking, at the wall. Neon blue afterimages of the idols and pictures of Hindu gods tacked up there appeared and floated over the white paint, and he watched them drift to the left.

The bright blue streaks began to spin in Max's vision, and his statement was an eruption of everything in his mind. *"I abdicate.* Right now, I *renounce* my place in the line of succession. I renounce all my titles and property. I renounce my goddamn citizenship."

Quentin said, "No. *No*, Prince Maxence, Your Highness. You *can't."*

"Oh yes, I *can*. Attorneys have advised me on how to do this. If I give up everything—my titles, my property, and my citizenship—you have no hold on me nor jurisdiction over me. So, *I renounce."*

"Your Highness, you *cannot,"* Quentin said.

Max's voice rose. *"No. I renounce. I* renounce it *all."*

"You would renounce your birthright so you can be *a priest?*

"To be a *Jesuit.* I will be a *Jesuit,* not a parish priest. And *yes.* I want nothing more in life than to be a member of the Jesuit order."

Quentin Sault's voice became a bit dry. "If I may be so bold, sir, you are *not* cut out to be *a priest,* Your Most Serene Highness."

Max would not relent. If he renounced, he *might* survive. And if he did convince Sault and his men not to murder him, the assassins would not look any farther in the inn to eliminate witnesses to their assassination. He said, "St. Augustine struggled with worldly temptations, as do I. It's not unusual. He wrote, 'Lord, grant me chastity and sobriety, *but not yet.'"*

Sault said, "I won't take your abdication back to the Crown Council."

Maxence whipped his head around and stared at Quentin Sault. Violence rose in his chest. "You can't *refuse* to accept it. You're a military officer and the director of the intelligence service. You have no *authority* in the government. You aren't in the line of succession or even the royal family. *You* can't refuse my abdication. Legally, no one can, but that won't stop them."

Quentin told him, "Your Serene Highness, my prince, you *need* to go back to Monaco to stand for the Crown Council's election of the next sovereign prince."

"You *can't* refuse to take my abdication back. I'll turn on my phone and call Pierre to abdicate. He might accept my renunciation, and maybe he'll countermand your order to kill me."

Sault's gray eyes flared open. "What are you *talking* about?"

"My brother, Prince Pierre, will accept my renunciation now that my uncle has died. Uncle Rainier has died, right? Dear God, *please* tell me his suffering is over. The doctors said his stroke was neither survivable nor recoverable. He should never have been intubated or had that feeding tube placed. It was *cruel*. Pierre insisted on doing it so he would have time to consolidate his position with the council."

Quentin Sault said, "That was *a month* ago. No one notified you when your uncle passed, either?"

Either?

No one notified him when his uncle had passed, *either?*

That was an odd choice of words.

The commandos by the exit hovered their hands near the oddly square bulges in the side pockets on their pants.

Maxence barreled on, determined to convince Quentin Sault that there was no reason to execute him. "Besides, Princess Flicka has returned to the palace. I saw that before I turned my phone off. Pierre has had more than enough time to dispel any stray rumors about divorce and ensure he has enough votes when the Crown Council finally meets. I'm surprised he hasn't called for the vote already. Pierre can do it without me. I've told everyone I've left that life behind and plan to take Holy Orders as soon as Pierre allows it. I will do it *tomorrow* if Pierre informs His Holiness. *I will not stand in the way of Pierre taking the throne. You don't have to do this."*

Sault asked, "Did you say you turned your phone off?"

"Of course, I did," Maxence said. "There's no mobile phone reception out in the Himalayas. My phone has been shut off for a month."

"For *a month?*" Quentin asked, his voice breathless. "My God. You haven't heard. I thought you must have seen it on the news and *decided* not to come back, or thought it too dangerous, or had been threatened. That's why we're here to *escort* you home *safely.*"

At that, Maxence turned and examined the ashen tones under Sault's complexion. His voice was low, and his words came out clipped with anger. "What happened?"

Sault shook his head like he was shaking off a shock. "Prince Maxence, Your Most Serene Highness, my prince, I regret to inform you that your brother, Prince Pierre Grimaldi, shot himself a week ago."

Maxence frowned at Quentin, utterly dismayed at why he had come all that way to tell Max this. "Is he all right?"

Quentin blinked, an exaggerated flapping of his eyelids. "I'm sorry, Your Highness. His Serene Highness, Prince Pierre Grimaldi, has died."

Impossible.

Rage flew up. "You were supposed to *guard* him. You were supposed *to take care* of him."

"I am aware of that," Sault said.

"What the hell happened?"

Quentin Sault drew himself up ramrod-straight,

and the troubled creases around his eyes could have been sorrow or shame. "Pierre's wife, Princess Flicka von Hannover, fled with her bodyguard and announced to the world that she had divorced Pierre. They confronted each other at Castle Marienburg in Germany in, what I must admit, was a masterclass of strategy on her side. Someone has been reading Clausewitz. When it became clear there was no path by which she could be returned to the Prince's Palace, by either persuasion or force, Pierre placed my gun under his chin and committed suicide."

The bleak vacuum of the room sucked the breath from Max's lungs.

He swiveled back and leaned on the counter, resting on his elbows, and tried to breathe.

His chest moved.

His lungs expanded.

But he did not seem to be able to gasp air.

Finally, Max choked out, *"Suicide?"*

"I'm afraid so, Your Serene Highness. I am prepared to tender my resignation after you arrive back at the palace, but I felt it should be my final duty to see you back home to your rightful place in the line of succession."

Maxence had always ruminated on new information at length, which was one of the reasons Father Moses had recruited him to be a Jesuit instead of a Franciscan as he'd initially planned.

Max tried to draw in the thought that his brother no longer lived. His grief was formidable, and it weighed on the crown of his head and his shoulders and constricted around his chest.

Pierre was one of the few people in the world who knew Max had spent months held hostage on that tanker ship, and they shared blood and genes and parents, who were also gone.

Another great sucking hole had been ripped in the atmosphere.

Max had always thought Pierre might eventually order his execution, but now he couldn't.

And Pierre would not betray any more of their friends nor threaten or abuse Flicka ever again.

Horror washed over Maxence that the world might be a better place without his brother in it, but *he grieved* at the loss.

The path of his future, once constrained like a dark tunnel, was now a boundless, terrifying void, but it seemed to snap shut when he tried to peer into it.

His soul could not settle on an emotion and thus they all assaulted him, but a flash of blond curls by the stairs caught his eye.

He looked over.

Dree was standing in the door to the stairway, her backpack lying on the floor at her feet.

The two commandos by the door whipped guns out of their clothes and pointed them at her.

Maxence covered the few feet of floor before his thoughts caught up. He spread himself across Dree, shielding her and looking back at the two commandos. "Put the guns away. *Sault,* tell them to put them away."

Quentin Sault raised one fist in the air like he was signaling someone to halt.

The two commandos lowered their weapons, but they kept them at the ready.

Sault asked, "Who's this?"

From behind him, Dree asked, "Maxence, what's

going on? Did you renounce your vows as a deacon in the Church?"

Oh, *those*.

Those holy vows further complicated the situation.

Maxence told her, "These men aren't from the Vatican."

"You renounced something, but I don't understand what's going on. Did someone commit suicide?"

He turned and looked down at Dree and thought he might fall into the blue of her guileless eyes. "I would say that I haven't told you some things about myself, but I think I've told you everything. I told you they were stories I'd made up."

She raised one of her blond eyebrows. "I have no idea what you're talking about."

"Monagasquay."

Dree shifted her weight onto one leg, bracing her fist on her jutting hip, and gazed up at him with a knowing, ridiculously cute grin. She said, "Monagasquay isn't a real country."

She was so adorable that he wanted to bite her. Just a nibble.

"It's Monaco," Max admitted. "Everything I told you is true, except the country's name is Monaco. It's a small principality on the Mediterranean Sea that cuts a small chunk out of southern France."

She squinted at him, dubious. "I thought Monaco was in Africa, not France. Isn't that where *Casablanca* takes place?"

"That's *Morocco*. *Morocco* is in North Africa, on the southern coast of the Mediterranean Sea. *Monaco* is in Europe, and it's a tiny city-state chipped out of the coast of France, north of Italy. *Monaco* is where James Bond films take place, in the Monte Carlo casino."

"Oh." She frowned. "You'd think twelve years of Catholic school would've taught me geography better than that. But you almost fooled me with Monagasquay, so I guess not."

Maxence said, "I was second in line to the throne of Monaco after my older brother, Pierre Grimaldi—"

"Wait, you mean *Prince* Pierre, the older brother from your stories when we were in France?" she asked, squinting at him.

"Yes, *Prince* Pierre, but now I'm the heir apparent to the throne of Monaco since he committed suicide. I am His Serene Highness, Prince Maxence Charles Honoré of the House of Grimaldi of Monaco."

Dree stared up at him with those fathomless, unblinking blue eyes, and he could practically see the machinery cranking inside her head.

She said, *"Nuh-uh."*

If you'd have asked Maxence, he would have said that absolutely nothing in the world or the universe could have dispelled the grief-stricken shock that permeated him, but Dree's canny refusal to be fooled by nonsense shattered his composure.

"You're right. You're right!" His legs weakened, and he sat on the floor at her feet, pulling her down to sit beside him. "This is the most absurd situation in the history of absurd situations. All my life, I have been denying any interest in the throne and insisting that I have no ambition other than to become an itinerant Jesuit who travels the world with nothing more than a rucksack to hold one extra black robe and a spare rosary, serving God and the Pope, not necessarily in that order."

She squinted at him, concern written in her pinched eyebrows. "Max? You okay?"

He gestured with an open hand at the three Monegasque men who had tracked him to the lobby of a run-down inn in the rural district of Jumla in the foothills of the Himalaya Mountains of Nepal, which was *insane.* "And now, Quentin Sault—the director of Monaco's intelligence services and an officer in our military, the bane of my existence whom I believed would hunt me down and murder me one day—shows up out of nowhere and tells me that my psychopathic brother has offed himself, which makes him more of a narcissist than a psychopath, I think. But Pierre's suicide makes *me* the heir apparent to the throne of Monaco."

Dree took his hand between her soft, tiny ones. "Max, honey, do you need a paper bag to breathe into?"

He waved her off. "Seriously, Sault might as well have shown up here and said, 'You're a wizard, Harry,' but instead, he says, 'You're the prince, Max.' Absurd. Utterly absurd. *Immeasurably absurd.*"

He shook his head and ended up with his head in his hands, finally breathing through the inappropriate laughter because every other reaction seemed more like a lunatic.

"Are you telling me—"

He nodded, flopping his head forward like a loon.

"You're *serious.* You're, like, a royal guy."

"'His Serene Highness, Prince Maxence of Monaco.' I kid you not. Oh, hey. I'm also the Duke of Mazarin and the Count of Polignac. Look me up on your phone."

"The WiFi still doesn't work for me," Dree said.

"Fine. When you get somewhere. But it's true. It's horribly, undeniably, unbelievably *true,*" he sighed.

"Maxence, Augustine, I don't know what to say."

"I went from thinking I was about to be executed—"

"Wait, *what?*" she asked. "You were serious about that?"

Max nodded. "Oh, yes. Quentin would have killed me if Pierre had ordered him to. Wouldn't you have, Sault?" He glanced over.

Quentin Sault was staring out the windows, his jaw set hard.

Max threaded his fingers through his hair. "Yeah, I thought so."

"So, everything you told me was true. Like, when you were kidnapped and the pirates and the tanker boat? *That* was real?"

From over at the counter, Quentin asked, his voice sharp, "You told her about *that?*"

"*I* can tell people." He turned back to Dree. "Anyway, my morning has gone from my imminent execution to my life upended. I am at an absolute loss for what to do."

Quentin spun and stared at him. "You're going back to Monaco and calling a Crown Council to elect and certify a new sovereign prince, and you're going to make sure it isn't Prince Jules Grimaldi."

Maxence shot back at Sault, "What if I don't go back? What if I take Holy Orders like I planned?"

Dree's fingers tightened on his arm, and he pressed his hand over hers.

Quentin sighed. "Then everyone will assume Prince Jules threatened you in some manner, and you ran."

"Why would he—" Max stopped.

Max's uncle, Prince Jules Grimaldi, had over a billion reasons to remove or kill anyone between him and the princely crown of Monaco, and Max was the first of three people who stood in his way.

Dree was still peering at him, her head tilted, like she was dissecting him with her gaze. "Why would a guy who is a *prince* want to be a *priest?*"

He sighed and flipped his fingers in the air. "It's a complicated story."

"Tell me."

Her questioning had become more brisk, even efficient. He was reminded of their conversations in Paris about Flicka, when Dree had said out loud what Max had not admitted to himself.

Afterward, his mind and soul had felt cleaner.

So, Max did his best to answer her. "I'm drawn to the church."

"Like a moth to a flame?" she asked, her clear blue eyes examining him.

"More like a prisoner to freedom. I've wanted to be a priest from the first time I read about the second sons of monarchs becoming priests. King Henry the Eighth planned to join the Church and take a run at the papacy until his older brother died, and thus he became the King of England. The sacerdotium was my entire ambition. I never wanted to rule anything."

"Was that just because your brother would have

to die for you to be the prince, or did you really not want it?" she asked.

"You did psych rotations, didn't you?" Max asked her.

She nodded again, briskly. "Psych rotations are standard in nursing school, but when you're a nurse, you see a lot of people who are fooling themselves about what is making them sick. I can detect anybody's bullshit at five hundred yards. I am a living, walking, breathing bullshit detector."

Maxence suspected this did not bode well for him.

She asked, "So, did you *really* not want it?"

He burrowed down into his mind, deeply examining what he wanted and what he *thought* he wanted, until he said, "I *didn't* want it, even if Pierre had abdicated his position instead of dying. Lots of royals have abdicated. He might have. He had several personal situations where he might have done it or have been forced to, and I'd already made plans to abdicate and leave if that had happened. Ever since I could remember, though, I wanted *out*. The priesthood was a way *out* that no one could question, and thus I wanted to join the priesthood."

Dree said, "There are other ways out. You could have just renounced it a long time ago."

"My uncle Rainier told me, flat out, that he would not accept my renunciation unless or until Pierre had produced two *legitimate* sons from a Catholic, dynastic marriage. There's that whole problem with the treaties of France. If there isn't a sovereign prince, Monaco will cease to exist."

"Yeah, I remember that about Monagasquay."

"What the hell is Monagasquay?" Quentin Sault demanded.

They ignored him.

Dree said, "You could have just signed up with the Catholic Church and found someone to give you Holy Orders. Not a lot of men want to be priests these days. They pass out Holy Orders like candy if you ask nicely."

Maxence shook his head. "Pope Celestine the Sixth told me he would never allow me to be ordained, even if my uncle or my brother consented. And if I were, he would declare it invalid."

She squinted at the ceiling, thinking. "Isn't he the Pope Emeritus now, and that's how we got Pope Vincent de Paul?"

Max smiled. "Yes."

"But you're a deacon now. You already took the first level of Holy Orders."

He nodded. "His Eminence Pope Vincent de Paul allowed me to take those."

"If you've had the sacrament of Holy Orders, you can't get married. If you can't get married, you can't have legitimate kids. That's a problem for those treaties with France you were talking about, right?"

Maxence sighed and dropped his head forward into his hands. "My vows were made to be broken. There are liturgical methods for laicization for deacons and priests who want to quit, even for cardinals, but everyone knew I was a special case. Pope Vincent de Paul wrote the vows in such a way so that he can call me on the phone and laicize me in five minutes. That's why Father Booker was poking at me that my sacrament probably wasn't valid, and he's probably right."

Dree nodded slowly, obviously thinking hard. "So, you can just walk away from being a deacon. That's why you've been holding onto it so tightly."

His skin chilled like all his clothes had been ripped off in the Himalayas in December, leaving him exposed. "I don't know. Maybe."

"But you haven't been allowed to walk away from Monaco and the royal family."

"It's not like that. I'm not just rebelling for the sake of it."

She shook her head, still thinking. "No, I don't think you would rebel just for the sake of it. It's not mere oppositional defiance. You're not like that. There's more." She looked at him more intently, even leaning toward his face and scrutinizing him. "So, why don't you want to go?"

He blinked. "Why don't I go where?"

"Why not go to Monaco and lobby that council and be the prince? What's stopping you?"

Wan winter sunlight barely glowed from the front windows of the inn's lobby, and the air was saturated with gloom.

Three photocopied pictures of the Hindu gods Ganesh and Shiva were tacked to the wall behind the desk, and rustic hand-embroidered tapestries depicted scenes of gods and shepherdesses from the Vedas in violet and red.

The cold wind whistled outside the front door, a clock on the opposite wall ticked loudly, and one of the commandos scraped his boot on the floor.

Herbal incense smoke, grilled chicken and lamb from last night's supper, and the cucumber and rose scent of Dree's soap like an English castle's kitchen garden filled his nose.

The ceramic tile on the floor chilled his butt and the backs of his legs. The thin December air needled his forehead and the inside of his nose when he breathed.

Dree's fingers were warm.

She was still scrutinizing him, waiting for an answer while he calmed his mind.

He inhaled hard, and everything in his soul tumbled out to her. "*You've seen* what I can do. *You've seen* what it's like when I read the Gospel or preach a homily. That must *mean* something. It *can't* just be a parlor trick."

She shook her head. "No one who has seen you preach thinks it's a parlor trick. Sister Mariam's religious friends went to Mass that morning for *you.* I was amused at first because I thought they were going just to ogle you, but they went to *hear* you, not look at you."

"Then *why* can I do it? What is that *light* that blows through me, that *pressure* that happens when I *feel* something, and then I can convince people of almost anything? It can't be an *accident.* It has to be *in me* for a reason."

Dree was listening to him, biting her plush lip and staring at the corner of the ceiling while she considered what he'd said. "But it's not only religious."

"But it's *something*—"

"But that time at the Castle of Versailles, at the party—when you convinced Sir Marvin Meriwether-Stone to invest in the company that your friend, Micah Shine, the guy with the pretty eyes, was founding—you did it then."

Maxence tried not to let his jaw drop. "You remember their names?"

She shrugged. "Nurses have to remember which patient is which and what drugs they were given and when. You need to know right away when a patient is crashing. A decent memory is part of the job. But the point is, you did it at Versailles, and you were doing it again at supper last night. It's not *just* in church. And you said you've been able to do it for a long time, like, when you were a kid."

"Yes, but—"

She pressed her lips together and nodded like she'd added something else to a list in her head. "How long have you been able to convince people of stuff?"

He shook his head. "I convinced the kidnappers to give me a boat and let me go because they believed I was one of them."

"Right. So it's *not* just about religion. Why do you *want* to be a priest?"

It was all too confusing. "It's my whole life."

"Have anyone ever asked you if you were sure about your vocation?"

He squeezed his eyes shut and laughed a tortured chuckle. "Every priest I've ever met has questioned me about it. Father Moses, Father Xavier, Father Gustavo Merino—"

"Who's that guy?"

"He took the pontifical name of Pope Vincent de Paul when he was elected pope."

"Oh, *yeah,* your *buddy,* the *Pope.* Wait, *hold on* a frickin' second. *The Pope* asked you whether you really want to be a priest?"

He shrugged.

Dree shook her head. *"Dude."*

"But I've *always* wanted to be a priest."

She ducked and growled at him, "But you *'slip'* every chance you get."

"Surely, not *every*—" He stopped talking because her blond eyebrows raised in disbelief. "But I *shouldn't.*"

"You keep asking God to grant you sobriety and chastity, *but not yet.*"

"It's a joke," Maxence muttered.

"I think it's one of those jokes where you're actually telling the truth. Would it be better for *Monaco* if you walked away from the throne?"

That caught Maxence under his rib cage like a meat hook, and he couldn't answer.

She said, "You've said that you want to be a priest because you want to make the world a better place. Would the *world* be better if you allowed your uncle Jules to be the Prince of Monaco?"

Maxence's teeth grated in his mouth. "No. The world would be very much worse if Jules had complete authority over forty thousand people and the power and wealth of the Principality of Monaco. He's evil."

Dree was staring right into Max's eyes, unblinking, not like a snake but like an angel, one of the cherubim whose righteous eyes could see everything but had no pity for flawed mortals. "You say you want to be a priest. Aren't priests supposed to, like, fight evil?"

Maxence couldn't look away. God, she was beautiful, like a blazing fire. "Yes, but I can do that without being the Prince, and surely I can fight evil if I am a priest. The very fact that the crown and

Monaco tempt me, that I want to take it and *rule,* proves that it is a sin to lust for that kind of power and wealth."

She glanced down at his chest, maybe even to his groin, and his cock jumped as if her eyes had stroked him through his clothes. She said, "Like you've never given in to temptation before."

His fingers found hers. "I was always meant to walk away," he told her. "That was my role, to support Pierre in his bid for the throne because he was older and it was his right. I was never meant to be the Prince, so I found something else to want."

Dree glanced at Quentin Sault and the two soldiers by the door. She leaned over and whispered to him, and her gentle breath feathered his ear. "No man who fucks like you do *wants* to be a priest."

He tightened his hand on her fingers.

Dree yelled over at Sault, "How long is this Crown Council thing going to take?"

Quentin Sault shrugged. "The palace is in chaos. Prince Jules has called for a council meeting this weekend, but Duke Alexandre and his faction have refused to attend anything sooner than three months."

"Can he do that?" Max asked him.

"There is a quorum requirement," Sault told him. "As long as enough nobles stand with Alexandre and refuse to attend, a new prince cannot be elected."

"So, it could take three months," Dree said, her voice firm.

Max said, "If it takes longer than that, France will rumble that the treaties have been violated, and their army will march in our streets."

Dree turned so that she was kneeling in front of where Max sat on the floor. She knotted her fist around one lapel of his black leather motorcycle jacket and pulled his ear closer to her mouth. "Hear me out. For three months, go back to Monaco and take care of business. Live as a prince again instead of a priest."

"I can't be trusted to do the right thing." He leaned back. His spine pressed against the wall. "I should not be trusted with that kind of power. I should be locked into a hierarchal organization where others define what I do with it. I am an unguided missile. I am a brandished gun."

"Max, you're smarter than that."

He muttered, "Even though I wanted to be a priest, I couldn't keep my cock in my pants."

"Which is proof they never really controlled you. Those weren't 'slips.' Those were *decisions*. You've always made your own decisions."

"Like when I—" He raised an eyebrow.

She grinned. "Oh, yeah. *Especially* that."

"Dree, you're funny. You're damn funny. But the decisions to break my vows were fundamentally wrong." He released his eye contact with her and stared at his heavily callused, deeply tanned hands clasped on his knees. "I never do the right thing. I should work harder on becoming a priest, not give in to *this*. I should take Holy Orders and go to a cloistered monastery. I should be locked inside the Vatican so I'm not tempted."

She raised an eyebrow again and whispered, "Men don't tempt you?"

He sighed, resigned to the fact that she was, indeed, a living, breathing bullshit detector.

"Yeah, okay." She whispered, her voice throaty and too close to his skin, "If you go back, if you break your vows, for three months, *you can have me.*"

Maxence looked up. God help him, he was weak. "I'm listening."

"Anything you want," she said, and her eyes glistened with excitement as she stared at him. *"Everything* you want, just like Paris, but for *three months.*"

"What—but why—" Formulating the question zinging around his head took a few tries. "Why would you do that?"

"Because you said I'm an angel," Dree told him, "and no one's ever said that to me before. Because angels fight evil, and if this guy Prince Jules is as bad as you say—"

"Worse," both Maxence and Sault said at the same time, and they glanced at each other, startled.

"Then I don't want him in a position of power," Dree said. "The world is awful and brutal, and we should have *kind* people running countries. The world should be better. *You're* a kind and good person."

"I'm not," he murmured.

"You're the type of person who should run the world, Maxence. You should rule Monaco."

No, he shouldn't. His chest clenched. A man with the ruined wings of a fallen angel tattooed on his back was exactly the wrong sort of person to become an absolute dictator.

"At the very least," Dree said, her gaze darting as she looked into his eyes, "you have to make sure it's someone other than this Prince Jules guy, and make sure it's someone kind and good, and not someone who's an evil, racist, bigoted jerk."

Maxence couldn't speak.

Sault glared at him from over by the front desk, and the left-side soldier was watching them with wide eyes while his gun pointed at the inn's front door.

Dree touched his chin and guided his gaze back to her. "I'll do whatever it takes to keep yet one more evil dictator away from the world, even if I have to do it *on my back.*"

He touched her cheek as tremors thrummed through his veins. "Dree."

She said, "Or lying face-down on a bed."

The image of her curvy ass in the air as he stroked into her made him lightheaded. "Dree. *Stop.*"

"Or *on*—"

She exaggerated the succulent movements of her mouth as her plush lips pressed together.

"*—my—*"

Her nose wrinkled as her tongue licked into view behind her teeth.

"*—knees.*"

Maxence grabbed her up in his arms and dragged her to his mouth to kiss her, his lips devouring hers, because the thought of her lips tight around his cock was enough to bring him to *his* knees.

She kissed him back, her arms tight around his neck.

His hands ran down the curves of her back to her pinched waist, and he pushed her back. Her lips were swollen, red, and wet, and her eyes were as dazed as his must be. She asked, "So, you'll do it?"

"Because you want me to, not because of what you bargained with," he said.

"I want to do that, too."

He dug his fingers into her hips, just curving his fingertips.

She smiled at him.

"Let's go," Quentin Sault said. "I've got a helicopter waiting. We can be in Monaco by tomorrow morning."

A man cleared his throat on the stairs above them.

Maxence turned his head.

Above them, on the landing five steps up, Isaak and Batsa stood and were watching them.

Isaak's expression was as plastic and emotionless as Max had ever seen him, but Batsa's eyes and mouth were wide and round. In just a second, he'd probably gasp and point at them.

Maxence swiveled his hand closer to Dree's waist because he was nearly grabbing her ass.

"Guys," Maxence said and stopped. He was going to say something like, *It's not what it looks like,* but it was even worse than it looked, especially if you included where he'd been the previous night.

Isaak said, "We'll notify Alfonso and Father Booker that you've decided to return to Monaco and that you're taking Andrea Catherine with you."

"This mission is over," Maxence said to him.

"Yes, surely," Isaak said, his tone very neutral.

"I'll contact you about the preemie pods and motorcycles, and about the grant applications."

Isaak sighed and nodded. "Those are important. When you return to Monaco and settle in, let me know. I'll start working on them when I get back to France." He shrugged and gestured between Max and Dree, who was staring at her hands in her lap.

"So, okay. I mean, it's not like we even had a chance to talk. I wish you the best. I wish you *both* the best."

Isaak turned and walked up the stairs.

Batsa said, "I'll make sure Father Booker and Alfonso get back to Kathmandu. Don't worry about us. I'll take care of them. Just, um, it sounds like there's a mess you need to clean up."

He shook Max's hand and then bounded up the stairs after Isaak.

Two more soldiers who had been stationed outside were dispatched to clear out Max's and Dree's rooms, probably because Sault wasn't letting Max out of his sight.

Ten minutes later, their backpacks were tossed in the backs of Sault's Jeeps—*how had he gotten Jeeps?*—and they were on their way to the tiny Chandannath airport, where a helicopter was warming up to fly them back to Kathmandu.

Maxence muttered to Dree as they walked across the cracked tarmac, "You were persuasive. You should have been a Jesuit."

Dree snorted. "Yeah, well, I lack a necessary member—"

He raised his eyebrows, repressing a grin.

"—ship requirement," she finished.

Maxence laughed aloud as the helicopter blades knifed the air, blowing the leather of his jacket against his body.

As they were climbing into the metal side of the helicopter, one with much nicer seats than the military-surplus chopper that they'd flown down on, Quentin Sault gripped Max's arm to get his attention.

He said, "Your Highness, sir, I want you to know

that I'll have airtight security around you every minute you're there. The two of you will be safe. Jules and his mercenaries won't get within a hundred meters of you."

Shock coursed through Max. "Mercenaries? Jules has *mercenaries* now? That's treason. It's in the Constitution that the other nobles cannot raise armies."

Quentin's lips pursed tightly. "Prince Rainier has been indisposed, and Prince Pierre has been distracted by chasing Her Royal Highness Princess Flicka all over the world. *No one* has been *in charge.*"

Maxence looked at the commandos standing beside the helicopter.

In a palace coup, which of the military would obey the chain of command and Quentin's orders, and which of them already had been threatened or bribed by Jules Grimaldi?

Maxence only wondered whether it would be a bloodless coup or the other kind.

If Jules had already paid for mercenaries, he'd make sure he got his money's worth.

"Thank you, Sault." Maxence boarded the helicopter.

As he buckled himself in, Dree asked, "What was that?"

He couldn't hide it from her. "Sault thinks this might turn violent. I don't want you in Monaco. I want you somewhere else, somewhere *safe.* I'll buy you a plane ticket to Paris, and I'll put you up at whatever hotel you want, for as long as you want. Forever, if that's what it takes."

She raised one blond eyebrow at him, and the morning sunlight made her hair glow like a halo. "If there's going to be violence, you're going to need an ER nurse to patch you up. I told you I'm going to Monaco with you."

"I don't want you in Monaco. It's not safe right now."

"*Nowhere* is safe for me, Max. If I go back to Phoenix, there are literal drug dealers who want impossible amounts of money or my hide. Probably, they want the money *and* my hide. In Monaco, at least I'll have trained men with guns between me and the murderers."

"But—"

"*No.*"

There was no use arguing with that woman when she'd made up her mind. Dree Clark might look like a tiny golden hamster, but her heart was more like a tough little desert rodent that wouldn't let go once it had sunk its sharp teeth into something.

He liked that about her. A challenge was always more fun than a dead lay.

Quentin Sault hauled the door shut, and the helicopter whined as the blades accelerated.

Sault handed out hearing protection earmuffs. Maxence began to settle his over his head when he caught Dree's eye.

She put her mouth right up against his ear, where he could feel the brush of her lips. "Are you sure this isn't a trap?"

Maxence turned and said to her, "*No.* No, I'm not sure of that *at all.* This might very well be a trap. Sault could be lying about Pierre being dead to get me to go somewhere so they can shoot me in the head in a ditch, or he might already be working for

Prince Jules and do exactly the same thing. I don't know if we're even going to make it to Kathmandu. Let me put you on a plane for Paris where you'll be safe."

"No." Dree's mouth was a hard line. "I said I'd go to Monaco with you, and I will. You're going to need back-up."

Maxence clapped the earmuffs on his head.

The helicopter noise diminished in his ears.

The sun was just rising over the immense peaks of the Himalayan mountain range, shining rays through the sky to the ground around them.

The helicopter tilted up and lifted off the ground, flying through the cold winter sunlight.

WHAT COMES NEXT?
PRINCE
By: Blair Babylon

Why would a guy who had it all—tall, hot, ripped, royal Maxence—say that he wants to walk away from the throne to be a priest?

He must be hiding something.